DEATH ON THE WEST HIGHLAND WAY

A SCOTTISH COZY MYSTERY

ADRIANA LICIO

The Home Travellers
Press

DEATH ON THE WEST HIGHLAND WAY
The Homeswappers Mysteries Series
Book 5

By Adriana Licio

Edition I
Copyright 2022 © Adriana Licio

Cover by **Wicked Smart Design**
Editing by **Alison Jack**

CONTENTS

1

THE INHERITANCE

In a carved wooden library in a Georgian house just outside Glasgow, an old solicitor, Henry Law of Law, Lorr and Morlore, was discussing the will of the late Sir Angus McGrouse. An only child with no children of his own, in death, Sir Angus had attracted a crowd of keen heirs. They had gathered in his study from the four corners of the world following an invitation sent out two weeks earlier.

The people in front of him were connected so remotely to Sir Angus that even Mr Law found it difficult to explain exactly how they were related to one another. The solicitor suspected Sir Angus had had some fun, dismissing some of his more obvious heirs and picking the ones he considered in need of a healthy injection of riches via an inheritance. Mr Law couldn't help noticing the not-so-subtle change in his audience's demeanour. Upon arrival, they had all appeared friendly and courteous, smiling at one another and chattering amiably, but as soon as he had announced that one and only one of them would inherit Sir Angus's substantial estate, most had stiffened and eyed each other malevolently.

"You mean", roared Lloyd de Beer, his face flushing to darken his tan, "my wife and I may have made the trip all the way from

South Africa to Scotland only to hear we're not going to inherit a thing? This is absurd!"

"The thing is," the lawyer said, raising one of his thick eyebrows, "you all, each and every one of you, have the chance to inherit. Unless, of course, you're too offended to take up the challenge Sir Angus set for you."

"A challenge? To benefit from what is rightfully ours? Ridiculous! But as we've taken the trouble to travel all this way…"

"…you might as well at least listen to what Mr Law has to tell us." A posh English accent cut through Mr de Beer's diatribe, not without a hint of sarcasm. Professor Alastair Hobbs glanced at the tall, slim young woman sitting next to him, who nodded silently in agreement.

"That's very much what I intend to do now," said Mr de Beer. "But let me assure you, you'd be just as resentful if you lived 8,000 miles away."

"It's not about the miles, it's about the attitude." These words were spoken in fluent if accented English. Amilcar Herrera wasn't too tall, but he was well built, his skin glowing and tanned from the sunshine of his homeland, Argentina. He had the confident air of a man whom women tended to fall for at first sight, despite – or maybe because of – a certain cockiness. "To me, this challenge is an opportunity. The sort of thing that doesn't happen twice in a lifetime, so I won't be complaining. On the contrary…"

"I've come all the way from the Netherlands," Wilfrida van Wetering interrupted loudly, her English as good as Herrera's with just a hint of a Dutch accent. A small woman, she had a fire in her eyes that suggested she wasn't to be trifled with. "A long trip, if you're not in the best of health. Still, I agree with Mr Herrera. It's an opportunity."

"But why not leave a wee bit to each of us?" Robert Gentle, a lanky and awkward red-haired young man, flushed as all eyes rounded on him. "I believe there'd be enough to go round…"

"That would mean diluting the inheritance," the lawyer explained. "But it's something you could agree upon, if you wish. It's not exactly what Sir Angus wanted, but you're free to draw up a contract stipulating that you will each inherit an equal share before you start on your venture."

"Would we be required to participate in the challenge even in the case of such an agreement?" asked Mrs van Wetering.

"Absolutely," said the lawyer. "Because if none of you succeeds in the challenge, the whole inheritance will go to charity."

"What?" the woman cried.

"Now that would be a real snub!" Lloyd de Beer protested.

"Which charity?" asked Professor Hobbs.

"One organising visits to Tilda Island's gardens and castle, thus keeping legend and history alive." The solicitor was evidently enjoying watching the power that money – loads of it – held over some avaricious souls.

A sturdy lady, her rigid bearing contrasting oddly with her shabby appearance, spoke for the first time. "Turning Tilda's castle into another tacky attraction, I suppose," she snorted. "It would be abominable!"

"Those stupid tourists crunching crisps in the purple living room…" The second speaker looked so much like the first one – same sagging cheeks; same double chin; same frizzy long hair – they had to be sisters. And they were: Faith and Hope Hillock, the only difference between them being that where Faith's locks were turning more salt, Hope's were still distinctly pepper.

"…stubbing out their cigarettes in the orangery vases…"

"…or on the tombstone of an ancestor in the private graveyard…"

"Still," said Olive de Beer, looking at the lawyer for confirmation, "there's got to be something more in the inheritance than a small island in the middle of the Atlantic."

"It's not in the middle of the Atlantic!" Faith Hillock looked horrified. "It's part of the Outer Hebrides…"

"I don't even want to imagine what the weather's like there..." Mrs de Beer stopped abruptly as her husband waved a hand at her, indicating that he wanted her to listen to the solicitor.

"Well, Mrs de Beer," Mr Law stated, "I can assure you there's much more to Tilda than the gardens and castle. But the trust is set in such a way that it requires you – should you and your husband inherit – to live there for most of the year."

"Never!" she cried.

"That's preposterous!" her husband added. "We have to be allowed to decide the direction of our own lives."

"It's one point Sir Angus was particularly firm on." The solicitor seemed rather pleased with the idea himself. "For at least five years after inheriting, the heir must officially become a resident of Tilda Island."

"The old guy was having a bit of fun at our expense." Herrera smiled. "Nonetheless, I'd be happy to oblige. I'm sure there's a decent golf course and plenty of rooms for my guests."

"A very fine golf course, I'm sure, if it's ever dry enough to play," Lloyd de Beer sneered.

"I thought coming from South Africa, you'd be more adaptable and spirited," Alastair Hobbs said, running a hand over his neatly trimmed moustache and goatee beard. "As for me, I'm like Mr Herrera. I'd be happy to live on Tilda."

"But my health condition requires that I live near a hospital," grumbled the Dutch woman.

"Mrs van Wetering, in consideration of your health, there's a codicil expressly for you."

"Though I'd be happy to base myself in that large library at the castle." Mrs van Wetering backtracked, clearly concerned that she might have protested too much and talked herself into losing out. "And the isolation is exactly what I need for my studies and research."

"You will certainly be able to have a couple of qualified

nurses to assist you on the island. The sea can get rough and a return to the mainland is not always feasible..."

"I believe Tilda Island is meant for us true Scots," said Miss Faith Hillock. "People fantasise about Scotland; I've seen quite a few English people, not to mention those from the continent, coming here with their heads full of wild landscapes and romantic visions, certain that they'll find the isolation and inspiration here to write the book of a lifetime, only to scuttle away like rats from a sinking ship after a couple of weeks."

"They don't know what isolation is," agreed Miss Hope Hillock, "nor how strong the northerly wind can blow till they experience it for themselves."

"And nowadays, life in the Highlands and Islands is nowhere near as hard as it used to be. There isn't the same snowfall, and roads get cleared quickly anyway..."

"Not to mention we have TV and the Internet..."

"You remember how long power cuts could last?"

"I do, sister." Hope sighed, her face full of nostalgia. "Those times will never come back."

"I jolly well hope they don't!" retorted Olive de Beer.

Henry Law of Law, Lorr and Morlore had a quick look at his watch. "I will give you 15 minutes to decide if you want to take part in the challenge set by the late Sir Angus McGrouse, and if you want to make an agreement to share the inheritance should one of you be successful. Those who decide to participate in the challenge will be shown a video of Sir Angus explaining the rules of the competition."

"Sir Angus himself? So he organised everything before he died?"

"Indeed. He'd been planning this for months, recording the video almost a year ago and giving us precise instructions on what to do after his death – which places to book, which heirs to get in touch with, etcetera, etcetera."

"What a man!" said Herrera, winking at the only other person in the room apart from Professor Hobbs's companion who hadn't yet spoken – a stunningly beautiful woman who was too busy looking down at the floor to meet his gaze.

"Shall we share the inheritance?" asked Professor Hobbs. "But what do we do about Tilda Island in that case? Shall we take it in turns to live there, or can we simply sell the property and divide the proceeds among us?"

The solicitor regarded the Englishman solemnly. "As far as the terms of the will go, it will be enough that the property is inhabited by any one of you. And yes, five years after the inheritance comes into effect, you will be free to sell the island."

"I might write the book of a lifetime during those five years," said Amilcar Herrera, eyeing the Hillock sisters. "I don't mind sharing the prize and I volunteer to live in the castle."

"It would be more fitting if my sister and I as Scots took up residence," said Faith.

Herrera anticipated Hope reinforcing her sister's statement. "Of course, I don't mind sharing the place with you two lovely ladies."

"Live under the same roof as a man?" the two sisters cried in horrified unison. "That would never do."

"I promise not to molest you."

"Instead of refining the details of our plan, at this point, we should decide if we all agree to share," said Professor Hobbs before the altercation between the Argentinian and the sisters could get out of hand. His companions looked at each other hesitantly.

"Aye, I believe that would be the perfect solution," said Robert Gentle. "We would all have enough to live happily ever after."

"One eighth of the inheritance is not as good as the entire thing," said Mrs de Beer drily.

"But it's much better than nothing at all," replied Amilcar Herrera.

"And much worse than having the whole thing for yourself…"

"Not to mention," said Mr de Beer, "each of us having to wait for the consent of the other heirs before we can make any decision involving the property…"

"We'd end up in court sooner rather than later," agreed Professor Hobbs, "and thereafter spend most of our time in tribunals. In all frankness, I'd rather go for all or nothing."

"That's so very English, thinking only in extremes," said Herrera, but he was smiling, as if he knew full well it was a trait he shared. "But there are two young ladies who haven't said a word so far."

The woman who had spent the entire proceedings beside Professor Hobbs explained her position. "I'm Sue MacDuff," she said. "I'm not one of the heirs; Professor Hobbs here," she nodded at her companion, "suggested I come with him to Tilda Island to work on my dissertation. You see, I'm a research assistant, studying for my doctorate in Cultural Heritage and Tourism Management."

"It might take longer than you hoped to get there," said Mr de Beer, grinning.

"Miss MacDuff and I will decide what's in her best interests once this meeting is over," said Professor Hobbs, turning to the beautiful woman who was now the only person in the room not to have spoken. "But how about this young lady? What's your position?"

Sitting at the back of the room, a little apart from the others, the woman finally raised her eyes from the floor. Caramel blonde hair cascaded over her shoulders, while dark, shapely brows rose like seagull wings over large brown eyes. She reddened and muttered her reply in a voice so low, not everyone in the room could hear.

"I'm Grace Jelly. I'm related to Sir Angus on my mother's side. And I will take part in the challenge with you."

"Do you want to share the inheritance?" Herrera said gently, almost drooling at the simple beauty of the woman.

"I think we should decide that together," she muttered, her hair slowly descending over her face.

"Professor Hobbs is right," said Mr de Beer after a few exchanges with his wife. "It's all or nothing."

"I'm sort of lazy," confessed Herrera, "and wouldn't have minded agreeing to share so I could watch you taking up the challenge while I stayed in the pub. But when you mentioned disputes and tribunals, you changed my mind. It might take years to reach a solution to the simplest of problems, and years of fighting are much worse than a few challenging days. Let's take life as it comes. All or nothing – each to his own."

"Or hers," said Faith Hillock. "Being Scots, my sister and I wouldn't want to share, unless it's with each other. And we know the land and its secrets, so we're the most likely to win any challenge set here. I really don't see why we should use our knowledge to the advantage of foreigners."

"You're truly two good Samaritans," mocked Amilcar Herrera.

"The Good Lord certainly didn't mean we Christians to be stupid."

"Nor to put ourselves in a position where we'd be exploited by heathens ..."

"All the same, we could have helped each other..." whispered a tiny voice.

"Come on, my boy, you're also a proud Scot," said Herrera, interrupting Robert Gentle. "Just like these two good ladies here, you'll have a great advantage in your own country."

"It's not that I'm afraid of taking on the challenge by myself," Robert argued. "But it seems unfair on everyone else..."

Professor Hobbs cut him short. "Don't bother yourself, life is never fair. Do what you have to do."

Robert sighed but, in the face of the determination in everyone else's eyes, said no more on the subject.

"Do we all agree?" asked Mr de Beer, looking around the

room. "Should we vote?" Everyone nodded. "Who's for sharing?"

Only Robert's hand went up.

"Are the rest of you ready to compete for the entire inheritance?"

Seven hands went up immediately. Grace hesitated, then put her hand up too. As she wasn't an heir, Sue MacDuff stepped back and abstained from voting. Grabbing her husband's hand and lowering it back to his side, Olive de Beer reminded him sharply that she not he was the heir, so he had no more right to lay claim to or vote on the inheritance than Sue.

"I believe we can call Mr Law back," announced Alastair Hobbs. "We decided much more quickly than I expected, so let's hear what sort of challenge awaits us. I guess we will need to hire cars to drive up and down the country."

"I believe the challenge will take place in a contained area," said Olive de Beer. "Maybe on Tilda Island itself."

"Let's call the lawyer back," said her husband.

"THE WEST HIGHLAND WAY? WHAT'S THAT?" ASKED MRS DE BEER when the video message from Sir Angus had been played.

"It's one of the most popular hikes in Scotland," Robert explained. "It's 96 miles from north of Glasgow to Fort William in the Highlands."

"A hike?" repeated Amilcar Herrera. "Surely we will be allowed to use cars or it will take days…"

"It will indeed take days," said the solicitor, "as you aren't allowed to use cars, or any mode of transport other than your two legs. You can only use cars, buses or trains once you have reached your destination on the route each day if you want to look round and about. Like all West Highland Way walkers, you can't skip any part of the track, unless the challenge expressly asks you to do so. You also need to start walking each morning from exactly where you left off the previous day.

"At each point of departure, my junior partner, Mr Archibald Morlore," at these words, a mere slip of a man in his sixties appeared beside Mr Law and nodded, "will hand you the riddle for the day, which you will have to decipher in order to find that day's 'treasure'. Then he, with the aid of helpers in disguise, will monitor that there's no foul play and the rules are respected.

"There will be eight items of 'treasure' to find every day, all in the same place. They will be numbered one to eight, so when you find them, choose the lowest number available. That will be proof of your order of arrival, and the lower the number, the higher your rating for the day. In other words, number one will get eight points, two will get seven, and so on.

"However, be warned: not all days will be rated equally, but according to Sir Angus's opinion on the difficulty level for each day. Don't hide or deface the clues left for the other competitors as you will be kicked out of the game. Once in Kinlochleven – the penultimate stop – you will be handed the final clue. Whoever arrives in Fort William with the highest score will win the challenge and take the entire inheritance."

"How long is each stretch?" Herrera asked.

"Anything between 10 and 15 miles."

"*Fifteen miles?*" Olive de Beer cried.

"Goodness!" her husband added.

"And we can't drive?" Herrera asked, looking convinced there had to be a mistake. "Are you kidding?"

"Of course I'm not!" said Mr Law, frowning at Herrera having the temerity to call his integrity into question. "How about you, Mrs van Wetering?"

"Excuse me? Sorry?" the woman said. From the tone of her voice and the way she tilted her head towards the solicitor, her companions could tell she was a little hard of hearing.

"Will you be OK hiking such long distances?"

"Of course," she replied stubbornly. "I've got my digoxin",

she patted her bag, "for my dodgy heart, and I exercise every day anyway."

"When do we get started?" asked Professor Hobbs.

"Tomorrow."

"But we need to get equipped!" Hobbs exclaimed. "You can't walk that kind of distance without sturdy boots and waterproofs and rucksacks..."

"Are we supposed to camp along the way?" Herrera asked.

"No. Sir Angus has chosen specific accommodation for you at each stop. As for the equipment, you have the entire afternoon in Glasgow to get everything you need. You won't even have to carry your luggage; Sir Angus arranged for the Travel Light transport service to take your things from one stop to the next. Actually, you struck lucky; the driver we'd booked fell sick at the last minute and this is the high season, but we managed to find a replacement. Without luggage transfer, believe me, your challenge would have been much harder. Nonetheless, I would recommend you carry a rucksack with you containing all you need for the daily walk. The route is wild in some sections and will take you far from any facilities. Better you have food and water handy at all times."

"How about maps and compasses?"

"We will supply maps, a DVD of Sir Angus's video in case you want to watch it again and a guide for each of you so you know what to expect and can familiarise yourself with the history of the places you'll see..."

"Oh yes, who would concentrate on an inheritance worth millions of pounds when they could delve into Scottish history?" said the Argentinian sarcastically.

"That history, Mr Herrera, might turn out to be useful in solving the riddles."

Amilcar Herrera took the reprimand in good humour. "I see. Forgive my silly remark, Mr Law. Sir Angus clearly planned this meticulously."

"Where are we starting?" asked Professor Hobbs.

"In Milngavie, I guess," said Robert.

The solicitor nodded, explaining, "That's the start of the West Highland Way, not too far from here. We took the liberty of booking accommodation for the night there so you can be ready for an early start tomorrow."

"And where exactly will we be expected to go?"

The solicitor unfolded the map of Scotland he had on his desk. His finger made a small circle north of Glasgow, then moved from one spot to the next.

"From Milngavie to Drymen, then along the bonnie banks of Loch Lomond. From there, the road passes through Rannoch Moore, Glencoe and the Mamore Mountains up in the Highlands of Scotland, until you arrive in Fort William, the official end of the route, in about a week's time."

His finger tapped complacently on the last location in the heart of Scotland as all around him, the heirs of Sir Angus McGrouse tried to make sense of the long distance between where they were right now and where they needed to be.

2

THE BONNIE BANKS OF LOCH LOMOND

"Oh Etta, I can't believe it! We're here on the famous bonnie, bonnie banks." Dorotea Rosa Pepe – Dora to her friends – clasped her plump hands together and peered from beneath her pepper fringe at the boatyard in front of her.

"You've already said that at least a hundred times since we set off yesterday." Concetta Natale Passolina, known simply as Etta, was just as rotund as her friend, but her hair was a vibrant red. As she cast her green eyes around her, she affected an indifference she didn't really feel, but she didn't manage to sound as offhand as she wanted. On the contrary, the tone of her voice was rather indulgent, at least to the trained ears of her two companions. The day was beautiful, the scenery even more so, and their first two days on the West Highland Way had been much better than she had feared.

"I'm almost tempted to climb all the way back to Conic Hill just to enjoy the sight of the loch from up there again," Dora continued, enraptured at the recollection of their stunning first sighting of Loch Lomond the day before when they had arrived in Drymen.

There was no way the third member of the trio was going to agree to that idea, no way at all. Napoleon – Leon to his friends –

was the brave Basset Hound who had adopted the two Italian ladies one year earlier, having found them wandering lost and confused in a small but beautiful German town called Rothenburg. Or at least, that was how Leon remembered it. The truth was rather more sinister – his former human had been the victim of a particularly nasty murder, and it had actually been the two friends – against Etta's better judgement – who had adopted him. Over the year they had all been together, Leon knew full well that he had won Etta's heart, despite her brusque manner. He also knew she had a little more common sense than his gentler biped, Dora, and so it was to Etta he appealed now.

He wasn't disappointed.

"Today is meant to be about rest, relaxation and enjoying the place before we set off on the rest of the walk. I have no intention of climbing all the way back up there. You're welcome to do so if you wish, but I'd save your energy for the days to come. You're no longer a… young woman." Etta was going to say a 50-year-old, but the thought of acknowledging that she too was 60-something – and a generous something at that – would hurt her more than her friend.

"You're absolutely right," said Dora, hiding her disappointment. "But oh! When I think of that view. It was stunning, wasn't it?" And she closed her dreamy slate-grey eyes to relive it in her mind: the long expanse of Loch Lomond embraced by hills, its green islands dotted one after the other as if they were a giant's stepping stones to the western shore. "I sent a few snapshots to Arturo – he was amazed. I wish he could have come along with us and enjoyed part of our trip; he's been working so hard, the poor lad."

Poor lad? Rascal, more like. I hope he isn't having wild parties in our house while we're away.

Etta decided to keep her fears to herself; Dora was far too attached to her hapless nephew to agree. As far as Etta was concerned, Arturo was determined never to do a single day's work in his life if it could be helped; in her opinion, he didn't have a responsible bone in his body, but Dora had insisted on leaving him the keys to their home in Castelmezzano – a house they shared to make the most of their meagre teachers' pensions – while they journeyed north to Scotland in their yolk-yellow Fiat 500. During their time away, fellow members of the Home Swap International Club that Dora had managed to talk Etta into joining would be coming and going from their house. And Dora had decided that Arturo could take care of the house in between visits so it would be ready to welcome the next group of guests. So far, so good – visitors from Prague and from Cambridge had been happy with both the house and the town, delighted to use Castelmezzano as a base from which to explore Southern Italy, despite this entailing an arduous drive along a narrow and winding, if spectacular, road. Etta had feared their guests might get bored in the remote mountain community after a couple of days, but apparently, the beautiful surroundings, the good food and the locals' hospitality (and curiosity) were more than enough to keep them amused.

As if reading Etta's mind, Dora spoke softly.

"The broom will be in full bloom and Castelmezzano will be filling up with tourists."

"We'll miss the Maggio this year," said Etta, thinking of the popular 'wedding of the trees'. Based in pagan lore, these rites celebrated a new agricultural season and propitiated Mother Nature to ensure the land would be fertile. Lasting for over a week and involving all the small villages around Castelmezzano, the Maggio was always a great occasion.

"This is so weird," said Dora. "When we were in Castelmezzano, we thought only of this long trip." She laughed, remembering the hours she and Etta had spent in their house, giving private lessons to students to augment their travel fund. "And you put up with Costanza's son too."

Costanza Di Vitello, the huge butcher's wife, had a bully of a son who was as strong as he was stupid. And the more aware he got of his intellectual limitations, the nastier he became. Until he met Etta, that was. The teacher's fierce green eyes that seemed to see right into his soul, her hair more fiery than the Devil's lair, and her sharp tongue had miraculously scared him into submission minutes into his first lesson.

"Don't remind me!" Etta retorted, shrugging.

"The point I'm making is that after all that planning, I never thought I would feel a little homesick while we were here."

"A second ago, you were beyond excited about being in Scotland…"

"But I am excited!" Dora looked at her companion with a smile. "I'm so very grateful to be here, but at the same time, I can't help thinking of what we're missing back home."

Etta looked at her without saying anything. Strong and pragmatic, she was always logical when it came to feelings, as if her nature could never understand the conflicts of the heart and soul.

"You know," Dora continued, "I believe travelling makes you more aware of the things you would otherwise ignore and take for granted. When you're away from home, you realise there are plenty of everyday things you care about."

Etta looked at her in amazement. Dora had a knack for expressing in words the hidden things bothering Etta which she couldn't put her finger on; she'd perceive them as 'annoying' or 'disturbing'. While her own judgement seemed to be shrouded in mist, Dora in a few simple sentences had clarified exactly what had been in the back of her mind for days.

Yes, she was happy – make that proud that they, two ultra-sexagenarian women and one Basset Hound, had made it all the way from Southern Italy to Scotland. That was an achievement, especially when friends back home – even her daughter Maddalena – had insisted that the best a retired teacher could hope for from life was babysitting their grandchildren. And Etta would have been happy to oblige, except her only grandson lived in Granada. Now she realised that, after forty plus years as a teacher and almost as many as a single mother, she deserved to celebrate her freedom.

Meeting Dora had been a game changer. But it was also true that now, before the vast expanse of Loch Lomond, Etta missed home. At least a *wee* bit, as their homeswapper friend in Edinburgh would say. Dora was right: nostalgia and wanderlust could walk hand in hand.

Her inner ruminations came to an abrupt halt as movement in the water caught her eye.

"Nessie?" she murmured. "But she has nothing to do with Loch Lomond, does she?" Etta asked more loudly. "She's based in Loch Ness, isn't she?"

"Of course, which is why she's called the Loch Ness Monster," replied Dora. "Why do you ask?"

Etta pointed ahead of them towards the loch. Dora squinted her eyes. Leon leaned forward, his four short legs tensed, the tip of his nose aligned with the rest of his long body as he followed his biped's finger. Then he barked loudly – so obstreperously that his front legs bounced off the ground and his ears flapped up and down.

"Oh my goodness," Dora cried. "Is someone taking a swim?"

"Blow me down! Why would anyone bathe in these cold waters? We're not on a Greek island." Etta was baffled. The day before, she had dared to dip her hot, sweaty feet in the waters of the loch, only to remove them almost immediately.

Now the tiny figure in the loch looked like it was waving its arms. Did the swimmer need help? Etta realised it was time for action, not speculation.

"There!" she cried, hurrying towards the pier. "There are some boats and people." Shouting to attract the attention of the people, she raced down the path, Leon and Dora right behind her. In fact, Leon soon overtook her and ploughed into the legs of a group of walkers.

"What the heck?" cried one of the walkers, regaining his balance. "Watch out, you stupid mutt."

"You should keep him on a leash," a female walker reproached the two women.

"Someone is drowning, we must help," Etta explained frantically.

"We don't have time," the female walker said disdainfully and moved on.

"But someone is dying," Dora cried.

"Well, they're stupid for putting their life at risk," said the man, following his companion. "If you can't swim, keep away from the water!"

At the head of the group was a lanky young man. Upon hearing the barks and Etta and Dora's shrill pleas for help, he looked at the water, then turned towards a little rowing boat on the shore. One by one, his companions overtook him and continued on their walk. Snatching a lifebuoy from a larger vessel moored nearby, he joined the two women and one Basset Hound and threw it into the rowing boat. The three bipeds then pushed the boat towards the water.

Etta stood petrified on the bonnie, bonnie banks. The boat danced and rolled on the water, which all of a sudden appeared rough and dark. Dora, amazingly, didn't hesitate; she jumped into the boat. Well, she didn't exactly jump, but more clambered, helped by the lad.

The boat left the shore, the lanky young man doing a commendable job of controlling the oars, while Etta and Leon ran to the jetty for a better view. When the rescue party reached the swimmer, the young man launched the lifebuoy, then – despite the instability of the small boat – leaned over the edge to pull the victim to safety.

3

AN UNUSUAL RESCUE TEAM

E verything on the loch was still. On board the boat, Dora sat like a statue while the young man leaned over the side, maybe trying to explain to the incautious swimmer what he was going to do. It took two attempts, but eventually the swimmer was hauled to safety in the boat. Watching from the jetty, Etta saw Dora giving the swimmer her jacket, and as the boat got closer to the shore again, she realised her friend was massaging the swimmer to warm them up.

As she and Leon jogged back to the shore, Etta rummaged in her rucksack to find her thermos of hot coffee, stopping only briefly to tell a passer-by what was going on. He said he'd alert the loch rescue team, and then they both carried on their way.

Finally, woman and hound arrived on the shore. Getting the shocked and disorientated swimmer from the boat and on to dry land was almost as difficult as it had been to get them on board in the first place. It was only when they had both feet placed firmly on solid ground that Etta realised the swimmer was a she.

"The loch rescue team is on its way." The helpful passer-by had returned. "They can perform first aid, then transport her to Luss for medical attention."

"How are you doing, dear?" said Dora, still massaging the young swimmer's arms vigorously.

"I'm so lucky you saw me," she replied in broken English.

"It's good you're wearing your wetsuit."

"I had a cramp at the back of my thigh," the swimmer explained. "At first, I thought I'd manage, but then a current took me further into the open water and I panicked."

"You should never go swimming alone," the passer-by said sternly. "Always have a pal with you."

The lanky young man was more gentle with the swimmer. "At least you're now speaking words that make sense and your lips are a better colour," he said cheerfully after the woman had taken a few long sips from Etta's thermos. "You'll be okay. Tell me, where do you come from?"

When she announced she was Croatian, the passer-by couldn't help butting in with more well-meant but stern advice. "Scottish lochs are not the Mediterranean! You should take them more seriously."

"I was stupid," the woman admitted. "I have swum every morning since I arrived and each time I felt more confident."

"Don't worry," the young man encouraged her. "We all make mistakes – and that's the rescue boat coming. Thank you, sir, for calling them." Smiling at the passer-by, he then turned to Etta and Dora. "And thank you too, ladies."

"And thank *you* for not wasting any time before springing into action," said Dora, smiling. "You and your friends seemed to be in a hurry, so I'm so glad you stopped, unlike those other folks. At my age, I couldn't row as fast as you did."

"No hurry… we were just on a hike." But the young man looked uncomfortable and Etta wondered if he was speaking the whole truth.

Leon barked twice in the direction of the lanky young man, who flushed. He clearly realised it was the Basset's way of saying, "Well done, young chap!"

"Do you really think I need the rescue team?" asked the

shivering swimmer. "I could simply go and warm up in my room…"

"No!" said the lanky man, sudden authority in his voice. "Hypothermia should never be taken lightly."

And a few moments later, the team arrived. After a quick check up and a few questions for the swimmer, they then got an account from Dora, Etta, and the young man, interspersed with some intelligently placed barks from Leon, of exactly what had occurred. Finally, they guided the Croatian swimmer on board their sleek launch, which cut through the water towards the Western shore.

When the rescue launch was no more than a distant speck on the loch, Etta turned to look at her two human companions, particularly at the large wet patches on their clothes from their contact with the swimmer. "I'd say you'd both better come back to the hotel and warm up before you catch a cold."

"I'm afraid… ahem… I am in a bit of a hurry," said the lanky man, grabbing the rucksack he'd left on the ground before running to rescue the swimmer. But the confused expression on his face contradicted his words. The two women and one dog looked up at him expectantly. He turned to walk away, only to stop after a couple of steps.

"Oh, why bother?" he muttered. "I'll come last anyway, I always do. I don't think I stand a chance." Looking at the two women and raising the volume of his words a little, he asked, "Is your hotel this one here, or are you staying at the Lodges?"

"The Lodges; they don't accept pets at the Pier Hotel," Etta replied resentfully. After a lifetime of dismissing pets as useless creatures who peed all over everything, including the morons who loved them, and despising any public place that allowed them in, Etta had abided by equally strong but completely opposite views since the Basset Hound had joined the family: any place that *didn't* welcome dogs, particularly *her* dog, was simply unworthy of her patronage.

"Gosh, we just checked out of our rooms at the Lodges, but I'll come back with you. I'm Robert, by the way."

"I'm Dora, and this is my friend, Etta."

They shook hands.

"And who's this valiant fellow?" asked Robert, tickling Leon behind the ears.

"He's Napoleon, more commonly known as Leon," said Dora.

"A fitting name for such a proud dog," Robert commented as Leon's breast swelled with more air than it could possibly accommodate. Leon loved introductions – they were among the few times he heard his name in its imposing entirety.

"Are you walking the West Highland Way?" Etta asked Robert.

"I am."

"And you wanted to reach Rowardennan today?"

"Exactly. How about you?"

"We arrived in Drymen yesterday, but our Scottish friends had offered us an extra night in Balmaha to enjoy the area at a more leisurely pace."

"That sounds such a good idea. You don't want to be in too much of a hurry, otherwise it's like being caught up in the rat race even on holiday."

"I'm curious to see Tom Weir's statue and the gardens around it," said Dora.

"What a man," said Robert. "A keen walker and explorer, and friendly and personable too. He did so much to help us Scots realise how beautiful our country is."

"I've watched a few of his TV programmes on the internet and he was a delightful man," said Dora. Etta rolled her eyes; she had no idea who Tom Weir was and she felt left out of the conversation.

They arrived at the series of lodges just a little higher up the road and stopped to take in the view. Then Dora went to change, while Robert, obviously too shy to accept the offer of using the women's lodge, went to the public toilets to put on some dry clothes from his rucksack. As the sun was warm and pleasant, they decided to take their lunch outside when he returned.

"I thought after our cooked breakfast, I wouldn't be able to eat lunch," confessed Etta, biting into a prawn and mayo sandwich with gusto. "But this is delicious." Robert ate like a starving man, while Leon discovered just how much he loved prawns too.

"Where's home to you ladies?" Robert asked them between one huge bite and the next.

"We come from Southern Italy," explained Etta.

"Did you fly here?" asked Robert, looking at Leon and clearly wondering how they'd managed on an aeroplane with a Basset Hound, even one as noble and intelligent as he.

"Oh no, we'd never take a plane with Leon or he would have to travel with the luggage," said Dora.

"We'd never take a plane full stop. Not for pleasure, at least," added Etta, imagining herself taking business trips to the US or Australia one day and having to overcome her phobia of being airborne. Now Dora had added a new fear to her old one: having her Leon tossed around in the cargo hold. "We drove!"

"Wow! It must have taken some time."

"We had a few stops on the way…"

"And we will have more going back."

"We're travelling through Europe."

"You must be very rich," said Robert, grinning impishly.

"Not likely!" said Dora. "We do home swaps."

"And drive a little Fiat 500, which is so much more economical than a large car."

"Home swaps?" Robert looked baffled.

"Yes – we invite guests to stay at our house in Italy, while we travel to wherever they live and stay at their place."

"You're swapping with someone from the Lodge?"

"Not exactly," explained Etta. "Our homeswapper hosts in

Edinburgh had a gift card for a stay here and they were kind enough to pass it on to us."

"So after a week in their Edinburgh home…"

"…my dear friend suggested we should not simply enjoy a comfy stay in Loch Lomond before our second Scottish home swap in the western islands, but go on a crazy adventure along the West Highland Way…"

"We've been walking a lot in preparation…"

"…as if driving all through Europe isn't adventurous enough for us," concluded Etta as if Dora hadn't spoken.

"You're two brave women," said Robert, his voice full of admiration. Leon barked in protest. Wasn't the man forgetting someone? Robert laughed. "Of course, having such a valiant dog by your side ensures your safety."

Appeased, Leon sat in front of him and Robert patted his back as if he really was a superhero. Overall, Etta observed wryly, Leon had decided he liked this chap.

"And what has brought you on the West Highland Way?" Dora asked Robert.

"Well," said Robert, inclining his head and rubbing his hands over his thighs as if uncomfortable about what he was going to say, "I'm on a kind of treasure hunt."

"Oh my goodness!" cried Dora, clasping her hands in excitement.

All sorts of childish things hold power over her – when will she ever grow up? Etta, as usual, was more down-to-earth.

"What kind of treasure are you hunting for?"

"We have to solve riddles each day in order to find daily 'treasure' – the first one to the treasure gets the highest number of points, and the one with the most points in total by the time we reach Fort William will win a… rather rich… ahem…" Robert blushed so red, Etta wondered if the cook had drizzled hot chilli into his dessert instead of raspberry syrup "…inheritance and… ahem… Tilda Island in the Outer Hebrides, along with its castle."

"A whole island and a castle?" Dora was now so enchanted, Etta feared her friend might start levitating at any moment.

"I've never heard of it," she said bluntly – her way of countering Dora's excitement.

"At the moment, it's private property and access is forbidden to the public," Robert explained. "A pity as it's a beautiful place. I'd love whoever wins it to allow public visits; it'd be a shame to keep the place for the enjoyment of a single person."

"And are those people we asked for help all part of your group?"

"They are, yes: distant cousins and other relatives..."

"They will have a massive head start over you by now."

"I know, but at the same time, I don't mind. Well, I do and I don't..."

"You don't care about your inheritance?" Etta looked at him in surprise. From the way he was dressed, she didn't think he was very well-off. How could he not care?

"The thing is, I'm no good at this kind of thing. I mean, I've never done well in any form of competition..."

"How can that be true? You were fast enough to spring into action and rescue that girl earlier on."

Dora sent Etta a look of approval. And why not? She had just made a good point.

If possible, the guy's blush became even deeper than it had been before.

"That was an emergency and I had to help. But ever since I was a child, I've never come first in any kind of competition..."

"Is it just sports you don't excel in?"

"No, not only sports. I didn't do well in any subject at school, even the ones I enjoyed. I'm just not a very ambitious guy as I never really cared about coming first... until now. In this competition, I do care, but a part of me knows it's impossible. I'll get there after all the others, especially as they're all so motivated and determined."

Etta and Dora exchanged a glance. After years of teaching

hundreds of pupils, they knew exactly what the other woman was thinking. There were students ready to lie and cheat to get the best marks ever; there were those who would spend hours and hours studying to impress their teachers and schoolmates; and then there were the talented but insecure ones who could excel, if only they'd just apply themselves. Instead, no matter how much they knew, they'd self-sabotage. They simply couldn't cope with the pressure of competition.

If Etta were a doctor, she would have prescribed a good dose of 'trust-in-yourself' for Robert, to be taken every morning. But she was not a doctor, and anyway, that medicine had not been invented yet.

"How have you scored so far?" Dora asked eagerly.

"Poorly; the others are too determined to win and I can't compete with that."

"But surely it's important to get a high score from the outset," insisted Etta.

"Not necessarily. The solicitor said that not all days are rated equally, I guess because some will be harder than others. These first two days have been relatively easy. We arrived at the treasure pretty much at the same time and the others were pushing and shoving. I just let them go ahead and take the treasure before me."

Etta felt like banging her forehead with her hand, but a glare from Dora told her to contain herself.

"If you're supposed to reach Rowardennan today, hadn't you better make a start?" she said instead.

"Actually, we were supposed to stay in Balmaha tonight, but we all woke up, got the daily clue and set off from our Drymen hotel so early, we'd already solved it and found today's treasure before we reached Balmaha. When two of my companions saw another couple in our group sneak from this very hotel, which was where we were supposed to stay overnight, we enquired at reception and found out they'd decided to check out and go directly to Rowardennan, our next stop. They'd asked if the concierge had their daily clue, which he did, and then left. Of course, we all felt obliged to do the same."

"I see," said Etta. "The one with the strongest legs will win the race. They might even decide not to stop in Rowardennan, but carry on further still."

"Yes, if they find the treasure and get given the next clue," said Robert with at least a ton of resignation in his voice.

"And what's the clue the concierge gave you?" Dora asked, eaten up by curiosity.

The young man produced a white envelope held closed by a large ruby seal. He looked at his watch.

"It's almost time. The concierge told us we could take the letter in advance, but not to open it until 2pm."

"Who would know?" asked Etta.

"We were told there would be people along the route, making sure we didn't break the rules. It's not worth the risk of being eliminated; it's only a matter of waiting a few more minutes."

"What if those other people reach Rowardennan and the treasure is hidden close to Balmaha? They will have to walk all the way back."

"The first treasure was in Drymen, our first stop, and the second was here in Balmaha. So we all assumed the third would be near Rowardennan."

"But what if it isn't?"

"That's what I told them, but once you see your competitors getting ahead of you, it doesn't leave much room for reasoning."

"What's that you were saying about a rat race?" asked Etta, shaking her head in disapproval. Robert, his eyes glued to the floor, nodded as if he had just been found guilty of a heinous crime.

From indoors, they heard the solemn chimes of a grandfather clock. One. Two. It was finally time to open the clue.

4

CLUES AND COOS

"Now, let's look at your clue," said Dora as eagerly as a child waiting to open a Christmas gift.

"Yes, it's time." Robert, clearly less impatient than Dora, read it silently, his lips moving. Then he smiled.

"Well?" asked Dora.

He read it again, this time aloud. "Never assume you can take matters into your own hands. You'll get your clue tomorrow morning, after a good rest in Balmaha; I'm sure you will enjoy the view and the lodge. That is, unless you proved yourself to be of a caring disposition."

The three looked at each other uncertainly, then Etta started to laugh.

"This means your friends, who by now will be well on the way to Rowardennan, will have to come all the way back here."

"I wonder how far they've got," said Dora.

"Not too far, but still a good two hours' walk," replied Robert.

Etta winked at him. "Which makes a total of four hours' unnecessary walking."

"I'd better tell the concierge that I will keep my lodge for the night. Hopefully they haven't let it out yet." He got up, but before leaving, he turned back to the two women and added, "Should I tell them that the others will be coming back, so they'd better keep their rooms free too?" Then he answered his own question. "Yes, I'd better do that."

"He's too generous, he will never win the challenge," said Etta. "The others wouldn't have bothered about him and his room."

"Never say never, Etta," Dora reproached her. "Kind behaviour always gets its rewards…"

"Sure, in fairy tales."

"Oh, come on, Etta, stop always trying to be the hard woman when I know full well you're as soft as a piece of bread and butter."

Etta was stunned. She'd believed her cover to be impenetrable, but she had no time to wonder what had given her away before Robert came back in a mood of great excitement.

"Good news?" Dora asked.

"Very. The receptionist said he never actually cancelled any of the bookings as Sir Angus's solicitor gave him precise instructions not to do so. Sir Angus left Law, Lorr and Morlore enough money to pay for all the rooms for tonight, no matter what we decided to do."

"That's not good news," snapped Etta. "I for one would have enjoyed seeing those uncaring people having to sleep under the stars for the night."

Dora frowned at her friend's vindictiveness.

"Well," said Robert, "to tell you the truth, that's not the only good news." He waved another letter sealed with wax under their noses. "Mr Morlore from Law, Lorr and Morlore was at reception, too, and he said he'd seen me helping the swimmer. As I was the only one to stop and help, I've got my clue early."

"Wow!" said Etta, avoiding Dora's gaze. She knew full well there would be a wide 'what-did-I-you-tell-you?' grin on her friend's face. But she couldn't block out Dora's voice.

"Your ancestor Sir Angus must have been an extremely good person," Dora rejoiced. "Goodness always wins in the end."

"I'm not sure about that," replied Robert. "Rumour has it that he was rather a hard man."

"I wonder how he knew something dreadful – like a young woman struggling against the current in the loch and needing our help – was going to happen," said Etta, pushing her large red-framed glasses up her nose, a sure sign her grey cells were running with various hypotheses.

"So, open it!" Dora, on the other hand, only had eyes for the next clue.

"Woof, woof, WOOF!" Leon had not troubled himself to follow the whole boring human discussion, but the excited tone of his gentler biped's voice told him that adventure might now be coming his way. As always, the bipeds had to be encouraged into action or they'd stay chatting and procrastinating all day long. Despite being a short-legged Basset, he was used to long walks. More importantly, he was determined to live life to the full... between a nap and a meal, that is.

"I can only assume the 'drowning swimmer' was a fake," said Etta, but her eyes, just like Dora's, were glued to Robert's hands as he broke the seal on the envelope and unfolded the paper from inside.

"Dig close to the red bull on the cow woman," he read.

"And?" asked Etta.

"That's it."

"Really?"

"Really." Robert had his eyes on the piece of paper. "This is rather cryptic; the previous clues were wordier and easier to interpret."

"The red bull? There must be thousands and thousands of them in Scotland..."

"Maybe on your walk to Rowardennan," suggested Dora, "you will find one close to the path and the message will become clearer."

"Maybe." Robert nodded slowly. "But at the same time, I'd feel more confident if I understood the thing before hitting the road."

"Shall we ask the people in the hotel if they know of any red bull of note? The message has to refer to a famous one."

"The clue also refers to the cow woman. What is a cow woman?"

"Maybe a woman who attends to the cows or heals them," said Robert, thoughtfully. "Here in Scotland, we used to have healers for the animals when there was no vet or it was too expensive to call for one..."

"You mean a witch doctor?" Dora loved local legends.

"Yes, sort of – a witch with a deep knowledge of nature, herbs and animal life."

"There's no such thing as witches," said Etta stubbornly. But the other two were too busy talking to pay her any heed.

"Let's ask at reception," said Dora. Robert smiled, clearly happy to have company in his quest. Etta guessed he probably wouldn't have dared to ask questions on his own.

But neither the receptionist, nor the hotel owner, nor the restaurant manager, nor even the 'wee lassie', as Robert called her, who had served at their table and was from Rowardennan, had a clue. Dora opened her guidebook, went through the section dedicated to the West Highland Way, but she couldn't find any reference to either a cow woman or a red bull.

"Shall we go back to the pier and ask there? Maybe the fishermen will know."

"Why would a fisherman know about cows and bulls?" protested Etta, rounding on her friend. She tended to get grumpy when she couldn't find a key to a puzzle. "Better to ask a farmer!"

"Any locals will do," said Dora, well used to Etta's mood swings. "The important thing is to do *something* other than just sitting here."

"Woof," agreed Leon.

"Thank you, all three of you," said Robert, winking at the hound. "I will take my rucksack with me. If we find nothing, then I'll be on my way to Rowardennan. Now that I have the clue, I may as well get started and not lose my advantage. As you said, the significance of those words might become clearer on the walk."

"That's clever thinking," said Dora, smiling as if she could already see a transformation in the good lad. "I'm sure you'll get there."

They left the hotel and headed back to the pier for the simple reason that the local folks seemed to congregate there, as if it were a public square. Surely someone would know the secret of the red bull and the cow woman.

5

CROSSING LOCH LOMOND

Despite asking everyone in sight, the three humans and one dog discovered nothing that would be of any help whatsoever. It seemed no one had ever heard of a cow woman, and while there were many cows – or 'coos' as the locals called them – and an abundance of red bulls nearby, as in the whole of Scotland, there was definitely not one that stood out.

Just as Etta was about to launch into a grumble at being thwarted so, a horn from the water announced the arrival of the Loch Lomond ferry. Instead of paying attention to Robert, who was taking his leave to make his way to Rowardennan, Dora had her eyes glued on the boat and the loch beyond.

"Oh, Etta, wouldn't it be a dream to have a ride on the boat? It's such a splendid day and we have plenty of free time this afternoon."

Etta looked around critically, evaluating the proposal. "As long as we're back in time for me to make full use of the Jacuzzi bath in our lodge. I doubt the rest of the accommodation along the way will provide this level of luxury." Her greatest fear on this holiday had been that she and her two companions would end up sharing dormitories in lousy youth hostels with a crowd of smelly hikers, but Dora had promised they'd always sleep in a clean and warm B&B at the very least. And Dora wasn't one for breaking her promises.

Robert tried to get a word in edgeways. "I need to leave if I'm to look for clues along the way..."

"Do you think this boat will go all the way to the far side of Loch Lomond?" Dora asked him.

"No, just to Inchcailloch," he explained.

"And what's Inchcailloch?" she asked, reading what was written on an information board on the pier.

"Och, that lump of green forest floating in front of you," Robert explained, indicating the island just ahead of them. "You can have a nice wee walk there, but take some water and a snack as I don't think there's any services on the island. So, enjoy the rest of your tour, as I'd better go..." but Dora was now too busy reading a second board dedicated to Inchcailloch and describing what to do on the island to pay him any attention. Leon wagged his tail at the young man as if to apologise for his biped's uncharacteristic lack of manners. And Etta for once decided to be a bit more Dora-ish in her friend's... absence.

"It's been a pleasure to meet you, Robert. We really wish you good luck. Remember to trust in yourself and not to think others are superior to you; they're simply better at pretending."

Robert sent her a shy smile, and then turned to go. "Bye, take care," he called over his shoulder.

"Maybe we will meet along the road," said Etta, nudging Dora with her elbow to encourage her at least to say farewell to the young man. But it was hopeless. Dora was entranced by the map and description of the island.

Robert left without his farewell.

Leon sighed with resignation.

Etta decided their pace along the West Highland Way was likely to be so slow, not only would they not meet the lad again, they'd be lucky to end their walk before they turned 99.

Dora was glowing with a sense of wonder when she finally turned around.

"Where's Robert?" she asked.

"He's gone. He left five minutes ago. Whatever parallel universe were you in just now?"

"He went without saying goodbye?" Dora was horrified. Etta and Leon looked at each other in despair.

"The poor lad did his best to attract your attention, but it seemed you were already on Inchall-whatever-island."

"But he should come with us! He *has* to come to Inchcailloch because that's where the *cow woman* is."

"*What?*"

Dora pointed to the small print at the bottom of the detailed information board. "*The name Inchcailloch might mean the Island of the Cowled Woman,*" she read out loud. "The clue has nothing to do with cows; I think it means this."

"How about the red bull?"

"Not sure about that one, but he too must be on the island."

"It doesn't make sense, but at the same time, it does…"

"Are you coming, ladies?" said the ferry Captain as he helped the last of the other passengers onboard.

"Of course we are," said Etta, trying to see how far Robert had gone. "But when is the next boat?"

"That's tomorrow, madam. This is the last boat today."

"Oh no! Please wait – one passenger is missing. Dora, you prevent the boat from leaving while I fetch Robert."

As Etta left, followed at speed by an unusually athletic Basset, the Captain spoke to Dora.

"It's time for the boat to depart, I'm afraid," he told her.

"I do understand. But the thing is… do you know who my friend is going to fetch?"

"I've no idea," said the man, readying the boat to leave and loosening the rope keeping it close to the pier.

"If you look up there, you might see him. He's the heir to an entire island in the Outer Hebrides and it's essential he gets on this boat. This might mean…" and she kept on chatting to the man as only Dora could, telling him all about the challenge and the other competitors.

"Unlike the others, Robert will share his beautiful inheritance with the community and open it up to visitors," Dora concluded with conviction born of desperation. The Captain stood there, partly enchanted, partly terrified. Was this woman before him in her right mind? For the first time in his illustrious career spanning almost 40 years, he was wondering if he could actually leave five or even ten minutes late. After all, what was more important? The passengers on board or an island for the entire nation to enjoy?

From the boat, a couple of passengers demanded to know what was happening, what the hold-up was. Snapping out of his reverie, the Captain confirmed they were about to leave.

"There!" cried Dora. "There they are!" and she pointed to the trio hurrying on to the pier in long strides, two on two legs and one on four.

"We can't keep the passengers waiting…"

But one of the people who had complained took one look at Dora's worried face and said, "Well, Captain, we've waited this long, we can wait a bit longer. It'll be our good deed for the day."

"Oh, thank you so much! If the world is still able to stop for an old woman like me, then it's not as bad as the news keeps telling us."

Captain and passengers exchanged a quizzical look, but Dora had somehow taken them all under her spell.

Leon arrived first in his proudest trot, doing his best to look like a seriously athletic hound rather than a short-legged comedian. The other two followed, with Robert helping an exhausted Etta to jump onboard to applause from all the passengers. Finally, the boat left, rolling placidly on Loch Lomond's shining waters. Etta wondered why the very waters that had looked so scary hours earlier now looked so inviting.

"That's His Majesty, Ben Lomond," said Robert, indicating a cone-shaped mountain towards the northern end of the loch.

"He's number 182 in terms of height among the Munros of Scotland, but in terms of prominence, he comes in at about 20th..."

"There must be an awesome view from up there," Dora said.

"You and your views, Miss Dorotea Rosa Pepe. I'd say it's time to read up about the island; I've asked the Captain, but he says there's no bull there, red or otherwise. But it could be a painting in St Kentigerna's Church."

"That's a good hypothesis," said a loud, throaty voice.

"Mrs van Wetering!" cried Robert, turning in surprise. "You're on the boat to the island, too. So smart of you."

The woman looked a little confused at his words. "I decided not to go to Rowardennan today," she explained, "just in case the clue wasn't there and I had to walk back. Because of my weak heart, I have to preserve the little energy I have. And as an anthropologist, I was curious to visit Inchcailloch to study the history of local communities there. Correct me if I'm wrong, Robert, but do you know something about the challenge that I don't?"

Robert's grey-blue eyes rested on the woman as if he were evaluating her. Etta tried to shush him, but Dora nudged her in the stomach with her elbow.

Etta harrumphed. *There they go again, the trusting and the gullible ignoring my advice and talking their way into trouble,* she grumbled inwardly. *Well, this time, I wash my hands of them.*

"Och, Mrs van Wetering," said Robert, his Scottish accent thickening as he blushed shyly, "I don't mind sharing ma wee secret with ye. Mr Morlore gave me the next clue in advance, in return for me helping out during a wee accident in the morning..."

"If we combine our efforts, we'd stand more chance of winning," Mrs van Wetering interrupted. "Thanks to my studies in anthropology, I know a lot of history, and I'm sure I can help you interpret clues and signs and complement your skills."

You're willing to help while he holds the all-important clue, thought Etta cynically. *I'm sure you'd be of a different mind if you had the clue.* She eyed the woman suspiciously, but again kept her sulky thoughts to herself.

Robert handed Mrs van Wetering the paper on which the clue was written.

"We thought the *cow woman* might be a play on words, meaning the island itself…"

"Isle of the Cowled Woman, I see."

Etta rolled her eyes. *How very clever!*

"But how about the red bull?" Mrs van Wetering asked.

Don't you worry, I'm sure Robert will let you know that part as soon as we discover it. Thanks for the insightful contribution.

"We think it might be a painted or sculpted animal on the church ruins…"

"That's a clever idea, and I can help you look for it."

It didn't take long for the boat to get to Inchcailloch. It followed the tree-lined shore for a short while until the pier came into view. The Captain guided the ferry on to the pier and secured it there.

"Please don't miss the boat in two hours, it's the last one back to Balmaha today," he said as the group of four people and one dog left with the other passengers.

6

INCHCAILLOCH ISLAND

E tta decided to ignore Dora's usual enthusiastic comments as they landed. The pier, which seemed far too long and precarious for Etta's liking, was to her friend the most romantic thing ever. Having managed to prevent Dora from wasting five minutes in hand-clasping ecstasy, Etta was frustrated once on solid land not to be able to find any signs for St Kentigerna's Church. Mrs van Wetering suggested they follow the ones for the burial ground instead, but not even this good idea could impress the sceptical Etta.

Dora unleashed Leon as there weren't too many people about other than the boat passengers, who had become good friends with the Basset during the short crossing. He was happy, running among oaks and yew trees on the path, sniffing long fern leaves still damp with dew, and smelling moss, earth and good things. When the forest thinned out and the ferns gave way to a cheerful purple carpet of bluebells, there was no stopping Dora from clasping her hands in delight. For once, even Etta stopped in admiration. Robert took some pictures – it was indeed a beautiful sight. Only Mrs van Wetering seemed unmoved.

Maybe she'd be more excited by a field of bones and skulls, thought Etta, inwardly confirming that the woman was not to be trusted. However, Mrs van Wetering's reaction did help bring the pragmatic Etta back to the task at hand.

"We'd better hurry up or we won't have enough time to explore properly."

Leon was happy to discover more, but with the exception of the Dutchwoman, the others were reluctant to leave the beautiful forest. In the end, though, they recognised the truth in Etta's words.

It didn't take long to get to the church, but to Etta's dismay, there was not much to explore. She had imagined at least a few vertical ruins, but instead they had to search in the grass for what was left of the walls.

"How about the churchyard?" asked Dora, looking at the enclosed area to the side of the ruins. "Maybe the red bull is on one of the gravestones."

"That's a brilliant idea," said Mrs van Wetering in approval.

And once more, you've proved yourself to be indispensable, thought Etta sarcastically. What other options did they have?

They moved on. There were a number of gravestones on which they could still read the inscriptions, the names MacFarlane and MacGregor being the most common. On some stones, beside the name and date, they could also make out a drawing. One looked like a bird and a cup; another depicted a skull with some bones beneath and the words '*Memento Mori*'.

"This must be heaven for you," said Etta to Mrs van Wetering, indicating the information boards by the graves. The woman joined her and, from her attentive expression, Etta guessed she had piqued her interest. She took in all details, whispered a few words; Etta wondered if she'd really share her observations with them or take advantage of Robert's trust. The woman looked around as if searching for something, then moved towards a larger board in the shade of a mature oak tree. Etta pretended to be absorbed in searching the churchyard, but she didn't leave Mrs van Wetering's side for a second.

Leon was having a great time among the gravestones, the only pity being that his two bipeds were strongly opposed to him peeing on them. Surely these splendid vertical objects were an open invitation to any dog to leave their worthy mark. But he was an educated quadruped, used to humans' weird requests. He complied, but his spirit remained critical.

"Here!" cried Mrs van Wetering unexpectedly. "I think I might have found it."

Dora and Robert rushed towards her from different directions; Etta, of course, was already at the Dutchwoman's side. Dora's eyes were shining; if anything, she looked more excited than Robert.

The information boards Wilfrida van Wetering had been reading were very detailed. One told them about the former church, the other about the gravestones.

"See here. It describes the Mitchell family enclosure – it must be that way," and Wilfrida van Wetering pointed in the direction Robert had come from. "They secured their piece of land in 1778, and the last burial dates back to 1933. The picture on each gravestone indicates the job of the deceased: a sheep for a shepherd; metal tools for a wright…"

"A bull!" cried Robert, his eyes jumping to the next drawing.

"Indeed, a bull for a farmer or a livestock trader."

"It won't be red, though," said Etta. The colour of all the gravestones was somewhere between grey and beige.

"This whole group of gravestones, except one which is white, is in red sandstone," said Mrs van Wetering, reading the text written on the board.

"Let's go and see!"

And there, in the small enclosure, they saw exactly what the panel had promised. The bull carved into the gravestone had not been erased by the passage of time and was easy to identify.

"The red bull on the cowled woman's island," said Robert.

Beside the slab, they could see that the ground looked freshly turned; Robert only had to dig a little way before he came across a collection of plastic folders. He picked up the first one and handed it to Mrs van Wetering, then picked up number two for himself.

"No, son," Mrs van Wetering said as he buried the rest of the treasure for the other competitors to find. "If it hadn't been for your willingness to share, I would never have found this out. One is yours, and I'll be happy with number two."

"Robert, you'll be doing quite well after this one," observed Dora.

"Och aye, it was just a bit of luck," he said, flushing as he did every time he was the centre of attention.

"We've still got a good hour before the boat's due," said Dora. "Shall we explore the island?"

"I hope you won't mind," said Wilfrida van Wetering, "but I'll take a rest on the beach near the pier. My stupid heart says it's better for me to preserve my strength for tomorrow."

The other three agreed to meet her at the pier in time to catch the ferry, then set off with Leon for the island summit suspended in the middle of the loch, taking in the view. Between the other islands dotted around them, green tongues of land dipped their toes in the water. Up north, Loch Lomond seemed to be closed in between imposing mountains, the most majestic of them the dark shape of Ben Lomond.

"Well, we're not really in the middle of the loch," Etta couldn't help correcting the over-enthusiastic Dora. "But it's breathtaking all the same."

"There's the boat," said Robert, stopping everyone's transports of delight in their tracks as they wandered around the summit and marvelled at the view. Even Leon's nose was upturned, taking in a whole host of new scents on the breeze. "We'd better hurry up if we don't want to spend the night on the island."

"Goodness!" cried Etta, wondering how spooky the

graveyard surrounded by oak trees would seem under a full moon with the water moving darkly nearby.

Leon, recognising the urgency in Etta's voice, gave his signature trio of barks: "Woof, woof, WOOF!" indicating that Dora would do well to come out of her latest rapture. Standing with her hands clasped and eyes closed, letting the view sink in and adding to her ever increasing store of memories, was all very well, but there was a time and a place. And now was not the time.

"I've told you over and over," said Etta, shaking her friend, "use your camera! You can even make copies in case the memory card freezes. No back-up available yet for lost memories."

WHEN THEY ARRIVED BACK AT THE PIER, THE BOAT WAS THERE. MRS van Wetering had begged the Captain to wait for her friends, who she'd insisted would surely be along in a minute. The man was not impressed.

"It seems it's you three holding us up – *again*," he reproached them, but despite his gruff manner, a certain gleam in his eyes showed he had taken their tardiness in good humour. On this day, three errant tourists had taught him that five minutes early or five minutes late made no difference in the grand scheme of things.

"But we're much less late than we were earlier, so we're definitely improving," answered Etta, smiling in satisfaction even as she panted to get her breath back. Silly moments like this had the ability to make her feel young again.

"Well, if you're improving," said the Captain as he manoeuvred the boat away from the pier and towards Balmaha, "then I might risk extending an invitation for this evening…"

Etta's green eyes sparkled with feline curiosity that extended well beyond her huge red-framed glasses.

"There's a cèilidh in Luss tonight," and the Captain pointed to a white dot on the Western side of the loch. "A number of guests at the Lodge have asked me if I would take them there, but there's still room on board."

"A *kelly*?" asked Etta, not too sure how to pronounce the word.

"Oh," said Dora, "they are traditional dances with jigs and reels. Will there be bagpipes too?"

"Indoors, it's best to go for smaller Scottish pipes, as there'll also be drums, flutes, guitars, an accordion and, of course, a good fiddle."

"I can't dance!" Etta said defensively.

"Sure you can, after a few drams…"

"Or you can just watch," Robert explained. "But I'm sure you won't be able to resist the music, and we Scots are happy to teach and share our fun with visitors. Please say you'll come."

"There's the tartan bow-tie we bought in Edinburgh for Leon…"

"You packed that for the walk?"

"Well, as it doesn't take up much room, I felt it'd be a pity to leave it behind, just in case he had an occasion to wear it along the way."

"Dorotea Rosa Pepe, you think of everything!"

Leon, who'd been enjoying a nap in the warm rays of the sun, stood up on all fours. An evening out? Surely, he'd find some cute she-dog to charm, especially in his new bow-tie.

In fewer than 10 minutes, Balmaha Bay, with its many boats bobbing gently on its peaceful water, welcomed them. Kissed by the sun and more cheerful than ever, they disembarked.

"What time does the ferry leave for the… thingy dance?" Etta asked the Captain, determined not to miss her dip in the Jacuzzi.

"At 6.15 prompt from right here," he replied.

"I guess," said Etta, looking at Dora's dreamy expression, "you can count us in."

"Mrs Concetta Natale Passolina, you're such a good sport," said Dora, hugging her reluctant friend.

"You'd go anyway."

"But together, it will be more fun."

"Count me in too," said Mrs van Wetering. "No dancing for me, though; I'm exhausted. But I can't miss a chance to listen to some traditional Celtic music."

7

KILTS AND CÈILIDHS

Dora, Etta and Leon were sitting in the main reception building at the Lodge, waiting for Robert to join them while silently contemplating the view over the loch from a couple of armchairs.

"I think we should save our energy for tomorrow." A strangely accented female voice cut through the peace. Even though the speaker was clearly making an attempt not to be overheard, she was loud enough to push her point home.

"If Robert has decided to go, there must be a reason."

Curiosity got the better of Etta and she peered around the pilaster that hid her and Dora from the speakers. The man who had answered was dressed in a kilt, but like his companion, he did not sound Scottish at all.

"Why didn't he follow the rest of us to Rowardennan?" the man carried on. "What does he know that we don't? Why did he decide to stay put?"

"Because he's a simpleton."

"That's for sure. Still, he did stop to help that foolish swimmer, and I can't get it out of my mind that Sir Angus might have appreciated..."

"Sir Angus is no longer with us! And if only you'd had this hunch earlier, we could have stopped here, too."

"It was only when we opened that wretched letter that I realised we'd made a mistake. Anyway, you're free to stay here, but I won't miss another opportunity to get ahead in the game. Imagine if Robert knows that the next clue is to be found in Luss..."

"OK, I'll come along."

A voice spoke from the corridor. "It was kind of you, Lloyd and Olive, to alert me to your suspicions. I don't like dancing and folk music generally, but tonight I may make an exception to the rule."

"Mr Herrera?" cried the woman. "You overheard!"

"Well, you were... over speaking. And I didn't think it was polite to interrupt such an intense conversation."

"It might have been polite to have made us aware of your presence."

"Really? I'll leave the good manners to the English gentleman... and here he comes."

Still peeping around the edge of the pilaster, Etta saw a handsome man, who looked like he had some kind of Spanish or maybe South American heritage, pointing towards a tall, distinguished-looking figure walking towards the group accompanied by a young woman. Despite being described as English, the newcomer was also dressed in a kilt.

"Are you having a meeting?" the gentleman asked, his words clipped.

"Yes," replied the handsome man simply, the South American tinge to his accent confirming Etta's thoughts. He pointed towards the couple and added, "Lloyd and Olive were suggesting it might be a good idea to follow Robert to this cèilidh in Luss, in case he knows something we don't."

"We were going for dinner..."

"What if the clue is in Luss?" argued the young woman.

"Hmm," said the gentleman. "Dinner on the other side of the loch might not be such a bad idea."

"Apparently, there's a boat leaving soon," said the handsome man. "As you seem to be dressed up for the occasion, perhaps I should get one of those kilts for myself too. If a South African can wear one, why not an Argentinian?"

South African, of course, thought Etta, chastising herself for not recognising the couple's accent from the start.

"Lloyd has every right to celebrate my Scottish heritage," replied the woman called Olive, glaring at the man she had addressed as Mr Herrera. "He's married into Scottish ancestry. So, who's going to this cèilidh and who isn't?"

"I guess we're in," said the Englishman after a quick exchange of glances with the young woman beside him. At this point, Robert joined the group. On learning that the other treasure hunters had decided to accompany him to Luss, he asked whether they should not extend the invitation to the members of the party who were missing. Etta caught the name Grace and a mention of some sisters.

"Certainly not," said the South African man who Etta had heard Herrera call Lloyd.

"I'm sure," his wife explained, "the Hillock sisters will appreciate a good night's sleep at their age so they can start afresh in the morning. We've more treasure to hunt, remember."

"How very thoughtful of you," said the English gentleman.

"I'm moved," added Herrera. "But what about Grace? I'm sure she's young enough to dance the night away and still have plenty of energy for tomorrow."

"I'll go and ask her," said the young woman, leaving the English gentleman's side and heading out towards the lodges.

Robert turned around and spotted Etta, Dora and Leon, greeting them as they appeared from behind the pilaster. The South African woman raised her eyebrows, her horrified expression suggesting she was wondering just how many more people had been eavesdropping. She then dropped her eyes to

Leon, clearly recognising him as the dog who had nearly upended her husband earlier in the day at the same moment Etta realised she was the belligerent woman who had suggested they keep the Basset Hound on a leash. Etta smiled coldly at her while Robert made all the introductions, finishing with Sue MacDuff as the young woman returned.

"Grace is too tired to join us," she said. "She prefers to rest."

Five minutes later, they all arrived at the boat pier. There weren't many other people there yet, and the Captain recognised Etta and Dora.

"Uh-oh, you're on time! Maybe my little trick wasn't necessary after all."

"What trick?"

"The boat is leaving at 6.30, but I told you 6.15 to make sure you'd be on time. My passengers get impatient when it's dinner time."

Etta glared at him. She could have soaked a little longer in that delicious tub. But Dora was amused.

"It's such a splendid evening," she said, pointing towards the loch. They could still see the sun, but the shadows were getting denser in the long pre-sunset of northern Europe. The air was just lightly chilly, a little breeze tickling their faces.

"Tea or Gaelic coffee?" asked the Captain.

"Is that a special blend?" Dora asked. In response, he handed her a glass containing a measure – a dram – of amber liquid. Of course: Scotch whisky.

The boat passed the loch's islands one by one, the dots of land linking one shoreline to the other. As they got closer, a small group of houses, surrounded by hills, revealed itself: this was Luss. Once ashore, the party followed a row of pretty cottages with windows framed by roses, surrounded by low stone walls, finally reaching the Royal Arms Hall. This was a hotel and restaurant with a long history dating from the XVII century when it was an inn for coaches on their way to the Highlands.

Dora clasped her hands when she was shown in to the old-fashioned wooden library that was going to be their dining room this evening. With its fireplace, leather sofas and tartan curtains, it was a worthy addition to her internal hall of memories.

"Well, look who's here," said a harsh voice.

"I knew you lot were up to something," added a second in an equally unfriendly tone. Two impressively ugly women dressed in old-fashioned tweeds were sitting at a small table near the fireplace. Robert introduced them to Dora and Etta as Faith and Hope Hillock, sisters to each other – Etta had already guessed that – and distant relations to him.

"Of course, Faith and Hope are also competing in the treasure hunt…"

"You shouldn't tell everyone," Faith reproached him.

"You shouldn't tell *anyone*," Hope added.

"You never know who you're dealing with…"

"Nor who might be listening…"

"Young folks can't keep a secret…"

"He's bound to be posting all about it on that Facebook thing…"

The two voices droned on, one overlapping the other so seamlessly, Etta could hardly distinguish which sister spoke which words. Not that it would make any difference to the long catalogue of moans.

They must be Siamese twins, separated at birth but still sharing a single brain, despite each one apparently having her own head and body.

Dora could evidently read her friend's expression. She winked at Etta, whose glare softened just a little in response.

"How did you get here?" Amilcar Herrera enquired of the sisters.

"We asked the luggage man – what's his name? Adam? – to pick us up…"

"We couldn't miss a cèilidh in Luss…"

"Well, thanks for inviting us," he replied sarcastically as the waiter invited them all to sit at a large table just in front of the two sisters. "It seems we're going to be dining neighbours all the same."

"We didn't know you had an interest in Scottish traditions…"

"Also, most of the group is here, but *you* didn't invite *us*…"

"Seems to me you deliberately did not tell us…"

"I'm sure there's been a misunderstanding." Dora, as usual, felt it was her duty to return peace to the world. "We don't know what to expect; actually, we're not sure what a cèilidh is. In our case – that's my friend Etta and myself, along with Mrs van Wetering and young Robert here – it was a last-minute decision; we were invited by Captain McFarlaine…"

Etta and Mrs van Wetering's eyebrows shot up in alarm.

"Captain McFarlaine? From the cruise and water bus service?" asked Faith. Or was it Hope?

"Yes," said Dora innocently, wondering why her two companions didn't seem to approve of her intervention.

"Why would he invite you?" The Hillock duo turned its gaze on to Mrs van Wetering, then to Robert. "Did you travel on the ferry earlier today?"

"We were on Inchcailloch Island this afternoon…" as soon as the words were out of her mouth, Dora finally realised her faux pas. Oops – she had just given away Robert and Mrs van Wetering's secret.

Robert looked up at Mrs van Wetering shyly. Despite her mouthing a warning, he decided to come clean in his typically honest way.

"Yes, we were there this afternoon. You see, after I left you all and rescued that drowning woman this morning, Mr Morlore told me I'd earned the right to get the next clue today, before everyone else…"

"How unfair!"

"We are on a treasure hunt! We couldn't have been expected to help someone in difficulty…"

"Especially as it meant going out of our way…

"God helps those who help themselves…"

Herrera laughed. "Then God must help you two all the time. Mean as you are, you still pretend to be devout Christians."

"You didn't stop to help either," Faith rebuked him.

"But I don't pretend to be anything other than a scoundrel of the worst kind. I don't attend mass on a Sunday, nor do I go say my prayers every day..."

"Not one of you went to church on Sunday," Faith snapped.

"Heathens!" added Hope, waving Herrera away as if he was talking the worst nonsense she'd ever heard. "So, the treasure is on the island, is it?" she asked Robert.

"I guess there's no point in denying it. And it's my way of giving something back to the family. I still think we should all help each other whenever possible."

"And what's the clue?" asked Faith Hillock

"I don't think you should tell them," said Wilfrida van Wetering, conveniently forgetting how she had benefitted from the young man sharing the clue with her. "It would be against the rules Sir Angus set. Robert, you need to be less naïve; I doubt any of them would ever return the favour..." She glared at the sisters, and then Mr and Mrs de Beer, as if excluding Herrera and Hobbs from the list of the selfish spongers.

AFTER AN ABUNDANT, DELICIOUS DINNER, THE BEST WAS YET TO come. The party was invited to move into a larger room where a dancefloor had been cleared and the music was about to start. Etta and Dora sat with the treasure hunters while Amilcar Herrera offered to fetch the first round of drinks.

As soon as the musicians struck up the first chords, Dora was so transported by the Celtic folk music, she found it simply impossible to stand still. When Robert asked her to dance as she tapped her feet to the rhythm, for a moment, she felt shy, uncertain what to do. But how could she ever say no to the dear lad?

Despite his lanky figure, Robert was a good dancer, and to her surprise, Dora felt as if she'd always known how to dance a reel. It was easy enough to copy what other people were doing, and she mostly let Robert lead her anyway. As a result, her feet knew exactly where to go.

Glancing around, she saw that Etta too had been invited to dance. Etta looked a little self-conscious and stiff, but her large kilted partner didn't seem to mind as he led her in the reel. As for Leon, the lucky dog had found a white Scottish Terrier, who was as cute as she was determined to be conquered in wee steps. She'd allow him to come close, then bark at him if he took liberties Her Ladyship would not allow. Then the canine Casanova would retreat with his tail between his legs, only to start all over again with a few glances from far enough away.

"My goodness!" cried Dora, insisting on returning to her table and refusing more invitations to dance. "I need a little rest, my head is spinning."

Etta joined her, cheeks red and eyes laughing. "I didn't know I could still dance like this," she said. "We had to drive four thousand miles to find out."

"And who was your partner?"

"Rufus McCall – he's from the Highlands and has come south to Glasgow to run some errands, but for tonight, he has decided to stay in Luss rather than the big city."

"He's a good dancer."

"Quite good," admitted Etta.

"And that kilt makes him even more attractive…"

Etta flushed all of a sudden. "What are you hinting at, Miss Pepe? I don't know and I don't even want to…" Then she burst into a mischievous chuckle. "But it's true, I never realised a kilted man could be so sexy."

"Leon always knew," Dora said, pointing at the dog. He sat with his head held high, glancing in the terrier's direction with a serious and heart-melting look on his face, displaying his tartan tie proudly around his neck.

The two Hillock sisters were sitting in front of Dora. It seemed they'd not had one single dance; maybe no potential partner had dared approach such a strait-laced pair. Finally, a kilted man in his forties came over to the two harpies... but no, it wasn't an invitation to dance, but to discuss their transport back to the hotel.

"Not yet, Adam," said one – Etta believed it was Faith, but wasn't sure she cared to remember which sister was which. "We wish to stay a little longer."

Etta growled. She instinctively knew that these two women and she were never going to be friends. But she had no time to worry about having to put up with their company on the return trip to Balmaha. Rufus, a large, benevolent smile printed across his face, invited her to dance once more. Etta – and it came as a surprise to her as much as it did to Dora – gave him an equally large smile, leapt to her feet like a young woman and lost herself in another mad series of swirls. The ever-patient Scottish dancers helped her to move around the room gracefully and never seemed to mind how hard she stamped on their feet. When she finally returned to Rufus, the man stretched out his right hand, inviting her to hold it, and crossed his other arm to grab her left elbow. Then he started to spin. At first, Etta went rigid as they gained speed, but as the man continued, she relaxed, throwing her head back and crying out with glee as they twirled around in a frenzy.

While Etta was having the time of her life, Mrs van Wetering was commenting to Dora on how 'the kilted man' reminded her of someone.

"Really?" asked Dora, wondering if Etta was dancing with a nobleman of some sort.

"Yes, but I can't seem to place him."

"It will come," said Dora. "Maybe after a good night's sleep."

"You can be sure it will come, I never forget a face," the Dutchwoman announced rather loudly, possibly to counter the volume of the music, possibly because that's how she always spoke.

The music stopped for a couple of minutes to give the musicians a rest, and Etta and Rufus returned to their table. Adam, the porter, took the opportunity to announce to the assembled treasure hunters that he'd fetch their luggage a little later than usual the following morning to transport it to their hotel in Rowardennan. After recommending they take plenty of food and water with them as there was nowhere to buy refreshments along the way, he then offered to get a round of drinks in.

"My treat," he said, gathering the order from his clients.

On his return with the drinks, Adam lingered for a while, making sure everyone was having a good time and picking up Mrs van Wetering's handbag; Lloyd de Beer in his hurry to be first to the drinks had knocked it from her chair. Adam cracked a couple of jokes on life in Scotland and generally behaved like a good host before announcing he'd better be on his way.

"Busy day tomorrow," he said as he bid the party goodbye. The group, including Etta and Dora, thanked him and toasted his good health. Dora appreciated that the Captain, as keen as he was on whisky, had reluctantly decided to stick to Irn Bru, the fizzy drink unique to Scotland, as he'd be the one taking them back across the loch. Dora herself was drinking lager because whisky seemed to have a strange effect on her.

"It really is quite potent," confirmed Mrs van Wetering wistfully, taking a long swig from her glass. "Alas, I'm limited to this gin and tonic that tastes exactly like my medicine."

"I thought you couldn't drink alcohol at all," Dora said. The Dutchwoman hadn't made a secret of her health conditions.

"If you listened to everything the doctors said," the woman replied, shaking her head, "you wouldn't do a single thing. That's not living; that's just existing!"

An hour later, the music had stopped for the night and the treasure hunters looked at each other, murmuring that maybe it was time to get back to Balmaha. The next day, they'd have to solve another riddle – true, Robert had given them a valuable clue, but even so, after visiting the island, they'd still have the seven-mile walk to Rowardennan to complete.

"It's not so bad," Captain McFarlaine reassured them. "Most people cover the Drymen to Rowardennan stretch all in one go. This way – staying over in Balmaha – you build your stamina for the longer stretches later on, and more importantly, you prevent yourself from getting blisters like those who are too impatient."

As they left, the mountains behind Luss were dark silhouettes in front of a bluish sky. Lights in the few houses sparkled like stars and the loch waters were reflecting the purplish clouds. The air smelled of fresh watery things. Back in Balmaha, their nostrils detected a light scent of woodsmoke coming from the chimneys. Even though it was June, the inhabitants clearly still felt the need to light a fire to warm their ancient homes.

Mrs van Wetering asked Dora to help her from the boat. "I may be half Dutch, but rolling on the water is not my favourite thing. I feel a tad seasick."

Once on land, she went directly to the bench near the pier. Dora accompanied her and had just got the woman seated when Mrs van Wetering went into convulsions. Gasping something that sounded like *my heart rate*, she collapsed on to the ground, as stiff as a board.

"Help!" called Dora, trying to hold the woman up, but only succeeding in slowing her fall slightly. "Help!" she cried, her horrified shout cutting through the cheerful laughter of those who had gone ahead.

8

NOT THAT TRUE

It was late the following morning before the walkers were finally ready to leave Balmaha. The night before, the local doctor confirmed it had been a heart attack that had killed poor Wilfrida van Wetering, brought on by the strain and fatigue of the challenge and accelerated by that last fatal drink. His theory was confirmed when he spoke to her Dutch doctor, who said that yes, she was taking digoxin to help with her heart troubles, but he had recommended that she be careful not to overtire herself.

The solicitor, Mr Henry Law, had been informed first thing this morning and had got in touch with her family in the Netherlands. He'd told them that as soon as the formalities were complete, Mrs van Wetering's body would be transported back home for burial. The rest of her group had stood around, as if uncertain what to do, but Mr Morlore, distributing the letters with the day's clue, had made it clear the sad incident would not interfere with the will's instructions.

"Just one less competitor," Mrs de Beer said to her husband in what she'd clearly intended to be a whisper, but her sharp voice carried to all nearby ears, including those of the solicitor.

Her husband nodded. "There's no point in pretending we're

sorry," he said to the shocked faces around him. *"Mors tua, vita mea –* that's as true for us as it is for the rest of you."

"Mors what?" asked Amilcar Herrera.

"Your death, my life," Etta translated for the people not familiar with the Latin quote. She and Dora had found themselves in the middle of the group, the doctor and police having wanted to hear Dora's first-hand account of Mrs van Wetering's last moments on Earth.

"Life's essence in just four words," Alastair Hobbs concluded laconically.

"But that's not true!" Robert protested. "There's so much more to life than that, and I would rather go without the inheritance and still have Wilfrida alive…"

"Pretty words," Lloyd de Beer cut him short. "Most of us think the other way round."

"He's only pretending to be generous," Lloyd's wife backed him up. "But in the end, he's competing like the rest of us…"

"Actually, he's ahead of us," Alastair Hobbs reminded her.

"We still need to go to Inchcailloch," Herrera added.

"But there's no ferry till 3.30. We missed the morning one because of Wilfrida's death, so we will get to Rowardennan rather late, I'm afraid."

"Just this once, we should pool our resources and hire a boat to take us there. After all, there are plenty of vessels moored at the pier."

At that point, the group had parted, the majority of treasure hunters heading towards the pier. Grace, whom Etta and Dora had only met for the first time that morning, had a chat with Adam, then scurried after them.

She seems such a friendly girl, thought Etta, *always making time for people whom others would just ignore or take for granted.*

As for Etta, Dora and Leon, they'd set off with Robert on the way to Rowardennan. Once past the boatyard, Dora had been happy to spot the bronze statue of Tom Weir, the legendary Scottish TV presenter and keen hiker, in his trademark beanie hat, binoculars hanging from his neck and the contented smile on his face of someone who'd found beauty and was keen to share it. A group of tourists handed them some red hats with white pom-poms, so reminiscent of Tom Weir himself, and took a picture of the four beside the statue. Leon sat with his head up, a serious expression on his face as if a photographer from *The Times* or *Vogue* had asked him to pose.

Upon looking at the picture on her mobile when the tourists handed it back, Dora allowed herself one of her large smiles of satisfaction. Such a great shot, one more gift for Memory Lane.

The four reached Craigie Fort, an elevated promontory just north of Balmaha, from the thick shadows of the oak forest. The view suddenly opened on to Loch Lomond, the tip of the now familiar Ben Lomond north of them and a few white sailing boats moving between the green islands.

"It's so peaceful, it's hard to believe that poor Mrs van Wetering passed away so suddenly," Dora said quietly. Her companions nodded, and even Leon seemed to pick up on the solemnity of their mood and was less buoyant than usual.

When they reached Milarrochy Bay with its tropical-looking white beach and a few trees with their roots immersed in the water, the little group decided the sun was too warm and intense for them to go any further without a rest.

"After all, Leon should have a few breaks, and the water will provide relief to his tired and weary muscles," said Etta. Leon was not a natural-born swimmer, but he soon decided there was nothing more pleasant than the cool water on his hard-working paws and tickling the lower part of his belly. Besides, it was fun to run on the beach where water and sand came together. The humans too enjoyed a good footbath, the wild dancing of the night before requiring a bit of aftercare.

~

ONCE BACK ON THE PATH, THEY SCAMPERED BETWEEN ROOTS, ROCKS and stones. The 11 kilometres between Balmaha and Rowardennan were not easy, but the four walkers stopped every once in a while next to a beach to enjoy their sandwiches with their feet immersed in the cool water. Each plunge dispelled any trace of a sombre mood and renewed their energy. Whenever they stopped, Etta would invite Robert to carry on at a faster pace – she and Dora did not want to slow him down. Every time, Robert had the same answer.

"I don't mind taking it easy today. Tomorrow it will be different – that stretch is longer and I have no idea where the next clue will take us. The solicitor won't give me the clue before breakfast time tomorrow, so there's really no need to hurry. For today, let me stay with you."

They chatted like old friends. Leon and the good lad played games in the water, while Dora clasped her hands at the vast swathes of bluebells. When they got to Rowardennan, they had plenty of time to shower and relax before dinner. Unsurprisingly, Dora and Etta were again staying in the same accommodation as the treasure hunters; the West Highland Way is something of a wilderness, so the places to sleep are few and far between. It is inevitable that walkers will encounter one another over and over again.

When the rest of the group of treasure hunters arrived, they found the trio busy reading and sunbathing in front of the hotel grounds, Leon snoozing at their feet. Robert had his nose buried in a guide, taking in all the details that might be useful the next day on the walk to Inverarnan.

Faith Hillock addressed him gruffly, as usual. "Having Wilfrida van Wetering with you must have been a great help in finding the treasure yesterday."

"Aye, she was invaluable," Robert answered.

"Did she mention anything that might be useful for the next stops?" demanded Hope Hillock.

"No, we were focusing on the Inchcailloch clue..."

"And you didn't discuss the rest of the treasure hunt?"

"We didn't really have time."

"Oh, I'm sure you'd share it with the rest of us if you had," Faith Hillock sneered sarcastically, turning as one with her sister to address a shadowy presence nearby. "And as for you, Grace Jelly, don't you know it's not nice to eavesdrop on conversations? You should make your presence known."

The shy young woman crept forward. "I wasn't eavesdropping. I was coming to join you and wasn't sure if I was interrupting…"

"A likely story. Anyway, you haven't interrupted much as Mr Heart of Gold isn't going to tell us anything. Come, sister, we'd better go and have a shower; it's been a long day."

As the Hillocks marched off, Robert shook his head.

"I'm sorry, they were so aggressive."

"Don't worry. But they're right, it has been a long day. I just want a little peace and quiet, but at the same time, I can't bear to be alone…"

"Because of Wilfrida?"

She paused, maybe surprised that Robert could read her so easily. "Yes, what an awful way to die when she was so determined to get the inheritance."

"Why don't you take a seat?" Robert invited her to sit on the bench next to him. He offered her a drink, and the inevitable questions followed. Soon, they were busy talking of their expectations and how they would love to restore Tilda Castle were they to inherit and preserve the island while keeping it open to the public.

"What are you two talking about? Have you had the next clue?" Miss Faith Hillock had returned and was eyeing them suspiciously.

"It would be grossly unfair to give him the clue in advance again," her sister argued.

"I'll get it tomorrow morning along with the rest of you," said Robert.

The two looked at him, and then left for the restaurant.

"I don't think they believed you," said Grace, smiling.

"I know," said Robert. "But what else could I say?"

"Have you been studying tomorrow's route?" Grace looked at the guide book by his side.

"A little…"

"So have I. I'm hoping the next treasure might be in Rob Roy's cave; there are no other landmarks of note."

"True, but that's on the lower path which is a bit more tiring to walk. The upper path would be a little faster."

"I'm sorry, I didn't want to mislead you…" The young woman lowered her eyes, tucking her rebellious blonde hair behind her ears.

"I didn't think that at all."

"Anyway, after the way yesterday turned out, we'd better wait until tomorrow to discover what the next clue is all about."

"True." Robert smiled at her, his eyes lingering on her little pixie face, the sweet doe eyes moving around as if she were always on guard against danger. "It was a pity you couldn't make it to the cèilidh yesterday…" Then he bit his lip and his cheeks turned as red as Etta's hair. "I mean, it was a good thing you didn't see what happened to poor Wilfrida, but the cèilidh was fun."

"Don't worry, I knew what you meant, and I'm sure it was fun. A pity I didn't know anything about it. Maybe next time."

"You didn't know about the cèilidh?"

"No. How did you find out about it? Did you see some brochures or posters at the hotel?"

"No, it was the Ferry Captain who told us. But didn't Sue come to your lodge and tell you we were going?"

"Sue? No, she never came to my lodge. Was she supposed to?"

"She said you'd told her you were too tired to join us, but maybe I misunderstood what she meant. Or… did you leave your lodge at all yesterday evening?"

"No... I mean, only at 8pm when I went to the hotel restaurant. As no one was there, I asked the waiters if I could take dinner in my room."

Robert was surprised, but decided against asking any more. There was already so much tension in the group, why add to it?

"Actually, talking of food, shall we go and eat? We could discuss our research further over dinner... Rob Roy, eh?"

"Yes please," the young woman answered with a sweet smile. "The smell coming from the kitchen is a real temptation."

9

INVERSNAID FALLS

Early the next morning, despite the thick carpet in the hotel's corridor, Etta could hear a stream of people passing by their door. Even Leon, who had slept soundly after the exertions of the previous day, raised his head above his paws, his ears pricked – well, as pricked as a Basset Hound's ears can get – and inclined his head. What was going on?

"I guess the treasure hunters are going for an early breakfast before getting their next clue," Dora whispered, as if afraid someone would hear her from the other side of the door. "The waiter said breakfast is served from 7.30…"

"…and Robert told me the solicitor will be around at breakfast time," Etta concluded, looking at her watch. "It's quarter past seven, so I guess the heirs want to make sure they'll set off with full stomachs."

"Especially as today's weather forecast is not as nice as yesterday's," Dora said.

That sent a shiver down Etta's spine. If Dora said something was 'not nice', this generally meant that for the rest of humanity, it was pretty awful. She rose from the bed, opened the curtains and looked at the gloomy sky ridden by rushing clouds, the rain rat-a-tattering against the glass.

"The last few days have been so lovely, I had almost forgotten we're in Scotland."

"Luckily, we have our waterproofs."

"Is it feasible to skip the walking and ask the porter to take us to the next hotel along with the luggage?"

"Concetta Natale Passolina! That'd be the equivalent of cheating."

"Cheating whom? We can be open about it, tell anyone who asks that on day so and so, the weather was so poor we decided not to walk." In truth, cheating was exactly what Etta had in mind, but she realised to admit that would cause further discussions and probably an argument, so she decided to concentrate on the essentials. Staying dry, at present, was all that mattered to her.

Of course, Dora was ready with an answer – the kind of answer Etta wasn't prepared for.

"Cheating ourselves, of course. We made this a goal: that even though we're in our sixties, we'd walk the entire West Highland Way no matter what."

Etta looked at Dora in astonishment. For almost as long as she'd know her, Etta had considered her former colleague and now dearest friend, Dorotea Rosa Pepe, to be a people pleaser with no backbone. When they had decided to move in together for the sake of economising so they could live on their meagre pensions and save money for travelling, Etta had felt confident she'd be the boss, deciding what they'd do and when, while complacent Dora would be only too happy to follow her lead. But the balance of power had shifted so rapidly, it had completely slipped out of her hands. After a year of their arrangement, they were travelling Europe in Dora's Fiat 500 having sold Etta's far more practical sedan; they had acquired a dog, despite Etta insisting that no pet, not even a goldfish, would ever live under her roof; she'd been home swapping regularly, something that had held no immediate appeal to her distrustful nature when Dora had first suggested it; and now she was walking 96 miles – 154 kilometres – not on the sun-drenched island of Crete, but in Scotland: the country of the four seasons in one day!

Had Dora turned from a sweet silly thing into a high-and-mighty tyrant? Or had that been her true nature all along and she'd simply kept it well hidden? Not at all. And this was the strange thing: how could someone so kind and gentle manage to get her own way on almost all the important issues so effortlessly? This was the one mystery Mrs Passolina – Etta loved to give herself her correct title in moments of introspection – had never managed to solve.

When they arrived in the breakfast room, it was full of people, Rowardennan being not only a main stop along the West Highland Way, but also the departure point for a good scramble up Ben Lomond.

"What's the point of climbing on an awful day like this?" Etta quizzed a group of friends who, while queuing with her for fried eggs and bacon at the breakfast buffet, were joking about the prospect of a soggy hike. "You won't be able to see anything at all from the summit."

"Och, madam, if we were to wait for the good weather, we'd stay put for months," a jovial young man replied.

"And it's just a wee bit o' rain," added another member of the group.

"It might even clear up every now and then."

"And if it does, we'll be up there, ready to catch a good view."

"Trust me, on a really bad day, the rangers would advise us not to climb on Old Lomond at all. It can be dangerous…"

"Dangerous?" cried Etta in disbelief. "It's not even 1,000 metres. My neighbouring village back home in Southern Italy, Pietrapertosa, lies at 1,088 metres and I've never heard anyone advised not to go up there. Indeed, my friend Dora used to live in that village and we still often walk between the two. Real mountains are something altogether different." For Etta, who lived in the Apennines, the 'real' mountains were the Alps, not the Trossachs.

The group of friends looked at her almost pityingly. "I hope you're not considering climbing while you're here…"

"I'm doing the West Highland Way."

The hiker carried on as if she hadn't spoken, "…because it's people like you, who arrive unprepared for our Munros, that need to be rescued because they underestimated these mountains – they did not realise they are *real* mountains."

Etta shrugged as her plate was filled with fried eggs and mushrooms, and then returned to the table. As she sat down beside Dora, Robert joined them, a letter in his hand.

"Good morning, ladies," he said cheerfully. "I came to wish you a safe journey. Hopefully, I'll meet you again tonight."

"We're staying at the Inverarnan hotel," said Dora.

"That's our next stop too." Robert smiled. "But won't it be too much of a stretch for this valiant fellow? It's almost 20 kilometres; I thought you'd stop in Inversnaid."

"We will have lunch in Inversnaid. From there, Michael, our porter, will take Leon the rest of the way in his van."

Robert nodded in approval. "The first half of today's walk shouldn't be as bad as the second half. The terrain gets quite rough and hard north of Inversnaid, so you made an excellent choice."

"That was Michael's advice, and our hosts back in Edinburgh recommended him to us."

Etta was listening to the conversation as she ate. If the weather continued to be as bad as it was right now, she was going to join Leon and the porter and skip the second part of the walk, no matter what Dorotea Rosa Pepe said.

"Is that your new clue? May I ask what is says?" Dora asked as innocently as only she could, but her eyes were glittering with curiosity beneath her short fringe.

"Aye, I guess it's no great secret as we all got the same…" and he handed her the message.

"*High lodged the 'Warrior',*" Dora read, "*like a bird of prey; Or where broad waters round him lay: But this wild Ruin is no ghost. Of his devices – buried, lost!*" She paused, then read it all over again, moving her lips as children do and softly whispering each syllable to herself. "It doesn't sound an easy one."

"It fits with what you and Grace were talking about yesterday," said Etta. "Is Rob Roy's cave near the waters of the loch?"

"Yes, the cave is just above the water. We will take the low road, even though it's tougher than the higher one…"

"We'll take the high road, you'll take the low road," Dora sang, adapting the lyrics of a popular Scottish song. The others chuckled.

"Where's Grace?" Etta asked. "I thought you'd be walking together."

Robert flushed violently, which was a common occurrence with this lad.

"I sat with her at breakfast, but I thought it'd be too intrusive of me to ask to walk together all day long…"

Etta felt like banging her head with her hand. These shy people were a disaster; she was pretty sure Grace would have felt exactly the same. She sent a look to Dora for help; after all, her friend was the expert matchmaker and Etta was just a newbie in comparison. But Dora didn't come to her rescue, instead throwing in some different words of wisdom.

"Shouldn't you get going?" she asked Robert, turning to look at Mr Herrera and Professor Hobbs, Miss MacDuff in tow as usual, who were making their way out of the hotel, the daily packs on their shoulders covered with a waterproof poncho. "You'll be last if you're not careful."

Robert grinned. "I have long legs." He took the message back and pulled a plastic folder from his rucksack, placing it next to a map and DVD contained within.

"What's that?" asked Dora curiously.

"That's the video my ancestor, Sir Angus McGrouse, made

before he died; the one in which he explains all details of the treasure hunt."

"Wouldn't it be better to keep it with your main luggage?"

"In case something goes wrong, I prefer to have it handy and well protected in my rucksack." Meeting Dora's gaze, he added, "Would you like to watch it sometime?"

"Oh," Dora's slate grey eyes opened almost as wide as Loch Lomond, "I'd love to."

"Then I'll be happy to show it to you one evening. See you up north."

"See you up north," echoed Dora as ecstatically as if he had promised to give her Tilda Island.

"See you up north?" gasped Etta, looking out into the rain as he left and dreading the cold and miserable day to come. "Are you really determined to do this?"

"Of course!"

Leon sighed deeply.

Etta sighed even more deeply.

"Then let's go. The sooner we get this over and done with, the better."

Once outside, Etta set off at a cracking pace, Leon trotting to keep up, while Dora turned back to say goodbye to their hotel. Even in bad weather, Loch Lomond was full of charm.

THANKS TO ETTA'S SUPER SPEED, THEY REACHED THE FORK WHERE the high and low paths split seemingly in no time at all. After an exchange of glances, they decided they'd stay on the less arduous higher path. The rain would make the rocks along the bonnie, bonnie banks rather slippery and the lower road would be too much for a Basset Hound, even one as willing as Leon.

Truth is, Etta thought, *my knees are grateful for the choice, even if Dora will be disappointed to miss Rob Roy's cave.*

After another brisk kilometre, a new group of people came

into view not too far ahead of them. It was a family of four: mother, father, and two children.

It must be their yearly adventure, thought Etta, wondering if the children might not have preferred to holiday somewhere – *anywhere* – else. The strange thing was that, although their waterproofs were running with rain, they were singing, chatting and laughing, and seemed in no hurry at all, despite the nasty weather.

"They remind me of the four hobbits leaving the Shire in *Lord of the Rings*," Dora said, still panting with the effort of keeping up with her friend. "They take it at a leisurely pace, don't they?"

It was then that Etta realised her waterproof jacket was keeping her warm. The rain that had looked so awful from the hotel was, in fact, rather gentle, and if she kept up her frenzied pace, she'd miss 20 kilometres of beautiful landscape without, as Dora would say, letting it all sink in: the peace of the forest; the perfume of thick moss, wet wood and earth. She slowed down and noticed that Leon immediately appreciated the change of pace. He was now able to give everything the thorough sniffing it deserved, while Dora was finally free to let her eyes wander over the large ferns and the dense forest. She started to hum, softly and happily, very much like a hobbit.

Silly me, I tend to forget that happiness might hide even under a wet coat on a rainy day. And Etta joined in Dora's humming and decided to use her memory instead of her camera to record it all.

Half way along the high road, they heard the sounds of people approaching them from behind.

"Hurry," commanded a familiar voice, "or we won't overtake them."

"Why didn't we leave earlier?"

"Because they'd get suspicious and follow us."

"But what if we're wrong?"

"We aren't. We're Scots and we know things."

"But *he* was English, not Scottish!"

"Shh!" As they passed Etta, Dora and Leon, the Hillock

sisters muttered a stiff "Hello", and then carried rapidly on their way.

"What are those two up to?" Etta wondered.

"And why didn't they want the other treasure hunters to see them taking the high road? Maybe the treasure is hidden on this path after all."

"No, they mentioned they want to overtake the others. I think they plan to hurry along this shorter route to be long gone by the time the others get to Inversnaid and find out the treasure's not there."

"Should we tell Robert that Rob Roy's cave may not be the right place?" But when Dora sheltered under an oak and took her phone out, she realised there was no signal.

"Why not message him once we reach the restaurant in Inversnaid? Although I guess by then, he will know he's not in the right place."

"Such a shame those two hags kept the secret to themselves…"

"Well," said Etta, smiling at Dora using such a strong word as 'hag', "I can understand it. After all, if you want to win, you can't be as generous as Robert."

"Generosity always gets its reward in the end."

"But only in Dorotea's world, I'm afraid."

"We'll see!"

"Is that a challenge, Miss Pepe?"

"I guess it is."

The two chuckled, and then carried on with their humming, the happy dog proud to lead the way and make sure the bipeds didn't end up on the wrong path. When, many songs later, they saw a few small buildings in the distance, the promise of warmth just as they started to feel cold and damp, the expectation of food making their stomachs growl, brightened their moods still further.

It is amazing, Etta mused, *the simple things that make walkers happy.*

The anticipation of a good lunch raised the trio's energy levels to such an extent, they decided to follow the path up to the waterfalls, just before they reached the hotel where they were due to meet Michael. These falls were considered the biggest attraction of the cute little hamlet, and even Etta didn't want to miss them.

"Better to see them before lunch, so that later, we can just carry on from the hotel."

"Good plan," Dora said.

But as they walked over the little bridge ahead of them, they saw a woman leaning out precariously over the rocks of the waterfall in the part closed to the public; it was too slippery and dangerous for tourists.

"Be careful!" Dora called out.

Too late. The figure slipped, lost her footing and fell...

10

WHO TO TRUST?

Leon barked and rushed towards the bottom of the waterfall, Dora and Etta following close behind. Thank goodness this part of the falls wasn't too high and the figure lying on the ground was already starting to move.

"Are you OK?" said Etta, carefully stretching out her right hand while Dora grabbed Etta's waist to stop her from slipping too. When the woman raised her head and turned towards them, they recognised Grace Jelly.

"Golly, how stupid of me," she cried.

"Can you stand up?"

"Yes, nothing's broken." Using Etta's hand for support, Grace managed to climb out of the falls and join the two women. "At least I've got this," she showed them a plastic folder. "It's today's treasure, number one – I'm the first to get here."

"You mean it wasn't in Rob Roy's cave after all?"

"No, I searched there and found nothing. Then I decided to carry on along the lower road to Inversnaid and explore a bit of the upper road before lunch. I wondered if the 'broad waters round him' might mean something other than the loch – what if Rob Roy had perched high up, here on the waterfalls, watching around the place like a bird of prey? As I leant over the falls, I saw the plastic folders the solicitors have been using to protect the treasure from the rain. Just as I caught hold of number one, I slipped and fell like an exhausted salmon..."

"That's a stupid place to put a clue; some of the others might take a worse fall than yours." But despite her concern, Dora couldn't deny that she was intrigued to know what was inside the plastic folder. Grace took out the envelope that should contain the details of when and where the solicitor would announce the next clue, but all she found inside was a crude painting of a red herring.

"How cruel!" said Dora.

"Argh!" cried Grace, massaging her bruised body.

"I think we'd better go down to the hotel restaurant and get some hot food," said the ever-pragmatic Etta.

"Woof, woof, WOOF!" barked Leon in approval. Even his red-haired biped made sense every once in a while.

As they left the falls behind them, the large white structure of Inversnaid Hotel came into view with its romantic windows facing the pier. Dora found it easy to be transported back in time to when the Duke of Montrose had commissioned the building of the hotel in 1820, the first tourists arriving to use the mansion as a hunting lodge. The restaurant was warm and filled with light, and a number of walkers were chatting happily over cups of hot tea and steaming dishes of food.

"A dream," said Dora, but Etta's attention was distracted by a loud conversation between two people at a nearby table.

"I told you we should have carried on," Mrs de Beer was yelling at her husband. "We've wasted time on the low road for nothing."

"So you keep reminding me," he replied sardonically. "But if we hadn't done so, we'd still be wondering if we'd made a mistake. Trust me, we've done the right thing."

"I'd love to believe you," Mrs de Beer snapped, making it clear that she didn't. "What next?"

"I'm not going to tell you now when all ears are on us..." He looked pointedly in the direction of Grace, standing in the middle of the room with Etta, Dora and Leon. "But I do have a plan."

At that moment, Sue MacDuff came in, followed closely by Amilcar Herrera and Professor Hobbs. They sat together and ordered hot tea with their food, making it clear to the waiter they had no time to waste.

"What about Robert? Do you think he's gone on already?" Dora whispered.

Etta shook her head. "He's a fast walker, but really, I have no idea. Have you seen him, Grace?"

Grace flushed gently. "Not since breakfast."

Etta shook her head in disapproval. *Those two young ones should stick together*, she thought. *It seems as if they have enemies all around.*

They picked up the menu and sat down at a vacant table. Etta and Dora decided on the soup of the day – vegetable – with a selection of sandwiches, and home-made apple crumble for dessert. A larger meal would await them that evening. Leon was treated to some toasted bread, on which a charming young waitress had spread a veil of kidney paté.

Och, such sweet lassies live in Scotland, thought the Basset, channelling his inner Highlander as he gazed at the blonde-haired blue-eyed woman who was patting him with an affectionate smile on her face.

"I'm still not sure I understand – what suddenly made you think the clue meant the waterfall?" asked Etta.

The young woman flushed again, and then explained. When she was approaching the Inversnaid Hotel, she had spotted the two Hillock sisters resting on a bench, unaware of her presence. She had slipped behind a tree and overheard them boasting about how clever they'd been not to have headed to Rob Roy's cave as they knew the clue meant the Inversnaid Falls.

"They agreed to use the facilities in the hotel before going to retrieve the treasure, sure that no one else would have realised yet that Rob Roy's cave was a red herring. So as soon as they went inside, I headed for the falls and... and you know how it went. That, it seems, was the red herring. It was a trap and I literally fell into it."

"How cruel those two harridans are."

"They knew full well you were there and only pretended to be unaware..."

"Also," said Etta, examining the message, "this isn't in the same style as the ones Robert and poor Mrs van Wetering found on Inchcailloch. Look – different paper; different ink; no wax seal. They must have reused the plastic folders from their previous finds."

"A fake?" asked Dora.

"Like Grace said, a trap. To get rid of one more competitor."

At that moment, the door opened and Robert walked in, his lanky body seeming a little incongruous in the romantic interior of the restaurant. He looked around the room, possibly searching for a quiet corner – not because he wanted to snub people, but because he was too shy to deal with the trauma of having to make conversation. But when he spotted Etta, Dora and Leon with Grace, his face split into a huge grin. He was such a charming man deep down and, Etta was sure, Grace was as drawn to him as he was to her.

He came over and asked if he could sit with them.

"Of course," said Grace.

"We're so happy to see you again so soon," Dora agreed.

Leon, busy licking his clattering bowl, wagged his tail in a frenzy to let the young man know he was as pleased as the others to see him, but was simply too busy to show it just now.

"Will you have something to eat?" asked Dora.

"Nay, I took a sandwich with me to save a little money," he

explained with his customary frankness. "But I will enjoy a hot cuppa and warm up a bit before going out again."

"Did you find your treasure?"

"I'm afraid I didn't. It wasn't in Rob Roy's cave."

"Nor at the waterfalls," added Grace.

"The waterfalls? Why would it be there? There's no reference to them in the message…"

"It was, I suspect, a joke played by two not-so-sweet ladies," said Etta. "A joke that could have ended in disaster."

And then, Grace explained what had happened.

"Och, how mean. But then, I'm sure they didn't realise how dangerous the falls could be."

"On the contrary, I think they knew full well," said Etta.

Robert sighed. It was clearly hard for him to admit that people could simply be mean for the sake of being mean, and not by accident.

"We expected you to be way ahead of us," said Etta.

"Och, nay. The lower road makes for tough walking and it takes longer than the upper road, not to mention the time I wasted exploring Rob Roy's cave and the area all around it. Then I searched a little way along the high road, and finally I stopped outside at the pier to eat my sandwich and make sense of it all." He produced the message he had been given that morning from his waterproof folder. "Despite having this clue, I'm clueless." He read it again. "I was really convinced the cave was the place to search."

"But what about the bird of prey?" asked Dora. "A cave doesn't seem the place for an eagle or a hawk."

"But the rest fits so perfectly: the warrior; the broad waters; the ruin that is no ghost…"

Etta opened her map and scrutinised every single place from Rowardennan to Inverarnan. Meanwhile, Dora picked up the hotel's brochure from the table and found a passage mentioning that Wordsworth and his sister had stayed there, when the poet was inspired to write the verses of 'Inversnaid, To a Highland Girl'.

"The poet!" she cried. "Wordsworth! Etta, he could be the *he* the Hillock sisters were talking about."

"I can't remember them talking about a poet at all…"

"Yes, you can – when they said, 'He is English, not Scottish', they meant Wordsworth. He knew the place almost as well as a Scot, and I bet the clue comes from this 'Highland Girl' poem…"

Using her mobile and the hotel Wi-Fi, Dora searched for the whole poem. Maybe there were more clues in it. But the poem mentioned in the brochure didn't match the verses in the clue.

"Could you read me the message again?" Dora asked Robert. "Maybe we should first understand who wrote those verses, and why."

The hotel Wi-Fi wasn't that fast, but after a while, the whole poem popped up. "'The Brownie's Cell'," read Dora. "And yes, it's by Wordsworth." But the verses that followed the quote in the clue didn't seem to shed any light on their search. Dora sat upright, her face unusually serious, her fingers drumming on the table as if they could help her concentration. Overall, Etta observed, she looked like Leon in his best attentive hound pose, when his tail was parallel to the ground, his nostrils quivering as if deciding which scent to follow, one front leg suspended ready to charge forward.

"So, what are you thinking?" Etta asked her, intrigued.

"When did Mr Wordsworth write this second poem?" Dora asked as her fingers ran over her mobile. It took a few seconds before the screen returned the search results.

"'The Brownie's Cell'", she read aloud, but not too loud, "is a poem the Master composed after a visit to Loch Lomond and the ruins on one of its islands."

"Another island?" said Etta in surprise. She had never imagined there'd be so many islands on Loch Lomond, but here she was contemplating visiting a second one.

"There's an island right across from where we are now," and

Robert pointed on the map, close to the western bank and the hamlet of Inveruglas.

"And are there ruins there?" Grace's eyes were wide.

"No," said Dora unusually petulantly, her teacher's spirit dismayed at the flaw in her logic. "There's also an island called Inveruglas, but I don't think it has anything to do with us."

"I hope not," whispered Grace, watching a couple leaving the restaurant and rushing towards the pier, possibly to get on the ferry. "The de Beers seem to be of a different mind."

"Listen," said Dora as she read from a website, "the poem was inspired by the scenic ruins of a castle the MacFarlane family built in 1570. After Inveruglas Castle was destroyed under Cromwell, the I Vow Castle became the seat of the MacFarlane clan. Later, when the elements tore this second castle to ruins, a hermit decided to live in what remained of the ancient tower and its vaulted cellar, and the place became the brownie's cell in Wordsworth's poem.

"Look here," and Dora unfolded Etta's map, her finger pressing against a little spot to the north, "just south of Ardlui on the other shore, there's this little place called Island I Vow. And there's the symbol of a castle. As we've read, it's in ruins and surrounded by water. Maybe it was the hermit, not Rob Roy, who Wordsworth meant when he mentioned 'the Warrior' – a man who could cope with being alone, facing the fierce elements and living in communion with nature and God."

"You're absolutely right!" cried Robert.

"Shh!" Grace pressed her index finger against her lips. "Don't draw attention to us."

But it was too late. Sue MacDuff stood up from her table and approached them.

"It sounds as if you have found something interesting."

"Maybe," Etta said, pointing to a menu. "In fact, I do have a confession…"

"What's that?" said Sue, eyeing the map that Dora had hidden between her arms suspiciously.

"I've ordered two portions of this wonderful apple crumble."

"I'm sure you were not discussing apple crumble. Look, the Hillock sisters aren't here; they've gone ahead. Mr and Mrs de Beer have taken a ferry who knows where, so they're out of the way. Isn't this the right time to form an alliance? Mr Herrera and Professor Hobbs were discussing that very thing..."

"I guess you ain't got a clue." Etta smiled malevolently.

"Maybe today we haven't, but how about tomorrow? And who are you anyway? Why are you meddling? You're not in our group, so mind your own business."

Robert and Grace, who had seemed to brighten up at the idea of a collaboration, were ready to react now that their new friends were under attack.

"The will's regulations do not exclude collaborations with others," said Grace with unusual vehemence. Robert, it seemed, was braver still.

"And it's a good job they don't," he said, holding Sue's gaze and for once not blushing, "being as you're not part of the family group either. You're only along at your professor's invitation."

Sue seemed to wilt under this two-pronged attack. "Enjoy!" she said, shrugging her shoulders, turning her back on them and returning to her table.

"They're waiting to see what we're up to," said Grace when Sue and her two companions didn't move. "Wherever we go, they will follow us."

"We're waiting for the van to pick up Leon," said Etta, "and I have a plan."

"Pick up Leon?" Grace asked. "Why?"

"The road today is too long and hard, so we decided he'd walk only halfway. Our porter Michael is coming to collect Leon and drive him to Inverarnan Hotel."

"I'm sure he will enjoy a good nap," said Robert, but Leon was not so convinced. He'd love to continue on the adventure, but when he thought of enduring even more rain after lunch, that did not excite him so much. Besides, you never knew who would be staying at the next hotel along the way. Maybe another generous lassie would offer him some good food, and if he was lucky, he'd have a pretty she-dog – maybe even a she-Basset – for company. The life of a hound is so difficult and full of choices that this time, Leon would let fate decide for him.

As if on cue, Michael McDermott entered the restaurant and greeted them.

"Leon, I'll be honoured to be your driver," he said to the dog. "Are you tired?"

"Not really," said Etta, as proud of the dog as she would be of her grandchild. "He's fit, is our Leon, far more so than we expected from his breed. He loves walking and exploring."

"It's all about the owners. Lazy owners mean lazy dogs."

Etta was struck by the observation. Maddalena, her daughter, had always been a strange child. Nowadays, she practised yoga each morning on her balcony in Granada, said hello to the sun and thanked the whole universe, believing in the energy of the cosmos and all that sort of weird stuff. Etta had never felt like a proud parent since Maddalena had stuffed her statistics degree into a drawer and become a tattooist, but now Etta wondered if she had perhaps done a far better job with her Basset Hound.

She passed the leash to Michael and patted Leon on the back, inviting the dog to follow him. Leon trotted obediently beside Michael, but when they had almost reached the van, he suddenly stopped and contorted his head in a strange manoeuvre in which he had reached the status of maestro. The collar slipped over his head so effortlessly that Michael McDermott carried on, unaware that he was no longer leading a dog until a suspicious clinking noise from the leash hooks alerted him.

Leon turned to face his bipeds, again assailed by doubts. Should he really leave those two all alone in an unfamiliar place? Women who had managed to get lost a mere 200 metres from their homeswap in Cambridge? They couldn't recognise a single smell, nor would they mark their scent. Could they be trusted to march through the Scottish wilderness all alone?

To his surprise, Etta approved of his trick.

"I think Leon is right," she said, going on to ask Michael if he would give them all a lift.

"Aye, there's plenty of room in the van," he said, a little surprised. Etta guessed after Dora's outburst that morning that most walkers adhered to a strict protocol: you could not travel a single mile of the West Highland Way on anything other than your own two feet.

Etta's companions, despite being just as surprised as Michael, decided to follow her anyway. But Robert was troubled.

"The others will denounce us for using a means of transport other than walking," he said once they were outside.

"We just want to fool them. They will have no choice but to leave and carry on along the path. Meanwhile, we will ask Michael to drop us a few hundred metres away. There's another path back down to the hotel, so we won't skip a single metre of the Way; all we need to do is let the three of them get ahead of us."

And that is exactly what they did, despite Leon looking deeply betrayed when the two women left him in the van with Michael. Useless was Dora's attempt to kiss him on the head; he'd never forgive such desertion. Though when the rain rattled furiously against the windowpane, he had to admit it was nice to snuggle up in the comfort and warmth of the van, listening to some gentle Scottish music and Michael's funny accent. When the pleasure of a well-stuffed stomach and expectations of great things to come got the better of him, he was soon sound asleep.

11

THE BROWNIE'S CELL

"It's all clear, let's go," announced Robert, returning to his companions who were waiting for him in the vegetation above the hotel.

"Did you see them leave?"

"No, but I asked a waitress and she confirmed the three of them have gone on their way."

"I wonder where they think we're going…"

"I don't care, as long as they don't spot us and follow us."

"We need to stay behind them, but not too far behind. As soon as Lloyd and Olive discover their mistake, they will head back here and we don't want them following us to the right island."

Drizzle turned into rain, then rain turned into a downpour, making it even tougher to walk on the dangerous combination of slippery rocks and moss-tapestried roots. The ups and downs and strange contortions of the path were hard on their ankles and, even more so, their knees.

"I'm so glad we've not got Leon with us," said Dora, wincing in pain. Robert held her arm as her foot slipped once more on a tangled mass of rotten branches, moss and slippery stones. Etta was too busy avoiding a spectacular fall of her own to remember she had one person to blame for her current situation: Dora.

"Let's have a wee stop," said Robert after a while. "We need to be clear headed while we're walking to avoid hurting ourselves."

"Sure, let's stretch our legs out in front of a fire and enjoy a good cup of coffee," replied Etta, furious that the rain had now started to make its way inside her waterproof and, worse, her boots. Robert led them all into a little corner sheltered by large rocks and oak trees, and then produced a thermos from his sack and invited each of them to take a draught of very hot tea.

"It feels marvellous," Etta conceded.

"True, there's nothing like a hot drink on a soggy day," Robert agreed.

They didn't stop for more than five minutes; the gusts of wind would soon have worked their way along the walkers' backs and cooled them rapidly. But it was the best five minutes' break Etta could ever remember.

Thirty minutes later, the rain returned to light drizzle, and again Etta could appreciate the alluring views ahead of her. Loch Lomond was enchanting on a sunny day, but its eerie charm could only really be revealed on a day as dark and misty and stormy as this. After one more scramble amongst the rocks, they saw the mists on the water clear at least partially and spotted what looked like a clump of trees floating on the loch between the eastern and western shore.

"I Vow Island!" Dora cried in excitement.

"That's an island? Really?" said Etta doubtfully. "It looks more like some trees swept up by the tide."

"It's just like on the map," said Dora, taking it carefully from her jacket, wrapped up in a plastic bag.

"I thought we'd see a castle!"

"Oh no, there are only the ruins," Robert explained. "And they must be hidden in the dense vegetation."

"I see," said Etta without trying to hide her disappointment. "How do we reach it? It's rather a long way from the shore."

Robert blushed. "Silly me, I should have thought to hire a boat back in Inversnaid."

"Where's the next pier?" asked Etta.

"Probably in Ardleish, which is only a couple of miles away. But it's so small, I'm not sure we will find a boat for hire there."

"But the map says it's a ferry stop. It can't be that small."

"It's not a real ferry stop," Robert explained. "It's just a service on request. You have to put the buoy out to signal there's someone to be picked up at the pier."

"Such a weird notion," commented Etta.

"Not that strange, if you think about it. It'd take hours for a car to get round to Ardlui, while by boat, it's just a matter of minutes. Thus ferry-on-demand is a way to avoid cutting this part of the loch off from the rest of the world."

Grace had been fidgeting with Dora's map. She now pointed ahead of them, beyond a group of rocks.

"Let's explore further up. It looks like there's a small beach; maybe we can find a boat or something there."

"Let's hope so." Etta's feet were getting wet and nothing could put her in a worse mood than that. Well, nothing apart from water trickling down her glasses and dropping on to her chin, and from there slipping inside her jacket. And that's exactly what could happen any minute.

On arrival at the beach, they found a couple of kayaks lying face down to avoid them getting flooded by the rain.

"Yes!" Grace cried in excitement.

Etta looked at the black waters ahead of her, then at the island that seemed so distant, and felt grateful there were only two kayaks.

"We will wait for you at the hotel. Can we order you something hot ahead of your arrival?"

"We'll be fine," said Robert. "Don't you worry; you go on and enjoy a hot shower."

Dora was shocked. "We're surely not going to leave them all alone?" she asked.

"Well, we can't wait here; we'll turn into icebergs!" Etta did feel vaguely guilty, but she was determined not to make her life tougher than it was already.

"Really, don't worry about us," insisted Robert, picking up the two paddles and turning the first kayak over. "You go on..."

"It's a two seater!" cried Dora triumphantly.

"So is the other one," said Grace, turning the second over.

Dora clasped her hands, overjoyed, while Etta's third eye presented her with an image of a grieving Maddalena, wondering at her mother's graveside how a sixty-something woman could have been so foolish as to launch herself into a mission she stood no chance of surviving.

"Miss Dorotea Rosa Pepe, are you out of your mind? Can't you see how rough the water is? Have you forgotten we'll be turning 60... um... something next year? This loch is not the Mediterranean; it's renowned for its icy cold water. And at this end, it's even deeper than it was in Balmaha. And there might be the nasty monster swimming around."

"I told you, that's Loch Ness, not Loch Lomond."

"All the same, she might have travelled."

"Mrs Concetta Natale Passolina, are you telling me you're afraid?"

"Of course not!"

"You are."

"I'm just being prudent, instead of pretending I'm still 20."

"Yoooμ aaaare scaaared!" Dora elongated each syllable triumphantly.

"Gimme that paddle." Infuriated, Etta snatched the one Grace was holding before turning back to Dora. "I'm sure the whole world will laugh at the news of two stupid retired sexagenarians drowning because they didn't know their limits. 'Oh,' they will say, 'if I were their age, I would have stayed safe in the warm with a cup of tea. But no, not these two *Italian* tourists…' because it's always more fun if the fools are foreigners '…from *Southern Italy*, where only morons live.' Well, what are you waiting for?" She screamed these last words at Dora, who had already seated herself on the front seat.

"Please put on your lifejacket," was all Robert was allowed to say. All his other protests went unheard. Of course, Etta would go with Dora if her friend was determined to put their lives at risk. There was no point in making it a collective sacrifice and putting the two younger ones in jeopardy.

Robert pushed the two-woman kayak into the open water, then did the same with the second before leaping in behind Grace. All through the crossing, Etta kept grumbling, mainly because whenever she shut her mouth, she felt her stomach churn with seasickness. But she was determined not to give anyone – the holidaying Nessie included – the satisfaction of seeing her sweet self vomiting her soul into the water. Instead, she railed against old age, her daughter, her former husband, her current predicament, her housemate and so-called best friend, Castelmezzano's mayor, Castelmezzano's priest, and anything or anyone else she could think of all the way to the island.

Etta did not throw up, but when Robert helped her out of the kayak after a heart-arresting landing, her legs were shaking as if they were made of soft ricotta cheese. But a mutinous flash in her eyes made it clear that no one was to comment on it.

"I think we all deserve another swig of hot tea," said Robert.

"Don't you have any whisky?"

"In fact, I do; I keep a small flask for emergencies."

"I'll take that!" and as the others drank the tea, Etta gulped down a long swig of whisky, only to descend into a coughing fit seconds later. But at least the fire water steadied her legs ready to start the exploration.

There had to be people visiting the island regularly, because even in the thickest areas of the copse, a path took them to the inner part of the island. Soon they were walking amongst the former walls, rooms and turrets of a castle.

"Like a bird of prey," recited Dora when they were standing on the highest part of the castle ruins. There, on the adjacent tower walls, was a number of plastic envelopes.

"They start with number three," said Robert. "Someone else has already picked up the first two."

"The Hillock sisters?"

"Who else?"

Robert handed envelope number three to Grace and took number four for himself. The woman protested, but it seemed Robert could be rather stubborn once he made a decision. He tore open the plastic folder and split the wax seal. Apart from congratulating the contestant on finding the treasure of the day and informing them that the next clue would be given out the next day at the hotel in Inverarnan, the message contained only one other instruction: to leave the kayaks – if kayaks had been used to reach the island – in exactly the same place as they'd found them, or the competitor would get penalised.

The return was not as bad as the outward journey, maybe because the whisky had a longer-lasting effect than Etta had realised. Or maybe she was feeling so wet and miserable, all she could think about was getting to the hotel. Once safely back on dry(ish) land, she wondered how far they had to go.

"Och, it must be about seven kilometres," said Robert softly.

Etta felt like banging her head against one of the rocky boulders strewn around. And in a downpour that got heavier and heavier, they trudged on.

As they passed the point opposite where Ardlui sat on the western bank, they encountered three more treasure hunters marching southwards.

"You've found your treasure, haven't you?" demanded Amilcar Herrera of Grace and Robert.

"We have," Robert confirmed.

"And it's on I Vow Island?" asked Sue. "A local told us where the poem originates from."

"It is. You will find a couple of kayaks on a beach just up the road from here…"

"Sue," said Professor Hobbs, "do you want to return to the hotel with these four? Amilcar and I will go on our own to fetch our clues, as there are only two kayaks."

"Actually," Robert explained, "each kayak is a two seater."

"Then I'll come with you," said Sue determinedly to Professor Hobbs. "I'm curious to explore the island as well. But," she turned to Etta and Dora, "where's your dog?"

"This was too long a stretch for him," Dora said. "We asked our porter to take him on to the hotel."

Sue gave Dora a funny look.

"We need to hurry," Amilcar reminded her. And with that, the trio left.

"It's a good job they bumped into us," said Etta. "I'm sure the sisters would have sent them the wrong way."

"But would they have trusted them?" asked Robert, chuckling.

"I doubt it," muttered Grace. "I'm the only one stupid enough to fall for their tricks."

"It wasn't your fault!" the young man protested.

Etta eyed her friend suspiciously. There was certainly tenderness budding between the two youngsters, but Dora, usually the first to match make, seemed indifferent to it. Was she finally growing out of her romantic habits? Would the West Highland Way become a place of change for both of them? What needed to be changed in Etta herself?

"Let's carry on to the hotel," she grumbled, unable to deal with her inner thoughts when they stormed her mind. "I can't stand it anymore, water everywhere!"

"Wait!" said Dora.

"What now?"

Dora didn't answer, instead pointing towards a couple of tourists on the pier who had hoisted the buoy up. A blue and white launch was making its way out of Ardlui Marina to pick them up. Dora watched, as enchanted as if she were witnessing a supernatural event, and refused to move until the boat had collected its passengers and disappeared from sight.

"Do you want to spend the night here?" snapped Etta, her patience, which had been low all day, finally having run out.

"Of course not," said Dora, blushing. From time to time, it seemed, she could be aware of her own follies.

"You're right to watch, though," Robert whispered to her. "This is the last part of the West Highland Way on the banks of Loch Lomond. Now we head north and leave it all behind."

Dora sighed deeply as if she were saying goodbye to an old friend. But finally, even she had to turn away and move forward.

12

DROVERS AND BOGLES

Etta would never have imagined that the sight of asphalt, the noise of cars, the smoke from chimneys could so gladden her heart. But that's exactly how she felt when her weary feet hit the main road and she saw the Drovers Inn, a three-storey building in rubble stone with two entrance porches sheltered under pitched roofs and an abundance of ancient case windows, ahead of her.

She and Dora entered the inn via the pub. It was dark but cosy inside, low ceilings supported by ebony beams, an ancient wooden floor, scorched tables with candles sitting in empty whisky bottles, dimmed lanterns hanging from the ceiling, a large roaring fire, oil paintings of times long gone, and stuffed animals all adding to the ambience. A noble eagle gazed down on them, while a large bear seemed to follow them with his curious eyes. At his feet lay a solemn Basset Hound, a reproachful expression on his face.

Etta and Dora looked in horror from the stuffed animals to the rigid form of their dog, unable to comprehend what their eyes were seeing.

"Look at the tail!" cried Dora finally, relief replacing disbelief.

Then, and only then, did Etta realise the otherwise still-as-a-statue Basset had a tail that was wagging so violently, partially hidden in the darkness, it looked as if it would fly from the back end of its canine owner at any moment.

"Leon, what are you doing there?"

The hound could resist no longer. Forgiving his two bad humans in an instant for deserting him, he hurtled towards them, his long body bouncing from left to right and back under the commanding power of a tail with a mind of its own.

"Och, the wee doggy has finally found his two humans," said the sturdy man behind the bar, smiling at them. "He's been waiting for ye since he arrived here; he's even refused any food." The man pointed to a bowl containing chunks of roast turkey.

"Really?" said Etta in surprise. She knew Leon had a certain affection for her and Dora, but he was usually such an independent dog.

"Oh, Leon, you should have known we'd never leave you for long," said Dora with suspiciously watery eyes. "What a silly dog you are."

"Even my Lulu," added the man, pointing towards a beautiful Border Collie sleeping on a tartan pillow, "could not cheer him up." At mention of her name, the Collie lifted her head, her black ears pricked as she watched the Basset wagging his way around two rotund ladies, the expression on her white face enquiring if this could possibly be the same motionless hound who'd arrived in the pub earlier that afternoon. Now, all of a sudden, he was receptive to all her invitations to play and run that had gone unheeded just five minutes earlier, asking the two women if they could go for a nice walk and a jolly time outside.

"Forget it!" cried Etta. "I'm walking no further than my bedroom, and if the stairs are too steep, I may even sleep down here beside the fire."

"Nae need, hen," said the friendly barman in his lovely singsong accent. "It's only one floor up and ye'll have a room with a comfy bathtub."

"That's the best news I've heard since we started our journey."

"And there's everything ye'll need to make yerself a nice cup of tea or coffee in the room. Dinner is ready whenever ye wish; we serve food all day long as hungry walkers drop by anytime."

"I'm in heaven…"

"I'll keep the table near the fire for ye!"

"Definitely heaven," confirmed Etta, "as you are an angel dressed up as a Scotsman."

The man handed them their room keys with another broad smile.

WHEN ETTA AND DORA CAME BACK DOWNSTAIRS WITH LEON, THEY felt so much better. A long soak in the bath had done each of the two humans the world of good; a little nap, which they were lulled into by light snoring from Leon, had restored their souls; and now the smell of food reaching their nostrils made them realise they were as hungry as a pack of wolves.

"I hope the food here is as good as the welcome," said Etta as they made their way downstairs. Robert and Grace waved to them from the table beside the fire.

"The barman told us this was going to be your table, so we hope you don't mind our company over dinner."

"Not at all," said Dora. "Did you manage to have a little rest?"

They both nodded. "Not for too long, though," Robert said. "I'd rather have an early night and a good, long sleep after dinner."

Etta, Dora and the young treasure hunters had just ordered their food when the Hillock sisters made their way into the pub from upstairs, their luggage in their hands.

"You gave us the haunted room!" croaked Faith with an

expression on her face that was more frightening than frightened.

"We've read your information pack and we know that number six is the room with all the ghosts," cawed Hope.

"But it's a large, comfy room," said the barman, "and the bogles don't make their presence known that often. And they're not the bad kind; they just like to greet our dear guests with some moaning, whispers and cries, but nothing really scary. They're responsible bogles; they know we run a business, after all, so they'd never do anything to jeopardise it."

"No way!" Faith Hillock was adamant. "We're not going to stay in a haunted room and that's that."

"We don't like bogles of any sorts. Not even entrepreneurial ones," snapped Hope.

Robert, as eager to help as ever, offered his room to the sisters; Grace did the same, but their rooms both had shared bathrooms. No, the sisters said sulkily, they needed private facilities.

Dora looked pleadingly at Etta, who gave her a death stare in return, its message clear.

"Don't you even think of offering our cosy room to those two harridans."

At that moment, the pub door opened and Amilcar Herrera, Alastair Hobbs and Sue MacDuff entered. They were completely drenched, their expressions less confident than they had been earlier.

"What's going on?" Mr Herrera asked, looking from the belligerent sisters to the still friendly but now not quite so jovial barman. As soon as the barman explained the problem, Herrera offered to take the haunted room, as long as it was cosy and warm and the barman would treat him to a dram of whisky near the fireplace.

"My pleasure, sir," the man said, clearly grateful to have such an understanding guest. "I'll send my daughter to clean the room for ye as soon as possible. This evening, we're fully booked so there's not much room swapping we could do."

Without a word of thanks, the sisters went to take possession of their new room, while Herrera came over to the four friends as they waited for their food by the fire.

"I need a hot shower," he said, "otherwise I'd join you. I'm literally starving."

"You'll feel great again after a good shower," said Dora, "but you can order some food in advance, so it will be ready on your return."

So Amilcar Herrera did exactly that.

"Will you be collaborating tomorrow with Miss MacDuff and Professor Hobbs?" Dora asked Herrera as he warmed his hands by the fire.

"That's a good question. Frankly, I don't know."

"You seem like a good team," said Etta.

"I know, but can I really trust them? Can you, Grace, trust Robert?"

Grace flushed. "Of course I can."

"And you, Robert – can you really trust her?"

"Yes," said Robert without any hesitation.

Etta noticed that Dora was watching what was going on closely, as if taking mental notes.

"Lucky you. I'm not so sure about my partners today."

"Why is that?"

"Come on! Most people – including me, to be fair – would do anything to get their hands on that kind of inheritance. It's a chance that only comes along once in a lifetime. And as for Sue, she only has her beloved professor's interests at heart, not mine."

"Your room is ready, sir," called the barman, and with that, Herrera left to take his shower.

∽

AFTER DINNER, THE INN'S OWNER JOINED HIS GUESTS. IN A beautifully mellifluous voice, he proceeded to tell them, at their request, stories about the spectres who had haunted the inn since its foundation in the 18th Century.

"Are any of ye staying in room six?" he asked in a stage whisper.

"I am," said Amilcar Herrera.

"Then I'd better not speak of ghosties and ghoulies," he concluded, as if he hadn't been doing so for the last ten minutes.

"I'm not easily scared," insisted Herrera. "I've seen worse things in life than a few spooks."

All the guests in the pub looked at the landlord expectantly.

"If this gentleman doesn't mind you telling the story, please do tell," said one.

"Are the ghosts malicious?" asked another.

"Nay, I can assure ye of that. For as long as we've owned this business – and it's almost a decade now – our bogles have behaved themselves. You might just feel an icy cold hand gently rubbing your cheek or your back, or see a flickering light undulating in the air as if floating on the loch, but that's all…"

"Then, tell us more," said a young woman, adding a few incomprehensible words in what Etta recognised as a broad Glasgow accent.

"I'd welcome those spooks better if I knew more about them," said Amilcar Herrera.

The landlord was evidently pleased to oblige. Like many Scots, he was a born storyteller, and practice had made him perfect. His strong voice became almost tender as he told of the young girl who'd drowned in the Falls of Falloch while playing with her doll, then boomed out the story of the cruel, unforgiving highland chieftain who had ordered the whole family of a cattle drover to be slaughtered after the young man had been drinking in the pub while the landowner's animals were stolen. As the stories went on, the lights flickered and dimmed – a normal occurrence in the Highlands, the landlord said. The candles were snuffed out by some mysterious draught and the guests were left with no illumination other than the light of the fire.

"Och, it happens every night," the landlord reassured the guests. "But it's the fault of Scottish Power rather than the spectres... I think."

"Shall we take candles up to our rooms?" one guest asked when the spooky tales came to an end.

"No need for that," the landlord said, winking at him. "You'll find the lights in the bedrooms work perfectly well."

The guests looked at him in surprise, then one or two of them noticed a little switch beside where he was sitting. As he turned it to the right, the lights flickered back on and the guests all burst into loud laughter.

"Maybe it's time tae go tae bed," said the Glaswegian lady. "Tomorrow is going to be a long day. Ta-ta for the night, and thank ye for the stories."

"You're welcome. I really hope you make it down for breakfast; we pride ourselves on serving one of the tastiest cooked breakfasts in the area."

"Why wouldn't we make it?" asked a woman. The other guests stifled a chuckle.

The host looked across at Herrera. "I'm mainly worried about this gentleman in room six, but he seems a brave sort."

"I'm not particularly brave," said Herrera. "But no one, flesh and blood or spirit, will manage to make me skip breakfast tomorrow morning."

But skip it he did.

13

BREAKFAST TIME

A cold, wet drill passed through the thick duvet. Into her fleece pyjamas it went, finally coming to rest on Etta's neck.

"My goodness!" she yelled, sitting bolt upright.

"What's going on?" cried Dora from the other side of the double bed – to Etta's dismay, no twin rooms had been available.

"It's that poor d-d-drowned g-girl, reaching for me," stuttered Etta. To her horror, the duvet that had been thrown aside when she was startled from her sleep started to move around, slowly at first, then becoming more frenzied.

"There she is!" she cried, pointing at the movement. "The poor child is looking for her doll..."

To Etta's amazement, Dora was looking in the direction her finger was pointing, but her reaction was all wrong. The silly woman was laughing heartily.

"It's just a thought," Dora said through her chuckles, "might it not be a ghostly girl, but Leon?"

Etta felt as if she has been drenched by a cold shower. With a shrug, she pulled the duvet over herself again and Leon emerged. Jumping and frolicking around like a baby goat, he only stopped when he felt the weight of Etta's glare. Then he sat on his haunches and looked down at the floor.

"Your cold, wet nose, again," snorted Etta implacably. The dog dropped to the floor beside the bed and tried to hide his nose between his paws in shame. "I don't believe your repentance is sincere at all."

"Oh, the poor doggy," said Dora with a smile, getting out of bed to console the miserable beastie. Etta too got up, her nostrils twitching at the most delicious of smells.

"Grilled sausages," said Dora.

"Fried bacon," said Etta.

"Woof, woof, WOOF!" said Leon impatiently. Why were humans so slow to recognise the important things in life, like food?

In mere minutes that felt like centuries to Leon, his two bipeds were dressed and ready to go downstairs. They took him outside, and there was Adam's van. Under the other porch, the treasure hunters' porter was speaking to Grace and stamping his feet against the cold. And cold it was – as soon as Leon had done his business, the two women called him over and they marched back inside.

Etta, whose usual morning fare was a simple Italian cornetto and cappuccino, had always despised cooked breakfasts. How could one eat eggs, sausages, bacon first thing in the morning? But being a walker on the West Highland Way, especially as their lunches en route tended to be rather frugal affairs, had adjusted both her stomach and her creed. Nothing but the full walkers' breakfast would suffice.

"I never knew grilled tomatoes could taste this good. Accompanied by sausage, I mean."

"And what about the mushrooms? Pan-fried mushrooms and eggs and bacon work miracles... I thought I had tired legs, but I already feel better."

Leon, his nose deep in a breakfast bowl of his own, decided he'd refuse any attempt by his bipeds, once they were back home, to serve him milk, yogurt and soya flakes. What was the point when such heavenly stuff as sausage meat existed? To think how long those two bad humans had kept the secret of a decent breakfast from him. Unforgivable! A dog can never trust a biped; not completely, at least.

The two Hillock sisters, who had probably been the first down to breakfast, had finished their food and were waiting impatiently for Mr Morlore the solicitor to arrive.

"We're wasting precious time," grumbled Faith. "Why can't he get here earlier than 8.30?"

"Indeed," agreed Hope. "A real walker would be out well before dawn."

Faith looked around at Robert, who was just heading for a table, so sleepy he didn't even see Etta and Dora. "I don't think these youngsters would have enough stamina for that!" she sneered.

"That's their problem. It's survival of the fittest."

A rapacious smile spread across the sisters' faces as Grace made her way into the room. She looked towards Etta and Dora, but Etta nodded towards Robert's table. The young woman took her cue and went to join him, but her eyes rested on the Hillocks.

"Those sisters really give me the creeps," they seemed to say. *"I'm sure they'd trample over anyone to get what they want."*

Sue MacDuff appeared on the threshold behind the sisters. As she walked into the dining room, Leon sprang up. What a charming Basset he was, stoically enduring more petting and rubbing than any dog could be expected to bear. At least this woman knew how to stroke him exactly where he liked to be stroked, and she asked permission first.

"Do you mind if I sit with you?" Sue asked Leon's bipeds. "I don't think I'll be welcome at Robert's table."

"Of course you can," said Dora. "Where's Professor Hobbs?"

"Still taking notes. He said he'll come down later."

"Did you sleep well?"

Sue pulled a face and shook her head. "I was so tired, but I could barely sleep at all. Then there was all that noise in the early hours…"

"What noise?"

"Well, maybe not noise exactly, but you know how it is when you can't sleep. Everything seems louder than it would be during the day. But there was someone walking about in the corridor."

"Maybe from the rooms with shared bathrooms."

"I guess so," said Sue. "Anyway, I must have fallen asleep after that, and by the time the alarm clock went off this morning, I could have gone on dreaming for another couple of hours. It was a tiring day yesterday."

"Today seems a little less wet, at least." Etta had scanned the area when she had taken Leon out before breakfast.

"I told you so!" Mrs de Beer's shrill voice broke through the ambience in the room. "Let's not jump to conclusions, otherwise we might end up walking further than we have to, like we did yesterday."

"But we need to arrive before the others." Her husband clearly wanted to lower the volume of the conversation, but was obliged to raise his voice in order to be heard. "It's vitally important in this game, can't you see?"

"Arriving in the wrong place and ending the day empty-handed like we did yesterday is what I call a rather dumb strategy," the woman cried.

"My goodness," said Sue, "do they ever stop bitching? I could not survive a relationship like that."

"Yes, it's draining," said Etta, half thinking of her former hubby. "But some people thrive on arguments."

"Have you seen Amilcar?" Sue looked around the dining room. "Has he not come down yet?"

"No, we've not seen him," said Dora.

"He was too rash in accepting the haunted room!" Sue giggled, welcoming a dish of scrambled eggs and passing a piece of toast and bacon to Leon.

Kindness of heart always gets its reward. Leon considered how right Dora was; after his gallant acceptance of all kinds of mawkishness from the young woman called Sue, it was only right she share her breakfast with him.

Professor Hobbs arrived, engrossed in reading something. He barely raised his head at the greeting from Sue and the two older women.

"I wouldn't even try to have a conversation with him when he's in this mood," whispered Sue.

At 8.25, Mr Morlore walked into the dining room. Most of the walkers had cleared every last crumb of food from their plates and were ready for him. At 8.30 precisely, the solicitor led the treasure hunters into a side room, booming that they would need to wait for Mr Herrera, the only one missing. Etta and Dora, who were heading back to their room to get their things together for the day, offered to knock at his door on their way past.

"Maybe he's overslept," Dora suggested.

"That's his problem." Faith Hillock's strident protest followed them into the hall. "I don't see why we should have to wait. Mr Morlore, carry on."

"I will announce the updated ranking after yesterday's hunt, and then wait five more minutes for Mr Herrera before handing you the next clue…"

Then the door clicked shut and Etta and Dora climbed back up the stairs to their room. Stopping in front of room six, Etta knocked. No reply. Etta knocked harder. But again, silence was all that came back in response.

"If he weren't walking the West Highland Way, I would have suggested he went out for a stroll, but no one in their right mind would add even 100 metres to their daily rations."

"Then why doesn't he open the door? There's no way he could have slept through your knocking."

"Let's ask at reception."

Downstairs they went again. At the reception desk, the genial man who had been tending the bar the previous afternoon greeted them and said he hadn't seen Amilcar Herrera. However, the key to room six was hanging from the wooden rack behind him.

"That's weird," said Etta. "He's competing in a treasure hunt; he wouldn't have left without his clue."

"Most strange," the friendly man agreed. "Even though it's the proceeds from Sir Angus's estate paying for the accommodation, guests usually check out personally. Let's go and check his room."

Up the stairs they went again. The receptionist knocked, knocked again, then hammered his fists on the door.

"Mr Herrera? Mr Amilcar Herrera? We're worried about ye, so I'm going to unlock this door and come into yer room. Say something if ye dinnae want tae be disturbed."

Nothing.

The man inserted the key and pushed the door open. Then he, Dora and Etta took in what lay beyond.

14

THE QUITTER

The room seemed to be in reasonable order. The curtains were drawn, the partially open window letting the chilly air in; the bed linen was creased as if someone had slept in it. But there was nothing left belonging to Amilcar Herrera: not a garment, nor a bag, nor a jacket hanging on the hook.

The receptionist opened the dark wooden wardrobe, but it was completely empty. Herrera was gone.

Then Etta noticed on the bedside table a sheet of paper. It was a handwritten note.

"DEAR DISTANT RELATIVES,

You know what? I'm bored of this game that I don't stand a chance of winning. I was hoping to strike up a collaboration with all or some of you, but you're all such individualists. Not that I can blame you for that; if I were a legitimate heir, I would feel the same. But I'm not, and I'm sure the solicitor will find that out, probably after I've walked the entire 96 miles for nothing. What a stupid waste of time.

Enjoy the rest of the West Highland Way,

Amilcar Herrera."

• • •

"He's retired from the competition?" cried Etta. "How is this possible? Why?"

The friendly receptionist shrugged. "I dinnae ken, I'm afraid, so I cannae really answer yer questions. The important thing is that nothing bad has happened to him; I feared he'd fallen sick."

Etta looked all around the room, but still, everything seemed to be in place. She caught Dora's eyes, noticing her friend looked a little confused. Even to Dora's trusting mind, this sudden departure must seem weird.

The three went back down the stairs and the receptionist knocked at the side room where the solicitor and the treasure hunters were. Then he handed Mr Morlore the note.

"I see," said the solicitor, reading it aloud to the rest of the group. The two sisters grinned at each other. The de Beers called a temporary truce in their constant sniping to celebrate this piece of good news – one less person competing for the inheritance. Grace looked lost and Robert surprised. As for Sue MacDuff, she looked up at Alastair Hobbs. Was it suspicion, or was she just wondering if he had an answer? Or was it something altogether different? Sue was a difficult woman to read. For his part, Hobbs didn't seem to know what to do. Was that why he wouldn't meet the researcher's eyes?

"What does it mean, he's not legitimate?" Faith Hillock piped up.

"Maybe he's not the son of our relative after all," Hope's eyes glittered with her customary avarice.

The solicitor was quick to explain he'd put the document on record and try to get in touch with the man later in the day to make sure there were no irregularities. And, of course, Law, Lorr and Morlore would look into the claims of the message. Then he looked at Dora, Etta and the receptionist, thanked them politely and made it clear that what he had to say next was not for their ears.

The three left. The receptionist headed back to his desk, but Etta was not yet ready to let him go.

"What would the man have to do if he wanted to return to the airport to fly home? Is there a train station in Crianlarich or closer?"

"Oh no, hen, the closest one is in Ardlui on the west side of Loch Lomond, just a couple of miles walk from here."

"I know where Ardlui is, but you said walk? Isn't there a bus? He'd have all his luggage with him."

"The first bus is at 9.15; I guess he didnae want to wait that long."

"And when's the first train from Ardlui to Glasgow?"

The man checked a sheet of paper next to the reception desk within the pub.

"That was at 6.51, which is maybe why we haven't seen him this morning. He must have left when we were all sleeping."

"Still, walking 2 miles with all that luggage must have taken some time…"

"Around 40 minutes, I'd say. But I didnae see how bulky his luggage was. Also, we locals are used to giving lifts to travellers, so he might have hitchhiked his way to Ardlui, or even Glasgow."

"Or called for a taxi?"

"That'd be a rather expensive option, I'm afraid."

"But still a possibility…"

"Yes, indeed."

"Is there a way to check if he's used his room phone to make a call?" Etta asked.

The man looked at her doubtfully. Etta feared he might mention privacy issues or some other silly argument; thank goodness here in the Highlands, common sense still prevailed.

"I can see no harm in that…" the man checked on his computer, then shook his head. "No; if he called for a taxi, he did it directly from his mobile."

"Wouldn't you have heard a taxi arriving?"

"Not likely. Once I'm asleep, I tend to stay asleep."

"But what about guests whose rooms face directly on to the road? They'd have been more likely to have heard a car coming and going early this morning."

"Well," he checked the computer screen again, "a lady from Glasgow and the two Hillock sisters have windows over the front courtyard; they might have heard something if they're light sleepers, but experience tells me hikers tend to sleep rather deeply."

"One last question: did Mr Herrera say anything last night to indicate he was planning to leave?"

"Not at all."

"Why were you asking all those questions?" Dora asked Etta after they'd bid the friendly man farewell and returned to their room to pack, which consisted mainly of putting any clothing that had got wet the previous day and had been drying overnight into their main luggage, and then filling their small rucksacks for the day. They checked that their socks were dry, as they had been advised to wash a pair every night to avoid having to pack dozens for the whole trip. Dry socks prevent blisters: that was one commandment from the *Wise Walker Handbook*.

"I don't know," said Etta, "but Herrera didn't seem like the sort of guy who'd give up on an opportunity such as this."

"But if he felt he wasn't a legitimate heir, he stood no chance of winning…"

"Only the solicitor can explain that; we will have to ask Robert later what he said. If we're done with packing, let's go back downstairs and ask the sisters if they heard a car arriving early this morning."

As they left the room, they came face to face with the Glaswegian woman who had so enjoyed the landlord's ghost stories the previous night. She greeted them with a big smile and cheerful, if somewhat unintelligible, words.

"Nooo," she said, making an effort to speak English the two

Italians could understand, "I'm afraid I didnae – didn't – hear anything early. But in the middle of the night, I heard doors opening and closing. I guess someone went to the toilet. I don't mind shared bathrooms, but in the wee small hours, they're a bother."

"What time was this?"

"It was 3am – I know because I looked at ma watch. It took me a while to go back to sleep."

"Did you hear them coming back?"

"Who?"

"The person opening and closing the door. If they went to the toilet, presumably they had to walk back to their room."

"Nay, I didnae – didn't – hear them coming back. Which is a bit strange, nou I think a' it. But maybe they were quieter..."

"Maybe. Anything else you noticed?"

"Nooo, I'm afraid not."

"Are you walking to Tyndrum today?"

"Nae; the day is so fine, I want to carry on tae Kingshoose... but ah'm not sure. Let's see how it gaws."

"Have a nice day," said Dora.

"The same to ye; it was good to meet two real Italians. I hope ye'll find some good spaghetti Bolognaise in yer next hotel."

"And I hope not!" Etta was horrified that anyone would think she was in Scotland in search of the most touristy Italian food.

"Take care, dear." Dora tried to cover up for her friend's abruptness. Etta was going to protest when she realised that Dora's eyes had gone watery; only Dora could become emotionally attached to someone she had only spoken to a couple of times.

Outside, the Hillock harpies were waiting impatiently for Adam, the porter. It wasn't easy to attract their attention, but once Etta adopted her I'm-your-teacher-and-boss voice and glare, she managed to extract some answers.

"No, we did not hear a car early this morning."

"Not a single one."

"How about the dead of night?"

"Why would a car have turned up then?" asked Faith, eyeing Etta suspiciously.

"Because your relation, Amilcar Herrera, must have used some means of transport to leave the inn."

"Maybe he walked. Simple."

"But he had all his luggage with him."

"Not that much, and if you want to leave without being heard, surely you walk." Faith looked even grumpier than usual; it was clear she didn't like to be questioned.

"Otherwise, he would have waited until this morning and used the bus," Hope jumped in to support her sister.

"He wasn't an honest man, or he wouldn't have run away."

"Maybe he was too ashamed at his own weakness."

"Weakness?" Etta enquired.

"If you give up on something so easily, you must be a coward," Faith explained impatiently.

"I thought you'd be happy he is no longer a competitor…"

"We appreciate the fact that the competition will now be simpler, but we don't admire cowardly people."

The familiar fanatical gleam glittered in two pairs of eyes. Again, the sisters seemed to be a single mind in two bodies.

"Those two are rather scary," muttered Etta as the sisters stalked away.

"Indeed," said Dora as Leon popped his head out from behind her legs only when he was sure the two witches had departed. "But why have they gone back inside?"

Adam, the treasure hunters' porter, called them back. Peering around the door, the two women and one dog heard him announcing to the whole group that he was about to pick up the luggage from the hotel in 10 minutes, so the treasure hunters could leave everything at the reception desk and they'd find it at their Tyndrum hotel upon their arrival.

"That's a shame," Etta commented. "I wanted to ask Adam a few questions, but not when he's in such a hurry."

"Adam?" said Dora. "About Amilcar Herrera?"

"Indeed."

Robert sidled over to them. "We have our daily clue and our next destination is Tyndrum. But I'm afraid I will have to walk fast today."

"Of course," said Dora, smiling.

"Woof, woof, WOOF!" agreed Leon. As usual, he'd be the one who'd have to take care of these two hapless women.

"Is Grace walking with you?" asked Etta, determined to take the matchmaking mantle from Dora.

"Indeed she is," Robert said, flushing.

"I'm so glad you'll have each other for company."

Dora flushed too, but for a very different reason. She could no longer contain herself. She was not only curious by nature, but she simply loved riddles of all kinds, and treasure hunts excited her now just as much as they had when she was a child.

"May I ask what the clue is for today? But if it is a secret, I'll understand."

"I don't think it's a big secret, especially as you're not competing against us," said Robert, pulling an envelope from his jacket pocket to read the contents. *"They threw them in the quiet, cold waters."*

The words might as well have been in ancient Aramaic as far as Etta was concerned, but as usual, Dora had studied the day's itinerary.

"That refers to the River Fillan, doesn't it?"

"Correct," said Robert. "And just above it, on the Western bank, there's a lochan…"

"A *what*?" asked Etta, disturbed by the fact she didn't seem to know as much as the other two.

"I beg your pardon," said Robert, blushing again. "A lochan is a small loch, and this one is in fact *very* small. Legend has it that it's where Robert the Bruce and his army were forced to flee after a battle against the Clan MacDougall. Robert asked all of his men to drop their weapons in the lochan, including his own 'claymore' – the large sword he used in his many battles. To this day, the Lady of the Loch guards those weapons."

Dora opened her map. She had a real passion for maps which tended to drive Etta mad. The North was never where Etta thought it should be – which was just ahead of her, of course.

Robert pointed his finger at Tyndrum on the map, close to the end of today's hike.

"That tiny speck there is the lochan."

"It's on the West Highland Way," said Dora excitedly, "so we will get a chance to see it too, and Leon will be with us at that point. He might smell the Lady of the Loch – I love a good legend. "

"I take it you'll be staying in Tyndrum too?" asked Robert.

"Yes, at Glenbarry Farm."

"We'll be at the hotel, but if the treasure hunt doesn't take too long, I will pop in to say hi."

"We'd love that. But now, my boy, it's time to go. Don't let us slow you down."

Sue MacDuff was waiting outside taking in the fresh air, her rucksack on the ground, her intense dark eyes set on the moor ahead of her.

"Will we meet again in Tyndrum?" she asked Etta and Dora as they emerged from the hotel.

"Yes," said Dora, "but we will be staying in different places this time."

What was that strange expression that passed through the woman's eyes?

"And is the hushpuppy walking all the way there?" she asked, but it seemed her mind was elsewhere.

"Of course not," said Dora. "Today's stretch is far too long and the terrain too hard for a Basset. We're waiting for Michael from our travel company to fetch him…"

"With your luggage?" said Sue sarcastically.

"Yes," Etta felt rubbed up the wrong way, "with our luggage. Leon is a mighty fine guard dog."

"And Michael and Leon are going to join us close to Crianlarich," Dora butted in gently, trying to reconcile the two. "The guide told us the second part of the walk through the forest should be pleasurable for him."

"No offence meant," said Sue with a pious smile.

"None taken," grunted Etta.

At that moment, Michael arrived. Leon made sure the women knew he was not at all happy with the arrangements; he glued his bum to the ground as he did not intend humans to make decisions for him, a Basset who knew what he wanted in life and was determined to pursue it.

"Don't worry," said Michael, "he will follow me," and he gently took the leash from Etta's hands and pulled on it lightly, inviting Leon to move on.

The Basset sat, unmoving as a boulder.

"Oh no!" cried Etta, now an expert on the fact a Basset's stubbornness is inversely proportional to the languidness of their droopy eyes. "If he's made up his mind, he will never budge."

"I know how to handle him." Michael winked at her. "Look, Leon, such a bonnie she-Basset."

Leon sprang up on all fours, looking around.

"Look, over there," Michael said, pointing to the car. But just a couple of metres away, Leon's nostrils squirmed at the scent of a big fat lie ahead of him. Without any more ado, he stopped, inclined his head, and the collar slipped off, once again leaving a disappointed Michael all alone with a drooping leash. Leon sat quietly with the air of a dog who knew victory was his. The two women couldn't help but chuckle, feeling a pinch of pride at being the slaves of such a worthy chap.

"Listen, Leon," said Michael, approaching him again with a

chastened look on his face and an imaginary tail between his legs, "I was wrong to try to cheat you. There's no Basset here, but there's a nice Westie in Crianlarich. And trust me, my friend, the road is long and tough, still wet from yesterday's rain. The ladies will be fine; there's no danger for them, and you will be with them for the last stretch when they will need your help the most."

Leon turned his eyes on Michael, baring and scrutinising, in typical canine fashion, the man's very soul. It was difficult to say if he was evaluating Michael's words or his submissive attitude, or something else altogether. Whatever the case, he got up and crossed over to the car, waiting for his latest servant to help him in while casting a concerned look at his two bipeds.

"Michael is a good guy," said Dora, waving her hand.

"Perfect to serve Emperor Napoleon." Etta sighed, knowing that she would have behaved as submissively as the man and wondering why people insisted on calling her and Dora 'dog owners' when it was patently obvious it was the other way round. But that, she guessed, was the power of the dog.

15

NOT ONLY FOR THE SPIRITUAL

Etta and Dora pulled their rucksacks on to their shoulders and finally left the Drovers Inn, Dora as usual almost in tears at having to say goodbye to the genial receptionist-cum-barman and the old building.

"I told you it was a mistake for us to do this hike," retorted Etta. "If we had stayed in one place, you would only have had to cry once."

Dora replied almost immediately. "It is better to have loved and lost than never to have loved at all," she said seriously.

"Well, that's me told. Was it the scenery that inspired such a profound thought?"

"Nope," confessed Dora, passing her friend a Bacio Perugina, the Italian chocolate with wrappers that each carried a romantic message, "just a sweetie."

They were still chuckling loudly when their ears caught the murmurs of falling water. A sign told them they had reached the Falls of Falloch. Etta looked around, remembering what had happened to Grace at Inversnaid and the poor girl in the story the landlord of the inn had told, but today, everything seemed fine. They were free to enjoy the sight of nature – the mossy stones; the gurgling water; the large fern leaves – coming to life in the summer air.

Further north, they passed over a bridge on the Falloch River and found themselves on the Old Military Road. It was then that they realised how much the scenery had changed, from smooth and curving to sharp, mountainous and edgy. They were now very much in the Highlands of Scotland, and even Etta's heart swelled.

They decided not to walk through the village of Crianlarich, but to follow the West Highland Way and meet Michael along the course of the River Fillan, where the path met the A82 just beyond the town. Leon was hugely relieved to find his humans alive and kicking; he had enjoyed the pub in Crianlarich immensely, especially – just as Michael had promised – the company of a very cute Westie, but a dog's heart is large enough to accommodate his humans too and he had left the pretty she-dog to do his duty. Now, the trio was ready to walk the last stretch to Tyndrum all together.

"You know, ladies," said Michael, as cheerful as ever, "you're more than half way."

"Half way?" asked Etta, intrigued and belligerent at the same time. "I thought we were much closer to our hotel than that."

"In that, you're correct; I mean you've walked more than half of the West Highland Way. Somewhere above Crianlarich is the half way point, and you're well past that."

As the porter left to transport their luggage to Tyndrum, Etta was buzzing.

"Half way? Think of that!" She'd always believed this whole West Highland Way idea was madness, an unrealistic adventure that Dora had decided to plunge the three of them in to. And Etta had been waiting for them to hit a wall so she could finally let Dora know exactly what she thought of her madcap idea. She'd imagined herself lecturing her dreamy friend with one of her favourite 'I told you so' comments.

"How could you ever have believed that two women our age could walk so far?" she'd say. *"And in a place as bleak and barren as the north of Britain. What chance would we have? We should never have come in the first place, just driven our car through the glens."*

But the words that came from her lips were quite different. "Half way!" she repeated. "Wait till I tell Maddalena; she won't believe me. In fact, I will send her a few pics tonight." Etta had not been in touch with her daughter much since they had left Balmaha; Maddalena had disapproved of the idea of two elderly women undertaking such a strenuous hike all alone.

Elderly, my eye! thought Etta, her strides automatically becoming longer and quicker – so much so that Leon had to trot to stay behind her. She, who back in Castelmezzano would be panting after a walk along a short, albeit steep, alley, was turning into a serious hiker.

When the West Highland Way had crossed the main road, a stone bridge took them to a path along the edge of some pastures and an enclosure filled with sheep. They passed a whitewashed farm with grey gables and roofs, at its side a sort of mound surrounded by a low dry-stone wall all covered in moss. Ancient weather-beaten gravestones were leaning over as if worshipping the mountains that were embracing them.

Dora clasped her hands in ecstasy. "Oh, Etta, imagine being buried here so the farmer, day in, day out, can pass by and say hello to you. I wonder what dawn looks like from here. If there's anywhere I'd like my old bones to rest, it is a small, well cared-for place like this."

Etta was horrified. Not only did she not like to be reminded that life comes to an end, but she also found it rather morbid to indulge in such thoughts. Life isn't easy, but you never know what's beyond. What if the priest was wrong and before you get to Heaven, you have to face up to all the things you have done wrong?

She shrugged away her own silly fears, took hold of Dora's rucksack and pulled her not violently, but not softly either.

"Didn't you say you wanted to visit that local or lochan or whatever it was that Robert mentioned this morning?"

Dora awoke from her daydreams. "I'd love to!"

Even Leon sighed in relief. When Dora descended into one of her trances about the wonders of the world, you never knew how long they would last. After a morning of rest, he was impatient to get going; to sniff, to trot and to bark at any silly male dog who had the temerity to cross his path without showing due respect. He reserved a very different greeting, of course, for she-dogs of all breeds.

"This is interesting," Etta said, reading a noticeboard erected by the Hills and Mountain Research Centre.

"What does it say?" said Dora, too busy taking in another view to read it for herself.

"That here, there is an annual average precipitation of 2.5 metres of rain."

"Is that a lot?"

"It says five times more than Edinburgh, so there's no point trying to compare it to what we get in Naples or Palermo..."

"That is a lot," said Dora, joining her friend. But, of course, the eternal optimist had to find something good to say about the board's warning. "Look, it says that June is the month with the least rain."

"I hope this week will prove its point." And, as if by some sort of cosmic perversion, it started to rain. Their heads disappeared under their hoods. Etta was back in marching mode, but it seemed everything was destined to catch Dora's attention, even in the wet.

"What's that?" she cried in wonder, as if she'd spotted a huge turreted castle.

Etta backtracked to see what she was looking at. "It's just a ruined wall."

But, of course, the stubborn woman wanted to have a better look, as if the rain didn't concern her at all.

"This is St Fillan's Priory." Dora, who didn't wear glasses so had no experience of foggy lenses hit by large rain drops, read the latest information board to cross their path. "He was a Saint who came all the way from Ireland to spread the Christian word..."

"Maybe reinforcing his point by using the same sword Robert the Bruce dropped in the pond that we will never reach if you keep stopping everywhere!"

Dora pretended not to hear and went closer to inspect what was left of the priory's walls. Piles of stones were embraced by the trees and fully covered by a thick layer of verdant ivy, but there was something endearing in the overall atmosphere. It was as if a benign presence lingered there and invited walkers to take heart and use this close contact with nature to cleanse their souls, and maintain that peaceful message once they were back home.

But Etta was not of a mind to share such a tender feeling.

The Basset trotted ahead, the light rain seeming to excite him. Maybe he could smell rabbits and hares having fun in the fields all around them. When they reached the main road again, Dora pointed to a little trail leaving the path.

"Another diversion?" growled Etta, recognising the top of a church ahead. "Don't we have our fair share of religious buildings in Italy? Do we really need to look inside each church, graveyard and ruin here?"

"You will love this one!"

Etta growled again, this time in despair. As for Leon, he put his super-sensitive nose to work and realised the gentler biped had a good point.

A cream building appeared ahead of them, its windows long and narrow. Its entrance was a Gothic arch and it had a white bell tower on the side. Such a cheerful building in the middle of the wilderness – Scotland had her moments of poetry when you least expected them. But what Etta found, to her surprise, went beyond poetry. Under the victorious scrutiny of Dora, she realised the church was actually a café, and the most wonderful smell of baked goodies and freshly brewed coffee hit her nostrils.

It was unexpectedly warm inside the converted church. Once she had defogged her glasses, Etta loved what she saw: cupboards and windows displaying artisanal crafts; a series of comfy chairs around wooden tables; a selection of pies and cakes that made her instantly hungry. Chattering people were sitting all around with the happy, glowing faces that only walkers have as they appreciate the small pleasures of a warm room, a good scone and a steaming cuppa.

Etta tuned in to some of the conversations, all of which had a common theme. Walkers, it seemed, would gloss over the great views, the amazing places they were seeing, the itinerary and how many days they were aiming to complete the West Highland Way in, before turning the conversation inevitably to one body part: their feet. How many blisters they'd suffered; how many plasters they'd used up; how sore their toes were; what kind of socks were best for protecting their heels; what kind of cream or other unguent eased the pain – on and on it went. Even here in the church café, while biting into a scone or a golden pancake, all the walkers discussed the same subject. One even went so far as to remove his boot and invite his companions, with an unmistakable degree of pride, to count the number of blisters he had collected.

Feet dominated all the conversations in the room – except one.

"I don't think so," a familiar harsh voice retorted.

"But where else if it's not there?" snapped its equally harsh twin.

"But that means walking back…"

"It's not that far. We can do it as long as the others are well behi…"

Faith Hillock interrupted herself as Etta approached, getting close in a shameless attempt to eavesdrop. Giving the sisters her best innocent smile, she then turned to examine a shelf filled with delightful tins of biscuits.

"We'd better keep our mouths shut," Faith whispered to her

sister, loudly enough that Etta would be sure to hear. "Italians are notorious for not being able to mind their own business!"

16

LOST SWORDS AND DROWNED SAINTS

E tta didn't feel able to respond to the slur on her nationality; it would have shown that she was indeed trying to listen in on the sisters' conversation. Looking around, she saw that Dora had sat down at a table. Leon was beside her, waiting longingly for a waitress to bring him something nutritious.

"That sponge cake looks marvellous," said Dora as Etta joined them.

"With a hot cuppa, it will be a real dream." And the dream arrived just as the sisters paid their bills and left.

"I wonder what those harridans are up to," said Etta as the door slammed shut behind them.

"They should have been much further ahead of us."

"They mentioned having to backtrack…"

"To where?"

"They didn't say," Etta told Dora. "They realised I was listening."

"Let's hope Robert is well ahead of them…"

"And Grace," said Etta, giving her friend a curious look. "Maybe they're already at the hotel."

The strong, hot tea had come in a porcelain teapot decorated with painted white and pink roses. Dora fell instantly in love with the thin teacups, each in a different style and design. The sponge cake, the waiter informed them, was made with eggs from a nearby farm, the fresh cream was from a local dairy, and the jam was produced in house. As for Leon, he was served a savoury pancake with cheese that made life a little less tough for this adventurous hound.

Dora gazed at all the things she would have loved to buy, but would not have been able to carry. In the end, she settled for a few postcards for friends in Castelmezzano – she'd write them in the hotel – and some homemade fudge. And this made her just as happy as if she had bought the whole shop.

Once refreshed, they ventured back outside. The rain was still falling, but it was more of a gentle drizzle creating a feeling of nostalgia that well suited the place.

"We're not to be spared our share of the 2.5 metres of rainfall, I guess," said Etta.

The path now followed the Fillan River, taking them near what looked like a pond surrounded by ferns on three sides and on the fourth – the side opposite them – by a wall of dark fir trees. Carved into a stone were the words "The lochan of the Lost Sword", while another stone depicted a long weapon: the claymore of Robert the Bruce. Dora peered into the lochan, as if expecting to catch a glimpse of metal. But under the leaden sky, the water was dark and impenetrable.

The hair on Leon's back suddenly rose as he launched a powerful volley of "Woo-woo-woofs" in the direction of the copse, alerting any potential intruder that a whole army of ferocious dogs awaited them. He took a few involuntary steps, but like all good pretenders, he stopped his forward momentum, just in case something really dangerous lurked out of sight.

To his consternation, something did move in the thicket of trees.

"It's us," a familiar voice said. "It's only us." And Robert and Grace made their way through the branches and came into full view.

"What the heck are you doing in there?" asked Etta as soon as she could breathe again.

"Is everything OK?" asked Dora, visibly relieved.

Leon ran towards them, his tail wagging in a friendly greeting; had he known it was his young friends, he wouldn't have made such a scene. Had he scared them too much?

"Leon, you're such a splendid guard dog," said Robert, scratching his back. "These two ladies are fortunate to have a companion and protector like you." Of course, Leon agreed with everything the man said.

"We thought you might be at your hotel already," said Dora.

"Solving the clue wasn't as easy as we expected," said Grace.

"The treasure isn't here," explained Robert. "I thought it could be next to the other lochan," and he pointed across the land on the opposite side of the Fillan River. "You can't really see it from here, but there lies Lochan nan Arm. Some believe it's where the claymore was really thrown."

"We went back to the main road and cut through the fields to the lochan," said Grace, her expression disheartened. "But we simply could not find the treasure."

"We met the sisters," said Etta, telling them about the short encounter. "Maybe they were heading to the same lochan as you."

Robert opened his map, his long, knuckly fingers pointing to each place as he spoke.

"No, they can't have been," he said. "To reach the Lochan nan Arm, you don't need to go as far south as the café. The diversion is well before it."

"Then where were they heading?" wondered Grace.

"At this point, I really don't care."

"Wait," said Dora. "Would you read the clue out loud again?"

"Of course," and Robert did as he was asked.

"Are we sure it means the weapons?"

"What else could it mean?" said Robert.

"I read near the priory that St Fillan himself was thrown in a lake," said Dora.

"True," Robert agreed. "The Saint was born with a stone in his mouth, which was believed to be a bad omen. And his father, in shame, threw him in a lake."

"That's it!" cried Etta triumphantly, as appreciative of Dora's discovery now as she had been impatient when Dora had insisted on stopping at the ruined priory earlier. But both Robert and Grace shook their heads.

"But that happened in Ireland where the Saint was born," explained Grace.

"Not in Scotland," confirmed Robert.

"What happened?" asked Dora.

"He was saved by a Bishop," Robert said, showing how clued up he was on Scotland's history, "and raised as a Christian. Then he moved to Scotland and founded the Monastery in Auchtertyre. You must have seen the ruins of the priory that was erected by Robert the Bruce to thank the Saint for his mission…"

"We did," said Dora meditatively. "So the Saint was thrown in water as a small child. In Italy, we often have ongoing traditions attached to these kinds of legends."

"You're right, I'm sure I read about something like that." Grace pulled a guide from her rucksack, heedless of the rain, and riffled through its pages with uncharacteristic impatience. "Here! It says Fillan is the Patron Saint of the mentally ill. It was a tradition to bring those poor unfortunates to the river, plunge them into the icy Fillan water, and then tie them up for the night in the cold chapel. In the morning, the monks checked the ropes; if they were loose, it was a sign the insanity had been cured."

"Goodness!" cried Etta and Dora in horror. "So maybe it was those poor souls and not the sword that the clue meant," added Etta, recovering from her shock. "Maybe there's a particular spot along the river, close to the priory."

"Let's go back!" Robert said, his face eager.

"You could ask at the café," Dora suggested. "Maybe the people there are familiar with the legend."

"That's a good idea; they might indicate the precise spot."

"Are you coming too?" Robert asked the two older women and one dog eagerly. Dora and Leon looked at Etta with their faces full of expectation.

"I guess so," she said. "We're close to Tyndrum anyway, so we can't miss all the fun."

Dora hugged her friend for once again making it possible for her to participate in a real treasure hunt.

On the way back to the café, the group stumbled into Professor Hobbs and Sue MacDuff, who were also coming back from a thorough search of Lochan nan Arm. Tiredness and confusion showed in equal measure on their faces.

"We're going back to the priory," Robert said. Then, to the horror of his companions, he told Hobbs and Sue about their theory. "I'm not sure we're right, but I can't see any other possibilities."

Hobbs eyed him suspiciously. "Why are you telling us?" he asked.

"In case you want to join us."

"How are you going to win if you share your secrets with your competitors?"

"I'm sure you would have got there too. Why would I make you go round in circles?"

"Because if I get overtired today, it'll be to your advantage tomorrow."

Robert shrugged, as if all this thinking was unimportant compared with finding the treasure.

"Anyway, we're going," he said. "Feel free to join us."

Alastair Hobbs seemed to be evaluating whether Robert was pulling his leg, as if the young man might have found the treasure already and was now attempting to put him off the scent. Sue, whom Professor Hobbs had not consulted, not even with a look, decided to air her opinion.

"I'd follow them if I were you."

"Would you, indeed," said Hobbs.

"Yes, Professor."

"So this woman trusts you," he said to Robert.

"Or maybe she just knows a generous offer when she hears one," growled Etta, still unhappy with Robert's decision, as if she were involved in the competition. Grace seemed to share Etta's mindset; she didn't look happy at all about Robert's generosity.

"So, where is the place?"

"We plan to ask the people who run a nearby café in a converted church if they know more about the tradition," said Dora.

The people in the café were indeed familiar with the place where the mentally ill had been treated so cruelly in the name of trying to cure them. The Fillan River turned a corner at that point, creating a quiet basin in a branch where the water flowed much more slowly. A little path would take them straight to St Fillan's Holy Pool.

"It might be June, but for the life of me, I would never take a dip in those waters," cried Etta once they reached the place.

"Och, ye should try it," said Robert. "In summertime, it's a grand place to bathe on a sunny day."

"It seems to me the sun doesn't make its way this far upcountry," Etta answered.

"It does," said Sue. "You can't imagine how it all changes and lightens up. You should see the range of colours in the mountains, the moor and the lochs."

"You're right," admitted Etta. "I can't imagine it."

"I hope you will see what we mean when you reach Loch Tulla," said Robert.

"In the meantime, let's look for our clue," said Professor Hobbs, clearly indifferent to the potential charms of Scotland.

They searched the area. Sure enough, under a willow tree

stretching over the calm water, they found the treasure. Robert offered number three to Grace, who hesitated, then took it.

"Numbers one and two have already gone," said Robert.

"The terrible twins, no doubt," said Professor Hobbs. "Young man, you take number four, and I'll be happy with five. The South Africans can't have arrived here yet."

Beyond his apparently fair behaviour, the man must be thinking what a piece of luck it is that Mrs van Wetering and Mr Herrera aren't competing any more, Etta thought. All of a sudden, a cold chill passed down her spine as she sensed danger. How much more relieved would the professor be if people with high scores – like Robert and Grace – were no longer in the game?

The wind picked up, slashing the increasingly heavy rain into their faces. It was time to head for Tyndrum.

17

BEINN DÒRAIN

G lenbarry Farm proved to be the perfect place to stay. The women each enjoyed a long bath followed by an excellent dinner, and by 9.30, they were in bed. Leon too was happy and satisfied; he had managed to scare a few of the hens that strolled around the farm before returning to their coop for the night – that was, until a cockerel, wings outstretched and eyes protruding menacingly, had tried to break his nose, letting him know his stupid jokes were not appreciated. Leon had retired quietly, hoping no one had seen a clever Basset such as he defeated by an overgrown sparrow.

In the morning, the farmer's wife welcomed Etta and Dora to a deliciously abundant breakfast.

"But it's just the two of us," Etta cried, looking at the many dishes the woman kept bringing to their table. "How can we possibly eat all of this?"

"Ye cannae walk on an empty stomach," she replied with a smile.

And 20 minutes later, to Etta's dismay, nothing was left on the table, nor under the table where Leon had made his precious contribution. When the hostess mentioned the eggs had come from the farm's very own free-range hens, the hound had wondered if he really wanted to taste them, remembering his shame the previous day. But when his eggs came scrambled and scattered with a few pieces of bacon, he decided to be brave. After all, how would the chickens or, worse, the fierce cockerel ever find out?

Leon's bipeds had just fastened their luggage when Michael arrived to pick up their rucksacks. And Leon himself. Michael's busy day wouldn't allow him an opportunity to meet Etta and Dora and drop Leon off, so he would drive the hound directly to The Inveroran Hotel on Loch Tulla.

"Just in case, I asked that chap who's portering for your friends, Adam, if he'd be available should you need him, and he said he will. He's done a good job of standing in for the normal driver, considering he was called on at such short notice."

Etta and Dora nodded; they too had heard positive comments about Adam. Michael spread the map out in front of them and explained what they'd see during the day's walk.

"You've done such a good job so far, I'm sure you will find today's stretch easy. Just nine miles…"

Etta's brain made the calculations almost instantaneously: 9 miles meant just shy of 15 kilometres. And any walker will confirm that there's a huge difference between 15 kilometres and 20; not all kilometres were created equal, and those final 5 require more effort than all the rest put together.

"Also," Michael added, after having pronounced the most jaw-breakingly difficult names of the highest peaks they'd meet that day, "I hope you'll have a clear view of the viaduct when you get *here*," he pointed. "See how the railway almost makes a U-turn between Beinn Dòrain and Beinn a'Chaisteil?"

"Is that the Hogwarts Express viaduct?" asked Dora, already imagining living that particular dream.

"Och, nay; you mean the Glenfinnan Viaduct. You only get to see that if you take the train from Fort William to Mallaig."

"Really?" cried Dora, overjoyed at the news.

"Will you be heading there after you've completed the Way?"

"Yes, our next homeswap is in the Western Isles."

"You'll be three real Scots by the end of your holiday," said Michael. And it did not take much for Leon to imagine himself dressed in a kilt, a bonnet on his head, a claymore hanging from his waist and a bonnie lassie-Basset at his side. He'd be a real Highlander, defending his castle and his one true love from any enemy.

"Oh, I almost forgot," said Michael. "If you need anything for the next few days, you want to get it here in Tyndrum before you leave. You're heading for Rannoch Moor, then you'll pass through Glencoe and the Devil's Staircase; there won't be any more shops until you reach Kinlochleven in two days' time."

The legendary endlessly weather-beaten Rannoch Moor; both Dora and Etta gasped at the thought. They had been reading about that immense expanse of land swept by the north wind and felt a mixture of expectations about something so different from their home. A primeval fear went down Etta's spine at the thought of such a wild environment with no houses, not even any trees, to offer protection.

The day was dark, grey and wet. Etta had partly come to terms with the idea of walking in the rain, but she still felt there was nothing more discouraging than getting wet from the very moment your nose poked out into the elements from your warm and cosy accommodation.

"We should reach the Bridge of Orchy in three to four hours," said Dora as if reading her thoughts. "We could have our lunch there, find a place for coffee and cake. Then it's only an hour maximum to Loch Tulla…"

"Then let's go this very moment, or I will run back to my bed and not even a hoist will get me up again."

Despite their host having prepared a generous packed lunch for them, the two friends decided to pass through Tyndrum to buy snacks. They had learned a few things about hiking and food: one, you tend to get *very* hungry on the way; two, food can cheer you up even when it's raining cats and dogs; and three, your appetite is inversely proportional to the amount of food you carry. If you take no food, you'll be ravenous the whole way; if you take plenty, you'll probably leave half of it. Etta realised the last point was probably psychological, but it had felt very real when her stomach was growling every 100 metres and all she could think about was when she'd next get a bite to eat.

Tyndrum, just a little to the north of Glenbarry Farm, was a huge disappointment to Etta. To start with, she and Dora could not find their young friends; when they enquired at the hotel, they were told the treasure hunters had left much earlier. All the two women learned was that the clue seemed to expect the treasure hunters to climb Ben Dòrain. Etta asked at least four times what on Earth Ben Dòrain might be. In the end, the receptionist took a map and pointed to a 1,076-metre peak.

"It's the 64th highest Munro in Scotland," the man added, looking like the proudest of parents showing off his child's talents.

"But that's not part of the West Highland Way. How long will it take them to climb it?"

"From here, a good six hours, I'd say," said the man, further inflating his chest. "That is, if they're fit enough. From Auch, they will take the Southern access, which is the tougher ascent. It goes up, up and up relentlessly, but if they manage that, the descent on the other side to Bridge of Orchy will be easy."

"Poor guys!" said Dora. Etta rubbed her thumb and index finger together, indicating that as the 'poor guys' stood to win quite an inheritance, they might as well suffer a bit for it. Dora ignored her.

"So, where's the village?" Etta asked.

"What village?"

"Tyndrum."

"This is Tyndrum," answered the man, waving a languid hand at the road just outside the hotel.

"That's not a village," Etta answered, dismayed.

"Of course it's a village – we have hotels, a supermarket, a petrol station…"

"So it's a rest area." Etta could not contain herself. She'd seen the ample parking in front of the petrol station, but to her, a village needed a church; a main square where people could meet and chat; an old town hall; at least two bars. Mostly, villages did not develop along a road, but in tiny streets circling around the historic centre.

Her scepticism seemed to irritate the old man, who had been patient and kind so far.

"We also have a train station and a community hall," he snapped, "with a kitchen and facilities."

"It will no doubt be in some dreary building. You should not claim in brochures that this is a village!" And she left, indignant that some people seemed to struggle to appreciate what to her was patently obvious.

"I apologise for my friend," Dora said to the angry man who was muttering things in a language she simply could not understand. "She's just received bad news from home and she's upset." This was totally untrue, but it was the only thing Dora could come up with to make sure the man would not hate all Italians from that day onwards.

"I prefer rain and wilderness to a crossroads." Etta was still muttering and grumbling about Tyndrum when Dora joined her outside and they spotted the signs for the West Highland Way.

As they resumed their walk, the rain was still falling, but every now and then, it'd stop. The sky would light up in a sudden brilliant blue and the mountains would sparkle with luscious green. When a prodigious double rainbow sliced through the sky, the mountains seemed more imposing than ever, the meadows larger. Dora stopped, her hands clasped. Everything was so perfect… until it started to rain again.

It was during one of the rainy spells that they came to a little stone cottage surrounded by a few oak trees. They were the only trees for miles around and were dominated by the mountains that embraced the landscape.

"It's so lovely," said Dora, hands clasped again.

"It is, but I'm not sure I'd be able to live here, so far from anyone else," answered Etta, relieved that her friend had not stopped in contemplation.

After a bend, the trail marched on straight ahead towards the pyramid shape of Ben Dòrain. At just over 1,000 metres, it rose up, like many mountains in Scotland, from ground level, towering above its surroundings.

"My goodness, I'm so glad we don't have to do the climb," Etta confessed. Dora nodded in agreement; even for an adventurer like her, there was something forbidding about the mountain's stern look.

For her part, Etta was happy not to be doing the walk by herself. She would probably never have contemplated doing any such thing, and she recognised, not for the first time, how Dora's cheerful presence had made a difference in her life. How many things one can do with a companion; actually, two, as she could not leave the Basset out. Of course, she did not mention any of this to Dora, but she did start to hum. Dora joined in and they carried on, as happy as children in the wild surroundings of the Scottish Highlands.

"There's the viaduct," cried Dora some time later, indicating a point where the railway line left the West Highland Way on its left to cut through Glen Coralan and Glen Chailein at the feet of the three large mountains that had accompanied the walkers thus far: Beinn Odhar, Beinn a'Chaisteil and the now familiar Beinn Dòrain. The viaduct with its nine spans was highlighted by a ray of sun hitting the side of the Munro. And as if on cue, a train appeared from the south.

Dora held her breath, her hands clasped at breast height, her mouth open in wonder, imagining a steam train breathing its puffy smoke into the air as it chugged across the viaduct. It was

Etta who had to snap a photo, as her friend had descended into her trance state.

"Not bad, maybe I should send it to Maddalena," Etta said, scrutinising her snapshot as if it was a masterpiece, despite it being partially obscured by her hood; despite the horizon being somewhat inclined to the left, as if the weight of Dòrain had dragged the train tracks down.

Dora woke up from her daydream to remind Etta that the hotel in Inveroran had no Wi-Fi and hardly any phone signal. Etta looked down at the phone in her hand, confirming there wasn't even enough signal to make a phone call, never mind use the internet.

"Oh well," said Etta, still too proud of her photographic achievements to care. "She will discover her mother's talents when we're in Fort William."

After crossing a bridge made from wooden planks laid over rough waters in Auch, they saw the signs to a secondary path going up the mountain. That must be the one the treasure hunters had taken. It not only climbed rather steeply, but it appeared to twist and turn between crags and huge pieces of loose rock.

"Can you really walk up that expanse of ostrich eggs?" Etta cried.

"It won't be an easy hike, especially if it's raining..."

"It's windy here, I can't imagine what it must be like up there."

"Let's hope everything has gone well," said Dora reassuringly. "Who knows? Perhaps the man at the hotel was exaggerating and Robert and Grace will be waiting for us in the hotel at Loch Tulla after a peaceful day's walking."

18

LOCH TULLA

The West Highland Way continued on the Old Military Road, a large track flanked by Beinn Dòrain on the right and both the river and the main road on the left. Etta and Dora came to a small but pretty train station boasting a red-brick kiosk with white-framed windows and a red gravel platform. Surrounded by trees and decorated with flowerbeds, it looked as pretty as anything they'd find in the sweet south. Then the road travelled between a few scattered houses.

Their arrival in Bridge of Orchy came as another disappointment to Etta: once again, it was nothing more than a crossroads, a smaller carbon copy of Tyndrum. The name Bridge of Orchy had held promise of pretty cottages and a cosy historical centre with a real square. She sighed deeply, until Dora pointed out a white turreted building rich with gables and equally white French windows. Large sun umbrellas covered outside tables – as if people round here really ran the risk of sunburn – and the happy chatter from within, the sight of waiters coming and going with dishes of rich food, made Etta eager to sit and enjoy a cup of hot coffee and a slice of cake. The plentiful chips, shiny steaks, even the simplest of soups made

Etta regret that they had to save money and pick a spot to eat their sandwiches in the cold outside.

Dora noticed her companion's eyes fixed on the food.

"We will have a delicious dinner tonight. And with what we save on lunch, we can buy a nice gift for Armando." Armando was Etta's grandson. She saw too little of the boy because her daughter had decided to live in Granada with a strange man – a naturopath, whatever that meant. But it was nice of Dora to remind her that all missed opportunities in life led to other opportunities, and giving up on a proper lunch in a great place was a small sacrifice in the big scheme of things.

They consumed their packed lunch in the proximity of the hotel restaurant, grateful that the Glenbarry Farm hostess had a knack for making tasty sandwiches. Then, they moved into the restaurant for coffee. Etta was horrified when a waiter asked if they wanted to sit outside or in.

"Inside, of course," she cried, her eyebrows shooting far beyond the frame of her red glasses. Then she ordered a cappuccino and a huge slice of gateau, and felt reconciled with the whole world in the interior of the cosy bistro – to the point that when she glanced at the view from the window, she had to admit Bridge of Orchy did have its own charm, despite having neither a square nor a church.

"OH MY GOODNESS!" CRIED DORA, FREEZING ON THE SPOT.

"What?" Etta was a few steps behind Dora, feeling she could no longer cope with the strong wind blowing straight against her face. Especially now, when the path had started to climb, she needed to send oxygen to her lungs in a smooth breathing rhythm. Inhaling the icy wind wasn't exactly what she had in mind.

As for her companion, Dora was standing stock still. All she could manage by way of an answer was to raise her right arm slowly and point at something in the distance. There, at the peak of Mam Carraigh, the view opened up over flat lands surrounded by dark mountains in the distance. When her glasses defogged, Etta spotted a strip of forest, but it was only when a pale ray of sun hit the landscape that she realised what she had thought was a plain was actually Loch Tulla, the pine trees on its southern side almost reaching its water. Under the touch of sun, the water turned instantly from grey to a deep blue, leaving Etta as speechless as her friend. Give a walker a pretty view and you've given meaning to a whole day's hard work and sweat. And even though this view was partially hidden by the crags and trees below the Old Military Road, it was simply stunning.

They started the descent in a state of high excitement. Reaching their accommodation this early in the day would mean plenty of chances for rest and relaxation, but surprisingly, considering all the kilometres they had under their belt, both women were eager to discover a little more about the area.

After greeting the hound, who was as ecstatic to see them as if they had been parted for years, the two friends each took a shower, and enjoyed a little rest and a cup of tea in their room. Then Etta looked at Dora, Dora looked at Leon and Leon looked at Etta. A twinkle of complicity flashed in three pairs of eyes.

"Shall we have a wee walk outside?" asked Etta, enjoying the little Scottish word she'd learned.

"Absolutely!"

"Woof, woof, WOOF!"

In the foyer of the hotel, they met Adam, the treasure hunters' porter, who was explaining to the receptionist why he was so late. Apparently, he'd had trouble with his vehicle and had been obliged to make a long detour to a garage. Then, inevitably, he'd had to wait for a missing piece before the repair could take place and he could leave for the hotel.

"I'm happy to have caught you," said Etta, addressing the man so eagerly that he looked somewhat startled. "Can I ask you something once you've finished your conversation?"

"Certainly," said Adam with a grin. "I think I'm done here. The receptionist just told me that I'm ahead of my group, which is good news."

"Yes, we've taken the luggage into their rooms," the receptionist confirmed. "And we'll see you tomorrow morning. The group will be leaving early, but you can come anytime to fetch their things."

The receptionist returned to his duties, and Adam turned to Etta.

"What can I do for you?"

Etta wondered if she should embellish her weird request with a justification of some sort, then decided against it. The more you justify yourself, the more people will ask you all the whys and wherefores before answering. Better to use her speciality: the power that only comes from a 40-year career in teaching.

"I'm sure you remember Mr Amilcar Herrera. Did he have a lot of luggage with him?"

If the man was surprised by the question, he hid it well. "Let me see… he had a suitcase with him, not a very large one, and his daily rucksack."

"The suitcase had wheels?"

"Yes, it did."

"Was it heavy?"

The man gave the question a little thought. "Not particularly, but it wasn't light either. Maybe around 15 kilograms."

"How about Miss Faith Hillock. Is her luggage heavier than his was?"

"Miss Hillock's?" The man repeated, as if trying to follow Etta's strange questions. "No, um… hers is probably a little lighter than Mr Herrera's was."

"Did he mention to you that he was thinking of retiring from the competition?"

"Not a word. I only found out when I went to pick up the luggage the day he quit and the hotel staff told me there was one less traveller."

"Did he walk to the train station, do you think?"

"Maybe yes, maybe no... I've no idea." Then the man shrugged. "Why are you asking me all these questions?"

"I had agreed to exchange email addresses with Amilcar Herrera. Like me, he's a passionate collector of Wedgewood porcelain and we want to exchange photos of our best pieces. But he left without notice. Do you have any idea how I can get in touch with him?"

"Sorry, madam, but Amilcar Herrera was just one of the guests in the treasure hunt party. I hardly exchanged more than a few words with him. Perhaps you could ask the solicitor? I'm sure Mr Morlore has contact details for them all."

"That's a good idea, I'll try to have a word with him in the morning. Thanks a lot for your help."

"So," Dora asked as they left the hotel, "What do you think?"

"I wouldn't walk three kilometres with 15 kilograms of luggage," said Etta.

"But he was obviously keen to get away without explaining himself."

"True."

"Why did you ask Adam about Faith Hillock's luggage?"

"I wanted to make sure he's a reliable witness. In Rowardennan, her luggage was blocking my path and I had to lift it out the way, and yes, it was definitely lighter than 15kg. So I know I can trust what Adam says."

"You're an amazing woman, Mrs Passolina."

They had almost reached the loch when they heard a deep growl from Leon. Then the deep growl became a series of woRf, woRf, WORFs.

"I can see his tail," said Dora, pointing to a little white tip jumping around in the long grass ahead of them. They marched towards him.

"What is it, Leon?" Dora asked. The dog seemed relieved that help had finally arrived.

"WoRRRf, WoRRRf, WORRRF!" he hollered, his front legs

stretched and his long body almost genuflecting in a comical attempt to touch something with the tip of his nose while keeping the rest of himself well away from it. Whatever it was, it might be dangerous, even for a Basset.

Etta took Leon by the collar and gently moved him to one side. And then they saw it…

19

AN UNEXPECTED MEETING

There in the grass, a brownish mass of warts was looking suspiciously in the Basset's direction, its head tucked between its shoulders, its reptilian eyes, black slits in the centre of caramel, unblinking.

"WoRf, WoRf, WORF!" Leon repeated, unable to believe the thing would not run away from him. The hound was feeling more powerful than ever now that Dora was holding him back.

"It's just a toad, Leon," said Dora with a chuckle. "There will be hundreds around, so please don't bark at each one."

"Goodness," said Etta in relief. "For a second, I thought he might have found a corp... ah, nonsense."

"I thought so too," confessed Dora, goggling at her friend. "I think we've encountered too many dead bodies on our home-swapping adventures."

They laughed, taking in their surroundings: the moon rising in the still luminous sky; the water trembling as a cool breeze caressed it; an islet populated by a dozen Scottish pines, their branches shaped by the ever-present wind.

"Those are the Black Mountains," said Dora, pointing to a range of irregular silhouettes cutting the horizon just above the lake. "We'll pass them tomorrow when making our way across Rannoch Moor."

Once again, their Latin hearts skipped a beat at the mere mention of the legendary place. Maybe it was the thought of the moor, maybe it was simple tiredness, maybe the wind really had got stronger, but they suddenly both felt cold and hungry.

"It feels so good when you know a cosy place for the night is waiting nearby," said Dora. Unseen by Etta, she paused briefly, contemplating the beauty of the loch, her thoughts happy and dreamy as ever.

"I wonder if the treasure hunters have arrived," said Etta.

"Let's go back and find out," replied Dora, catching up with her dear friends, human and canine.

When they got to the hotel, they found the treasure hunters had indeed arrived; in fact, the restaurant was full of them. The only people Etta and Dora didn't recognise was a couple of German tourists.

"Please, do sit with us... if you would like to, that is," said Robert, who was sitting opposite Grace and indicating the two free seats next to them.

"When did you arrive?"

"About half an hour ago."

"And we have plenty to tell you," said Grace to Etta, whispering her words as if she didn't want to be heard by the other people in the room. Raising her eyes and looking past the Germans' table, Etta noticed that Sue was glaring in their direction.

"What's happened?" asked Dora. "Did you win the treasure hunt today?"

"No, it was Alastair who got there first."

"Wait," said Robert. "Let's order our food first; I'm positively starving." And they didn't only order their food, but ate it like a pack of wolves when it arrived. Scotch broth; garlic bread; grilled salmon; beef steaks with gravy and mustard mash; wild rice; neeps and tatties – which Robert explained were mashed turnips and potatoes, the traditional accompaniment to the uniquely Scottish dish of haggis. They all disappeared from the table as soon as they were served. Not a word was spoken as the four adventurers filled their empty bellies. It was only when the hour, although still fairly early, edged towards bedtime that Grace finally started to tell her tale.

"When we received our clue this morning, we realised we'd have to climb Ben Dòrain to find it. It was rather obvious, no great secret this time, so speed rather than ingenuity was the order of the day. And it was a tough climb."

"It's not a path up it, but loose stones, and it's very steep," said Robert, flushing as if embarrassed he had interrupted Grace.

"The wind got stronger and stronger, making it hard to keep our balance. Then after passing a rocky outcrop, we found ourselves completely surrounded by mist. We could hardly see each other…"

"And that was where the track was at its most precarious: just blocks of rock on which it was hard to balance, let alone walk. It was then that I heard Grace cry out, but before I could think of going to her aid, I felt someone grab my backpack and pull me over. It's a miracle I didn't fall from the path and tumble down the mountain. I got away with just a few bruises rather than broken bones, or worse."

"Goodness!" cried Dora.

"Gracious!" retorted Etta.

"Woof!" added Leon.

"I had also been pushed over moments before," said Grace. "And I too was lucky not to break my neck."

"We screamed at whoever was there to show their face…"

"But the only ones to come out of the mist were the Hillock sisters, who had been behind us. Then Alastair and Sue came back down – they had been further ahead."

"We all searched the area, but could not find anyone else there."

"What about the de Beers?" asked Etta.

"They had fallen behind during the climb. We waited for them to let them know they might be in danger, and then we all decided to proceed together, agreeing to distribute the treasure in the order we'd been in when Grace and I were attacked. Hence Alastair was first."

"Lloyd and Olive protested, saying that they would have caught us up, but in the end – after some bickering between the two of them – they decided to accept the proposal."

"Luckily, the treasure was not that hard to find. It was just near the summit cairn – the pile of stones that marks Beinn Dòrain's peak."

"But it was a hard scramble."

"So I take it you're still top of the leader board?" asked Etta.

"Yes, we're still top," said Grace, casting the sweetest look at Robert. As usual, he blushed, but it didn't matter as she did too.

"There's live music on in the pub," Alastair Hobbs announced as he and Sue approached their table. "A dance might help you young ones to sleep. As for me, I'm getting too old for dancing the night away; I prefer my bed. Who knows what's waiting for us tomorrow?"

"The treasure might be on the moor." If Sue was embarrassed at the fact Professor Hobbs was lumping her in with Grace and Robert as one of the 'young ones', she managed not to show it. "Or it might be on the mountains in Glencoe…"

"Another climb?" cried Mrs de Beer's horrified voice from behind Sue.

"The Glencoe mountains are not part of the West Highland Way," said Robert.

"Nor was Beinn Dòrain," replied Sue.

"At least it's not too long a stretch tomorrow."

"Only one mile more than today and we'll be in Kingshouse."

"But don't you think that leaves time for another diversion?"

"Hopefully not, but I guess we are getting close to the end."

"We'll be able to see the end point beyond the Devil's Staircase."

"What's that?" asked Etta.

"Another sharp climb just before Kinlochleven, our stop the day after tomorrow."

Mr and Mrs de Beer decided to follow Professor Hobbs's suggestion to retire early; the sisters had already gone up. Robert and Grace wanted to have a look at the loch under the night sky, while Etta and Dora were curious about the live music.

As they entered the traditional little pub, Dora's elbow landed sharply in Etta's stomach.

"Ouch!" Etta cried, rounding on her friend for an explanation. But when her eyes looked beyond Dora, she found it: Rufus McCall, the man Etta had so enjoyed dancing with at the cèilidh in Luss, was sitting at the bar. As soon as Etta's eyes alighted on him, he turned as if feeling the weight of her stare and started slightly at recognising the duo.

He rose immediately and came over to them, his eyes never leaving Etta.

"What a surprise! I had regretted not exchanging phone numbers with you, and now fate has decided we should meet again. What are you ladies drinking?"

The three of them sat at the bar, then Dora spotted Sue all by herself and went to keep her company. Leon followed her; it seemed even the hound didn't want to play gooseberry. Etta felt a little embarrassed at finding herself alone in Rufus's company, but he had such an easy manner about him, always quick with a joke or a friendly word, that before long, she was telling him all about her life. And not in her usual abrupt way, but in a smooth and humorous tone. The man chuckled loudly at her quips; he had a deep, velvety voice, and his laugh, spontaneous and hearty, sent an inexplicable thrill down Etta's spine.

"Did your daughter miss her father when he left?" he asked Etta after hearing about her failed marriage.

"I think Maddalena missed the idea of having a father in her life, but that had little to do with the actual man himself."

"You're a strong woman to have brought her up all alone,

and you don't seem to be embittered by the experience. I guess it takes great character to live through such things and retain a cheerful spirit."

Etta, for once, flushed violently. She, who was ready to tell a fib whenever the need arose, found it hard to pretend with this man. His eyes, as honest as a child's, held the deep shadows of someone who had gone through his fair share of happiness and sadness.

"Actually, unlike my friend Dora, I am rather bitter and sharp tongued," she confessed. "Although not all the time."

"I'm sure you aren't at all." He smiled at her. Etta felt concerned that her heart would melt unless she did something to rectify the situation.

"This is such a nice tune, shall we dance?" she asked.

"I was afraid to ask in case you were too tired after your hike today," but the man rose from his chair without hesitation and took her hand.

"Today wasn't a long or hard stretch," she said. "If it weren't for the rain, it would have been idyllic." She started to move her body to the rhythm, clumsily at first, but growing in confidence as she let him lead her. "We didn't have to climb Beinn Dòrain like the party of treasure hunters."

"The treasure hunters?" he asked as he got closer to her for the next dance.

"You remember – the people you met at the cèilidh in Luss."

"Indeed, I do. I believe one of the party sadly passed away later that night."

Etta nodded. "They do seem to be plagued by unfortunate occurrences," and whenever she had enough breath during the dance to allow her to speak, she filled Rufus in on what had happened to Grace and Robert on Dòrain that day.

"Now, I'm totally out of breath," said Etta when the music finally stopped. "I shouldn't have done so much talking."

"Well, we redheads – actually, I'm only a former redhead –

look our best when we're breathless and our complexion matches our hair."

Etta burst out laughing. "I'm not sure that's a very charming thing to say, but it's so true."

"Trust me, I wasn't teasing; it shows we're alive and kicking."

He accompanied her back to the bar. As soon as they'd sat, he picked up the story from where Etta had left it.

"So, have there been any other weird things happen to the treasure hunters?"

Etta thought it over, then mentioned what had happened to Grace on the falls near Inversnaid.

"Then there was another thing," she added, for the first time wondering if there might be a connection between all the things that had happened to Robert's party, or whether it was just a series of random incidents that one should expect during a strenuous hike such as the West Highland Way, "although it wasn't unfortunate as such, but in Inverarnan, Mr Herrera left the competition."

"What's wrong with that?"

"Well, probably nothing, except no one saw him leaving," and she told him all about her casual sleuthing that had turned up no evidence of foul play whatsoever.

"Didn't anyone try to get in touch with him?"

"The solicitor did, but to no avail. The man's phone was switched off."

The two looked into each other's eyes.

"You know, talking to you has made me realise there might be something wrong about this whole thing," said Etta. "I never considered connecting the dots before; I thought of them as unrelated happenings, but now I'm left wondering if I may have been rather naïve. Who knows the depths to which someone might stoop to win this competition?"

"You have a powerful sleuthing brain. I wish I'd had you on my team when I worked at Police Scotland, although back then it was called the Northern Constabulary, before all the fancy names arrived…"

"Were you in the police?" Etta cried in surprise, realising that while she had told him all about her teaching job, she'd not once enquired about what he did.

"Guilty as charged," he confirmed with a smile. "I retired after 35 years in the force; I'm an old man, I'm afraid."

She waved the comment away. Now more than ever, she didn't want to be reminded of trivia such as age.

"Who's most likely to win the competition?" he asked.

"So far, the young couple, Robert and Grace, are in the lead."

"Are they collaborating?"

"Yes, and there's some tenderness between the two of them. I'd be surprised if they didn't end up together after this adventure."

"Well, when large amounts of money are involved, you can never tell…"

"But those two live in a world of their own. They're not as ambitious as the others in the party."

"I see," said Rufus, caressing the stubble on his chin and taking a long pause. "We need to think this over. If what you fear is true – if these unfortunate occurrences are in fact linked – this young couple might be in real danger."

Etta shivered. She'd never thought of that; well, not in so many words, at least, but it could explain the light sense of unease and anxiety she felt every time she wondered how the youngsters were doing, whether they'd reached their next stop safely. And she knew Dora felt the same.

"Does anyone in the party seem particularly drawn to the money?" asked Rufus.

"They all do, apart from the young ones. The sisters are so greedy, it shows in their malignant eyes. Mr and Mrs de Beer will probably divorce if they don't get their hands on that money; I bet they'd do anything to win. But they are bottom of the leader board, so unless they plan a massacre, they stand no chance.

Finally, there's Professor Alastair Hobbs. He pretends to be rather aloof and detached, but he kept close to Mrs van Wetering, then Herrera, and now his assistant is trying to strike up a friendship with the young ones."

"Is that the woman your friend is speaking to?"

"Yes. Hobbs is her lecturer. I get the impression she's gritty and determined and knows how to manipulate people."

"Do you think she will convince him to marry her if he wins?"

"I think that's her intention. Despite the fact he tries to portray himself as a man in command, I bet she's the one who actually makes the rules."

"In a few words, you have painted a clear picture of them all. I might make a phone call to my contacts in the police forces around Loch Lomond. Do you know the full name of the man who's disappeared?"

"Amilcar Herrera. He's from Argentina, or at least that's what I understood. I could ask Robert for more details."

"Better not spread the word that we're doing a little sleuthing, but if you can ask on some innocent pretext, do text me and let me know. That way, you will have to exchange phone numbers with me."

And so they did.

"In the meantime, keep an eye on the young ones, and what's happening around them. I hope I will have some news for you about Mr Herrera upon your arrival in Fort William; I'll wait for you there."

They talked for a bit longer, then Etta said it really was time for her to go to bed, although she regretted her words the instant they were out of her mouth. She could have continued to talk into the night like a teenager, and she almost got her wish. Rufus, despite having a drive back home ahead of him, tempted her with an invitation to take a short walk before he left.

"I know you're tired, but I assure you it's worth an extra ten minutes. No longer than that, I promise."

Outside, the air was chilly, the smell of the water hanging in the breeze. They crossed to a path between the oaks, the way lit by Rufus's torch. Close to the loch, he switched it off, and once Etta's eyes got accustomed to the gloom, she realised it was not as dark as she had thought. A quarter moon shone dimly through the clouds and its reflection danced on the undulating water. The trees were silhouettes, their branches reaching up into the sky, and the cool, exhilarating perfume of ferns, heather and peat reached Etta's nostrils.

"That's the moor's breath," explained Rufus in his gruff but warm voice.

"It's reinvigorating," Etta murmured.

"Look over there," he whispered, his mouth so close to her ear that Etta would have hit him in the ribs if she'd stepped back. Looking where Rufus was pointing, she saw branches not only moving, but... walking! And in a rather singular fashion, too, like a large horizontal body spreading in all directions. Then she realised it was a group of deer on the shore. The higher 'branches' were their antlers, the lower ones their legs. The herd reached a spot illuminated by the moon, and Etta and Rufus watched them passing by before disappearing into the darkness of the forest.

"A group of deer between the water and the moon," Etta whispered, clasping her hands in a very Dora-ish fashion.

"You're both practical and dreamy, such an extraordinary woman," Rufus murmured, maybe thinking the wind would cover his words. Instantly, Etta brushed off her daydream and returned to her normal ways.

"We must go back now," she said, turning towards the path, only to stop a few metres later. Under the canopy of trees, the moonlight could not penetrate and it was pitch-black.

He took her by the elbow, gently asking her pardon. "Let's not use the torch; it's more special with limited light."

"Switch on that torch," she commanded imperiously. "I can't even see as far as my foot," but as she spoke, she realised it wasn't true. Every passing second, her eyes could make out more and more. A series of white stones on the gravelled path showed her the way.

Amazed, she discovered that walking in almost complete darkness sharpened her other senses. Her ears caught the lightest sound; her nostrils were tickled by the subtlest scent. Now it was moss, then fern, then a dampness drifting in from the loch. Even touching a wet tree trunk became a heightened experience – as did Rufus's gentle but firm grip on her arm. For some inexplicable reason, it sent shivers down her body.

Must be the cold, damp air, she thought.

20

KINGSHOUSE AND SALT SMUGGLERS

To Etta's great dismay, when she, Dora and Leon went downstairs for breakfast, they found no one remaining from the treasure hunting party. Enquiring at reception, they learned the party had received a call at short notice, and as early as 6.30, they had left. No cooked breakfast for Robert's group today; just a take-away coffee and a pack of sandwiches each.

Etta remembered what Rufus had advised about keeping an eye on the two young ones, but the treasure hunters had more than an hour's head start. There would be no chance of catching up with them.

"You're in room 23?" the woman at the reception enquired. "Mrs Passolina and Miss Pepe?"

"That's us."

"Well, it seems the people you're looking for left a message for you."

It was a note, written by Robert.

"DEAR ETTA AND DORA,

We left too early to give you a call, but knowing how much

you've enjoyed our treasure hunt so far, I'll share the next clue with you. Hope it gives you some fun along the way.

You'll cross Rannoch Moor today. It's a beautiful if bleak place, so stay safe and enjoy this stunning part of my country. I'll see you this evening at Kingshouse.

Sincerely,

Robert Gentle

"So, what's the clue?" asked Dora eagerly.

"'*It's closer than you think, but take my word with a grain of salt. And mostly, ask and it will be given to you*'."

"Ohhh," said Dora. "This treasure hunt is such a great idea, but today's clue is rather easy."

"Easy? It doesn't even sound like a clue to me," admitted Etta, who had no patience with quizzes of any kind.

"I believe I've read somewhere…"

"What did you read this time?" Etta interrupted, wondering how, when and why Dora found time to absorb all sorts of useful things. After each day's hike, Etta had barely had the energy to read the restaurants' menus.

"Apparently, the man who owned the Kingshouse Inn in the early 19th century made more money from smuggling salt than the tourist business, which he kept going only as a façade to cover his illegal activities."

"So you believe the treasure is at Kingshouse?"

"I'm pretty sure it is. When the clue says 'It's closer than you think', it could easily refer to the fact it's at the very place the treasure hunters will spend the night."

"How about 'Ask and it will be given'? That sounds almost like something from the gospel – the two pious sisters will be happy."

"I've no idea about that part. Maybe it means they should ask the people at reception in the inn. Maybe there's a key to the vaults where the salt was hidden, and that's where Sir Angus's solicitors hid the treasure."

"Sounds reasonable to me."

At that moment, Michael called to them from outside. "See what a gorgeous day it is? Rannoch Moor is waiting for you. How about my dear chap?"

Leon went to greet Michael. He liked this man, even more so now that Michael had stopped trying to put him on a leash or tell him fibs.

"If you make a start now," Michael added, "you'll be in Kingshouse by lunchtime, and this afternoon you could explore the area."

"I don't think I will want to walk much more once we arrive..."

"In that case, you can enjoy the nice view from the bistro, and the nice fireplace."

"This sounds much better!"

Leon followed Michael silently. Once again, it seemed, the humans did not trust this Basset's ability to hike the mighty moor and hunt for deer. Resigned to his destiny, he waited for Michael to open the car door so he could resume his essential work as a fearless co-pilot.

As soon as they had bid farewell to Leon and Michael, Etta and Dora started their walk, amazed at the sun shining high in the sky, bringing out the spectacular colours of the moor. There was water running everywhere: in streams and lochans, or springing from the ground directly under their feet. But they had not been walking long before Etta felt her half-uncovered arms pricking and itching, and so was her face.

Maybe, she thought, *it is my bare skin reacting to the sun it's not seen for so long.* But when she started scratching wildly and noticed her friend doing the same, she locked eyes with Dora as realisation dawned.

"It's them!" she screamed. "It's the notorious Scottish midges!"

These biting insects, these tiny terrors, they had been warned, swamped the moors and lochs of Scotland all through the summer. The sharp breeze had kept them at bay along Loch Lomond, and the relentless rain they had encountered since had made them disappear completely, but now the midges were determined to make their presence known. Soon, they were reaching the areas of skin hidden under the women's looser garments.

Dora stopped, extracted a bottle of magic potion from her rucksack and invited Etta to massage copious amounts over her skin. It smelled of eucalyptus and citronella, scents that are known to repel biting insects, but it took loads of it to keep the almost invisible beasties at bay.

After an hour of hiking, a rain shower surprised them. It was violent and heavy, and there was not a single tree to offer any shelter, but after 15 minutes, the wind had cleared the clouds away and the sun reappeared, creating a majestic double rainbow. After that, the walk was an endless round of getting too hot and sweaty, taking layers off, keeping the midges at bay with the magic potion, then covering up again as the next cold rainstorm hit.

Unexpectedly, Etta felt more exhilarated than annoyed by the erratic weather. The air smelled good, and when the sun shone, the sky took on a deeper blue than she'd ever seen. The fluffy white clouds gave depth to that infinite sky, and on a couple of occasions, they spotted a herd of deer crossing the moor, the younger ones having fun splashing in the water.

"I think I kind of love this country, despite all this rainy madness," she blurted out during one of the wet spells.

"Or maybe because of it," replied Dora with a chuckle.

21

NOT THERE YET!

It was in the pouring rain and freezing cold that Etta and Dora arrived at Kingshouse, the hotel on the threshold of Glencoe. They could smell the north wind blowing down from the mountains; it may have been June, but Etta wouldn't have been surprised to see a snowflake or two.

Leon was waiting for them in the hall. As soon as his bipeds appeared, he created his usual scene as if the three had parted years rather than hours earlier. But when Etta looked around as the dog's exuberance abated, she found the silence in the hotel hall rather odd. Where were the treasure hunters? Was the party still searching the inn? Or had they already found the treasure and retired to their rooms for a good shower?

Etta's eyes fell on the key case at the reception desk. It was obvious from just one glance that the room keys were all still hanging there.

"Excuse me," she asked the woman at reception, "but our friends – Sir Angus McGrouse's party – should have arrived by now. But I can't see any of them around."

"You're right, they've already been and gone."

"What do you mean, gone? Are they searching the area around here on their treasure hunt?"

"No, I mean that they've *really* gone: they won't be staying here tonight. We don't mind as Sir Angus's solicitor paid for the rooms nonetheless, but it's such a waste of space in high season. Why book the rooms if the guests were meant to stay somewhere else?"

"Somewhere else? Is there another hotel nearby?"

"No… I mean, there are a few in Glencoe, but they're not going there."

"So where are they going?" said Etta exasperated, wishing the woman would get to the point. For her part, the receptionist looked at Etta as if she were stupid.

"To the next stop on the West Highland Way, of course," she said as if it were patently obvious. "I thought you'd know that."

"You mean to Kin… heaven… whatever?" Etta tended to get confused with the simplest of names, so all the *Invers, lochs* and *kins* that appeared in Scotland were leaving her totally baffled.

"Yes, they'rrrre going to *Kinlochleven*!" said the woman, with the pleasure and pride many Scots take when rolling their Rs and pronouncing their impossibly throaty ch sound.

Etta limited her response to a roll of her eyes. "But, isn't that a good 15 kilometres away?"

"Is it?"

"*You* should know!" cried Etta in amazement.

"I only understand miles. All those foreign kilograms and kilometres mean nothing to me."

"It must be around 9 miles."

"Yes, that's it. Nine long miles, and you've got to climb the Devil's Staircase too. They should have stopped here."

"Goodness!" cried Etta, running towards their room where Dora was already busy unpacking *everything*, as she had done at each stop along the way. "DorAAA!" Etta bustled into the room. "Why don't you leave the stuff in your rucksack? We will be departing in under 24 hours."

"Well, dear," explained Dora calmly, as if answering the question for the very first time, "nothing gives me more pleasure than unpacking a bag in a new place. It makes me feel like we have arrived home, as if we are going to stay longer. I love finding a place for my toothbrush and toothpaste, my day cream; unwrapping the soap bar..." as she described the actions, Dora did those very things. "And placing even one t-shirt in the wardrobe gives me a thrill, as if we belong here."

Etta felt like hitting her head with her hand, but she had more pressing matters to attend to.

"Robert and the others," she blurted out breathlessly, "have gone on to... Kin... loch... Inver... what's it called?"

"To Kinlochleven?" asked Dora in disbelief. She stopped her unpacking abruptly, as if wondering what to do. During today's hike, Etta had shared her fears for Robert and Grace following her discussion with Rufus. Then Dora came to a decision. "Then we must go too," she said, repeating her actions in reverse. The t-shirt came out of the wardrobe, was folded and placed back in the bag. The day cream, toothbrush and toothpaste followed.

"Are you kidding me?" cried Etta. "It's 15 kilometres away and it's pouring with rain. We're already wet and as tired as those poor overworked donkeys you see in some holiday resorts."

Dora stopped for consideration. "Maybe we could catch a bus or hitchhike..."

"Hitchhike? Two drenched women and a dog? We'll have turned 80 by the time someone decides to pick us up."

"So let's ask the time of the next bus," and to Etta's amazement, Dora left the room to speak to the receptionist. She was back after a couple of minutes.

"The woman said we will have to pay for the room anyway, even if we don't sleep here tonight."

"She already has Sir Angus's payment for the treasure hunters' rooms, and surely she can fill at least some of them and get paid again. It's still only lunchtime. I hope she mentioned a heavy discount."

"I'm afraid not."

"Then I'll speak to her!" growled Etta. She left the room and marched directly to the carpark where a couple of cars had just pulled up, approaching the occupants and, in typical Etta style, demanding to know whether they wanted a room for the night. The first couple were just there for lunch, but the second were indeed about to enquire whether there was a room free.

"Such a shame you have to leave suddenly," said the woman in the car, "but yes, I will tell the receptionist that my hubby and I will take your room. Surely they won't charge both you and us for the same room."

But the receptionist was no pushover. "If you had stayed," she said to Etta, showing she could think at lightning speed where making money was concerned, "this lady and her husband would have paid for another room that I have empty and I would have sold all my rooms today. Now, I will be missing one room's rent."

"If you don't give us this lady's room," said the Scottish guest defiantly, "we'll drive somewhere where the people are eager to show the friendliness and hospitality we Scots are renowned for."

"So I'm not being hospitable?"

Etta and the woman both shook their heads.

"Then I'll show you. As Mrs Passolina and Miss Pepe have urgent business to attend to, but their bus doesn't leave until 3pm, we'll be glad not only to allow you to take their room, but also to offer them a free meal in our bistro."

"This is more like it," cried the guest. "I knew this place wouldn't disappoint, and I'll be sure to spread the word about your generosity."

The receptionist smiled, and Etta was delighted at the idea of a free lunch in a warm bistro. She thanked the receptionist.

The helpful guest winked at her as Etta passed on her way to fetch Dora, saying, "Enjoy your meal."

❧

THE BISTRO HAD WOODEN FLOORS, A FIREPLACE AND TWO LARGE glass walls that overlooked the short plain along the River Etive from where Beinn a'Chrùlaiste suddenly rose in all its imposing glory. It was a stunning, if humbling view.

"These Scottish mountains make me feel vertigo," said Etta as they took their seat. "This one is not even a Munro, but it looks so tall and dramatic."

The meal was delicious, enhanced by the stunning view from the huge windows. But as they started on their dessert, concern crossed Etta's face.

"Are we doing the right thing?" she asked. "Maybe we were too impulsive and should stay here after all."

"But we can't leave those two young ones to fend for themselves, Etta," said Dora, more decisively than you might expect from such a soft people-pleaser kind of person. But Etta had learned to recognise how strong Dora's determination could be on the rare occasions it showed up.

"The other thing is," confessed Etta, "I feel so sad that we have walked more than 115 kilometres, only to miss out a stretch of 15. Maddalena will be full of it, telling me she knew from the start I had no chance…"

Dora dropped her spoon into her pudding. It bounced on the sweet sponge, gaining momentum (as well as gathering some berry sauce) and ending up in a sticky mess on the floor. Leon's strong sense of duty took over and he immediately sprang into action, meticulously licking clean not only the spoon, but the whole area of contaminated floor.

Dora's face was also spotted by dark blobs of red berry sauce. Looking as if she had suddenly gone down with measles, she clasped her hands, opened her mouth, "aha"ed loudly in delight and surprise, and stared into Etta's face with such intensity, Etta shuffled back on her chair.

"What's wrong?" she asked, wondering if her friend had become possessed by a spirit.

"I knew, I knew, I knew it, my dearest Etta!" And Dora

stretched across the table to grasp Etta's hands and squeeze them.

"You knew what?"

"That it's just as important to you as it is to me that we finish what we started."

"You mean we should stay here after all?"

"No, we can't leave those two young ones alone. I mean we should walk, despite everything."

"*Walk?*" Etta exclaimed in disbelief.

"Exactly."

"Despite the fact it's raining, the Devil's Staircase is waiting for us, it's getting late and we could end up in the heart of those scary mountains after dark?" And Etta looked outside at Beinn a'Chrùlaiste, which now looked terrifying. "And how about Leon? He can't walk that far."

"WOOF!" cried Leon. Although he had no wish to walk *that far*, at the same time, he couldn't stand the thought of his biped assuming there were things a heroic Basset could not do.

"That's no problem. I phoned Michael and he said he could meet us at Altnafeadh." Dora opened out the map that seemed to have become an extension of her body as it was always by her side, even in bed, and pointed at a place where the West Highland Way left the path of the A82 and started its climb up towards the Devil's Staircase. "And on his way north, he can call in here first to pick our luggage up from reception."

"You phoned Michael? Why?"

"Well, we hadn't agreed on anything, but just before lunch, I was hoping you'd suggest we keep going. I wanted to make sure Leon and the luggage would be sorted if we did."

Etta tried to hide how disorientated she felt. How was it possible that Dora could foresee her every move when she herself had had no idea she was so determined to finish this stupid trail? But there was another thought working in the background of Etta's brain. It tried moving into her consciousness, but it was so weird and scary, she pushed it back.

Rufus. How proud he would be of her.

Bugger off, you stupid, stupid idea.

Etta dug into her apple pie with such vehemence that the knife cut straight through the pastry and screeched gratingly on the dish. She shivered and raised her eyes just as a group of four walkers appeared on the trail beyond the large glass wall. They were drenched and Etta could read in their eyes how glad they were to have arrived at their destination for the night. Was she really intending to go back outside and start walking for the second time in a single day?

Nonsense.

To her great shock, her tongue moved in opposition to her logic.

"OK, call Michael and tell him we're about to leave Kingshouse."

THERE'S SOMETHING WEIRD ABOUT RAIN, MUD, WIND AND COLD: they tend to seem worse when you're inside. Once you've found the courage to venture out into the elements, they never seem as bad. As long as there was Leon to lead the way, cheerfully providing them with something to laugh at, and they could tease each other about this mad day, Etta was sure she and Dora would make it to Kinlochleven.

"If only Maddalena could see me now, she'd think I had lost my mind and send me to a care home straight away."

"She'd never do that!" protested Dora.

"You don't know her as well as I do. Once she has me imprisoned, she'll have nothing to worry about. Anyway, I thought it had rained the full yearly two-and-a-half metres yesterday; how is it possible there's still any water in the sky? Maybe it's a daily, not a yearly measure."

As they advanced, the dramatic shape of Buachaille Etive Mòr dominated the landscape more and more. Despite knowing they weren't meant to climb it, Etta still felt apprehensive; the mere sight of that difficult mountain with its crags and indents, steep gullies and deep clefts, affected her in a way she could not explain. The Scottish scenery wasn't something innocuous you just looked at; no, it was active. It got inside you. It could do things to you.

"Tolkien must have got the inspiration for some of the places in *Lord of the Rings* here," she said, thinking of the epic hike of the Company of the Ring.

"Oh, Etta, you're so right. And look at how excited Leon is, as if he can smell hobbits or elves."

Etta growled. Yet again, Dora was being far too cheerful for her taste.

The path ran parallel to the A82 until the road turned east. Then they faced Glencoe, a place that took them back to what Earth must have looked like when it was shaped hundreds of millions of years ago; when its entire crust was dancing wildly, volcanoes and mountains popping up from the ground and, much later, glaciers coming and going, forming cliffs and ridges.

Even in the mist and the rain, Etta and Dora recognised Michael's van in a parking space. Leon barked, overjoyed to see the man again; he associated Michael with good food and a warm place to snuggle up and enjoy a rest. And after a three-mile walk, the Basset was ready for both.

"Are you sure you want to carry on?" asked Michael, pointing to the West Highland Way as it said goodbye to the A82 and climbed laboriously up into the rough, dark mountains.

"No, we aren't sure at all," said Etta, looking in horror at the isolated path that seemed to disappear into desolate solitude.

"We're *determined*!" said Dora at the same time.

Michael looked at Etta. "As Dora said, we aren't simply sure, we're adamant."

"You're a pair of gritty women," said Michael in admiration. "Look at it this way: you've already covered a third of the stretch from Kingshouse; now you only have 6 miles to go. Leon and your luggage will be waiting for you at Mamore Lodge. It's an excellent place to stay – a little out of the way, but stunning."

Etta looked back at the threatening Buachaille mountain. It had loomed over them, but now looked more like a molar tooth in the distance, a big depression separating the two tall peaks. Had some ancient glacier made its way down through that gap to where a small white cottage sat at the foot of the mountain?

"That must be one of Scotland's most popular photo opportunities," said Michael, following her gaze. As Etta acted on Michael's advice and took a few pictures, Dora stood beside her, opening and closing her eyes. Etta knew she was storing the view in her memory: the Goliath of the mountain and the David that was the little cottage. Then it was time to go. Having said goodbye to Michael and Leon, they set off on the ascent.

They moved up the path slowly; it was wet and boggy and slippery, and Etta felt cold and sweaty at the same time. Wind and rain smacked against their faces, despite the two women pulling their hoods down to their noses. A few times, they had to retrace their steps to find the track as they'd stumbled on to a secondary trail or been misled by a series of stone slabs that looked like they should be part of the West Highland Way, but weren't. With the wind so wild, it was hard to look ahead and check their direction, and even Dora had no wish whatsoever to pull out the map and risk losing it to the elements. No, it was easier to advance from signpost to signpost, even if it did mean taking the odd wrong turn.

Etta would have been glad to remove her glasses. They were so foggy and large drops of rain clung to them like long-lost friends, but without them, she'd hardly see anything at all. When she gave it a try, Dora had to grasp her arm and ask her where she was going – Etta had been just about to step off a crag. Better to see the world through the mist and the distorting lens of the raindrops than be almost blind.

It seemed as if they were not making any progress, just trudging on and on across the barren landscape. There was not a single tree in view; even when the mist cleared and Etta cleaned her glasses, all she could see was more of the same rocky ascent. The women's chatter had abandoned them; even Dora looked tired and discouraged, which scared Etta more than anything else. Dora discouraged? That was either an oxymoron or a sure sign things really stunk.

"Oh, Etta, I'm afraid I've led you too far this time," Dora cried eventually. "I shouldn't have insisted we walk on today; we could be enjoying the fire at Kingshouse."

"Even Miss Wordsworth," said Etta, paraphrasing one of Dora's favourite poets, "said that this was such an unwelcoming kind of a place. While don't thou like even the sound of the name... Mamore Lodge? Not to mention that we need to help our friends. Thou can't forget that."

"Of course not," said Dora, trying to smile at Etta's attempts to speak old English, but doing it with little conviction. Etta guessed Dora felt so frail, as did she, that she wondered what kind of help they could offer the two young ones.

Etta stopped, turning her back on the wild wind and inviting Dora to stand at her side and do the same. She dropped her rucksack and pulled out the thermos of hot coffee.

"Why do they make these things out of cold metal?" she grumbled as she had to remove her gloves to handle the slippery flask. "I would have covered it with rubber."

"Or felt," said Dora, smiling for the first time in a while at her friend's complaints. "It never gets cold, even when it's wet."

"But the stupid designers never bothered to ask us," said Etta, offering her friend the hot drink.

"Oh goodness!" Dora said after a long draught. Her cheeks felt almost rosy again. Etta took the flask from her and drank deeply, and it was pure magic. She had no words to describe how good it felt to have something hot and sweet going through her mouth, caressing her chest and warming her stomach. Heaven must be a place where she'd feel this good all the time.

When they had finished their drink, Etta offered Dora a piece of dark chocolate. "Let it melt slowly in your mouth," she advised.

"I feel much better now, Etta, thank you sooo much," but Dora still looked doubtful about how to proceed.

"Do you think we should go back down and call Michael to give us a lift?" Etta asked as they turned to face what was visible of the glen behind them. The mist was too low to appreciate the view... but what was that movement?

Something was emerging from the obscurity.

A rather large something.

And it was making its way directly towards them.

22

THE DEVIL'S STAIRCASE

From the fog came a man wearing a brilliant green windproof jacket, his red face partially hidden by the hood. He made his way towards them, and then stopped.

"Hiya," he said with a smile. "Not the best of days…"

The two shocked women shook their heads in agreement.

"Come on, ladies," he said with a chuckle. "You've made it all the way up here; you should be happy. Where have you walked from?"

"Last night, we were at Inveroran and maybe we've stretched ourselves a bit too much today," Dora explained.

"You've walked from Inveroran? That's a long stretch indeed."

"Maybe we should go back to the main road and see if we can catch a lift or a bus to Kinlochleven…"

"That'd make no sense! You're almost there."

"Really?" cried Dora and Etta in disbelieving unison.

"Well, not *there* as such, but you've conquered the Devil's Staircase…"

Etta and Dora started in surprise. They hadn't realised they had made such good progress; they thought the Devil's Staircase was still in front of them.

"Once you get to the summit," the man continued, "then it's all downhill to Kinlochleven. Come on, follow me."

Now, one of the many virtues of the Scottish people is that their mood is infectious. Granted, if they're sad, they can bring you down with them, but if they're happy, everyone around them will see the world through rose-tinted glasses. When they're as determined and positive as this walker was, you would feel duty bound to follow them. And follow the two friends did.

Before long, the walker invited them to raise their heads against the furious wind and look in front of them. On the other side of the mountain range, their eyes made out more misty peaks, more foggy slopes. But more importantly, they could see the grey gravel of the Old Military Road heading downwards.

"You're now north of the Devil's Staircase. All you have to do is follow the track downwards; you can't see Kinlochleven yet, but those mountains – the ones away in the distance – embrace it."

The two women nodded, their hearts thumping in their chests partly from the climb, partly from emotion.

"Those are the Mamore Mountains. Aren't they pretty and awe inspiring?"

"They are indeed."

"Now, can I leave you? I need to return to Kingshouse."

"What?" cried the two women in unison, Etta adding, "We thought you were staying in Kinlochleven too."

"No, I'm heading in the opposite direction."

"But you accompanied us this far."

"Yes, I spotted you in the mist and guessed you needed help. But now I've seen you're in good shape and were just a bit discouraged, I know you can do it."

"And you climbed all the way back up to help us?" Etta still couldn't believe her ears.

"We're on tough mountains, we need to help each other. And

I wanted to make sure you were on the right track; you can't miss your path now."

"But how can we thank you?" said Dora.

The man shrugged. "Pay it forward. We always meet someone in life who needs our help, don't we?" He winked at them before turning and descending in the opposite direction, where he slowly, slowly, slowly disappeared into the thick fog.

"How generous Scottish men can be – don't you think?" said Dora, smiling one of her happy smiles.

"Indeed," said Etta, feeling pretty happy herself now her friend had overcome her dreadful moment of desolation. But there was a strange look in Dora's eyes, almost a smirk on her face. And finally Etta understood. Blushing under her hood, she realised that Dora was referring to another Scottish man, Rufus McCall, and Etta could only agree. She was sure he wouldn't have been any less generous or cheerful than the friendly walker they had just met.

WHEN HIKING IN THE MOUNTAINS, ONE MIGHT THINK THE HARDEST part would be going up. But that's not necessarily true, especially when one's descending over a hard, rocky, uneven and slippery track. Etta's knees and ankles were in pain, her tense muscles crying out for rest and a hot shower. Her small rucksack seemed as heavy as a boulder. When going down a particularly high step, she experienced such pressure in her joints, her legs visibly trembled. She was grateful that her walking sticks helped her to distribute some of the effort into her arms, even though she had berated those same sticks as useless dead weight at the start of the walk. Despite the fact they exposed her hands to the cold bite of the North wind, she now appreciated how much they helped and couldn't imagine how awful the descent from the Devil's Staircase would have been without them.

Finally, the houses of Kinlochleven came into view. To Etta's delight, it was a real town, not just a road. The women's hearts cheered. As for their tiredness, it was maybe not forgotten, but it could certainly be dealt with.

They had been concentrating so hard on their footing that even Dora hadn't noticed the large Blackwater Reservoir in the distance, nor Ben Nevis emerging from behind the Mamore Mountains. For a long while, they even ignored the huge pipelines that until the year 2000 had carried water to the aluminium plant in Kinlochleven. Only when the path started to follow the pipelines did the women acknowledge their presence. But their joy and relief was still on hold; that arrived when the forest and the river led them into the town and they found themselves among the houses they had seen from up above.

They spotted a few B&B signs, an inn, a hotel, but no indication where Mamore Lodge might be. In the end, they stopped an old man and asked him for directions, but he replied in a thoroughly incomprehensible language. Then he slowly raised his finger and, to Etta and Dora's great consternation, moved it all the way up to point to the mountains surrounding the village on the other side from their approach.

"It's der," he said simply when his finger stopped at a little white dot. And 'der' it was indeed, up, up and far away.

"What?" growled Etta, wincing as if he had stabbed her.

"Der," he confirmed.

"You're a moron!" Etta cried, pulling her friend by her arm to drag her away from this idiot making fun of them. She marched the two of them over to a fish and chip shop and stopped in front of it. The doors were locked, but a woman was mopping the floor inside.

"Excuse me, madam," Etta called, tapping on the window and trying to look like the politest person in the world.

"Hiya," the woman called back. "We're closed, I'm afraid."

"I know, but we just need directions to Mamore Lodge."

"Och, Mamore. Nice place, isn't it?"

"We haven't actually got there yet."

The woman leaned the mop against the wall and opened the door on to the street. Then, to Etta's dismay, she looked towards the same mountain as the old man had done earlier on, pointing to the same faraway white dot.

"That's the Mamore," she said. "You get such great views from there."

"But how far away is it?"

"Och, nay more than a couple of miles. It's a steep private road, but on a good day, you get such a view…"

Dora must have feared that Etta would burst into one of her trademark 'Bugger your views!' retorts at any moment as she hurriedly asked where the road started and thanked the woman warmly. Due to the inclement weather and lateness of the hour, there were no people in the streets of Kinlochleven. Nor were the two exhausted walkers able to take in any of the village views. Like automatons, they trudged towards the main street to search for the road up to Mamore Lodge. When they passed a B&B, they caught a glimpse of a cosy living room, a lamp on a table and the fire lit. At that, Etta could no longer hold back.

"It says it has vacancies – let's stop here. Forget that wretched Mamore place!"

"What about our luggage, not to mention Leon?"

"I've always thought that those who say dogs are a man's best friend obviously give no consideration to a woman."

Dora smiled, knowing grumbling tapped in to Etta's reserves of energy.

A powerful clap of thunder surprised them both and made them shiver.

"Whatever next?" Etta wondered. The answer came sooner rather than later when a small road opened up on their right. It was steep and windy and, of course, wet as large drops of rain started to fall.

23

MAMORE LODGE

Mamore Lodge was in the middle of a large clearing in the forest, facing a parking area containing a few cars. A white Victorian manor house, it had long blue-framed windows, bracketed eaves in the same shade, a few gables and an abundance of chimneys. The smoke coming from these chimneys delighted Dora immediately.

The two friends walked around the building to the other side in search of the entrance. It was then that they realised the hotel overlooked the town below and a long, thin loch so enclosed by mountains, it almost looked like a Norwegian fjord. Dora's eyes, as tired as they were, appreciated the romance of the hotel. But before she could even think of clasping her hands, Etta dragged her up the steps to the entrance.

As they pushed the door open and entered, a furry torpedo hurtled towards them and burst into a long series of angry barks.

"WOOF, WOOF, WOOOOF!" Leon cried, reminding them just how long they had kept a poor Basset waiting all alone, and how concerned he had been.

A young blonde woman at reception addressed the new arrivals. "He was sleeping in your room for a couple of hours, but then I heard him crying and thought I'd better bring him down here to sit with me. He's been so worried, poor boy."

Caresses and hugs and crying and barking ensued as if this modern-day Argos had finally been reunited with his Ulysses duo after twenty years – Bassets have their own special way of marking the passage of time. But when a pair of quivering nostrils rose from the melee, they weren't Leon's.

"Is that food I can smell?" asked Etta, her stomach growling ravenously. Food had been her only thought for the past two hours, so much so she had made a contingency plan: if the wretched Mamore place didn't have a restaurant, she would invade the kitchen and prepare a supper using scrambled eggs, porridge, bacon and whatever else was available. If the provisions were intended for breakfast in the morning, it wouldn't matter to her.

"The kitchen is closing in ten minutes, I'm afraid," said the young receptionist as if reading Etta's mind.

"But we need a hot shower!" Etta was ready to fight for her rights, and would not hear any reason why she couldn't have her shower *and* dinner.

The young woman winked. "I have a plan, if you don't mind warmed-up food." She ran over to a door and opened it to reveal pine-panelled walls and a host of tables with the pleasant flickering of candles on them. Then she returned with a menu in her hands.

"Now, give me your order, then go upstairs and take your time in the shower. Once you're done, I'll warm up your food and you can have your dinner at the bar."

Etta and Dora looked at the woman as if she were an angel; there were no words to thank her. Then without further ado, they browsed the menu and ordered hot soup, main course and dessert. Running up ancient wooden stairs covered by carpet depicting heraldic symbols, their energy renewed and Leon in tow, they noticed their door sported the name Captain Frank Bibby. But the real surprise came when they entered to find an ample but cosy bedroom with three tall windows. Through these, they could admire a dusky blue sky, across which darker clouds passed at speed. On their right-hand side, underneath a wooden mantelpiece, a blazing fire was crackling. A few logs lay in a basket on the side of the stone hearth.

Outside, the storm was raging. Thunder, powerful and long, resonated around the large bedroom, making Etta's glasses tremble violently as if they were about to burst out of their red frames. Leon sidled closer to the two women; under certain circumstances, even useless bipeds could offer a little comfort to a frighten… I beg your pardon, a cautious Basset. With his ears so low, they could have swept the floor, he gazed up at Dora, who didn't look any less worried than he was.

Dora, her heart beating fast, looked at Etta.

"What's wrong?" Etta asked abruptly, realising her two companions were staring at her with pained looks on their faces, as if they'd each got a stone stuck in their throat.

"Wasn't that loud?" said Dora. "As if a cannon had been fired in the corridor."

"It's only a storm."

"Do you think they have lightning rods on the roof?"

"Of course, they do. Otherwise, the lodge wouldn't still be here after a hundred and more years."

"Glad to hear that."

"The thing is, I don't really mind the thunder," confessed Etta. "After all I've gone through today outside, there's nothing that can scare me now I'm in a warm, comfy place. Unless I don't get my dinner, of course."

Dora, strangely comforted by her friend's pragmatic spirit, marched to the window and stared outside into the troubled skies.

"What are you doing?"

"I'm counting."

"Counting what?"

"How many seconds there are between each flash of

lightning and the thunder," and Dora clasped her hands and stood still in amazement, giving the dumbfounded Etta ample time to take her shower first.

IN THE CORRIDOR OUTSIDE THEIR ROOM, AFTER BOTH WOMEN HAD showered, Etta, Dora and Leon encountered Sue. Her eyes glued to the door opposite theirs, the young woman was muttering to herself.

"What an oddball!" she said scathingly.

"Who?" asked Etta.

"My professor," Sue answered as the two friends invited her to come downstairs with them. "He went to his room without a word, even though today he won the competition and is ahead of the others. I can't imagine what he'd be like if he'd lost."

"Is he often like that?" asked Etta, leading the way downstairs.

"No, not that often. But neither is it a rarity. By the way, what are you doing here?"

"Are you forgetting we're walking the West Highland Way just like you?" answered Etta.

"I thought you'd stop at Kingshouse like most walkers."

"No," said Etta. "We decided to do it all in one day." Before she got the chance to ask Sue why the treasure hunters had also done the long stretch from Inveroran in one day, they reached the ground floor and Dora spoke up, effectively changing the subject.

"Aren't you coming to the bar?" she asked Sue.

"Not now. I need half an hour of peace and quiet, so I'm heading for the lounge," Sue replied, turning to the right. "There are plenty of books in there, but hopefully no people."

"WOOF!" protested Leon at seeing her go.

"You're such a spoiled brat!" said Sue, scratching the dog's back. Then she left without even looking at Etta and Dora.

The pub was panelled like the rest of the lodge. The floor was polished wood and hunting trophies hung from the walls, along with black-and-white pictures of famous guests who had spent a night here over the ages: Sir Henry Fairfax-Lucy, Viscount Churchill, King Edward VII; on the whole, the people who'd given their names to the hotel rooms.

Etta and Dora had just sat down as close to the fire as possible, Leon at their feet, when the young receptionist cleaned their table for them and announced their food was coming.

"Make it as hot as possible," requested Etta.

"Did you like your room?"

"It was such a surprise," said Dora.

"We gave you an upgrade since that room was vacant and Michael told us you'd walked extra miles today," said the receptionist with a smile. "He argued your case so nicely, and Leon's face did the rest."

As the woman left, Robert and Grace rose from a table near the bar and came to join them. They didn't look at all surprised to see them.

"I recognised Leon at reception earlier on," Robert explained, caressing the Basset with a complacent smile, "and they told us they were expecting you." Leon wagged his tail, always happy to see the good lad. "But why did you decide to walk so far in one day?"

"Do sit down," said Dora as three bowls of hot soup arrived, together with fragrant, warm garlic bread. One of the bowls was, of course, for Leon.

"We wanted to catch up with you so that you could tell us about your day's adventure. Was the treasure hard to find?"

"Not the first one," said Robert. "The clue I left for you – did you get it?"

The women both nodded, unable to speak as they tucked hungrily into their starter.

"But we had not one, but two clues today," said Grace. "The first treasure was near the Kingshouse Hotel, which we thought it would be. We guessed it was a reference to the salt-smuggling business of a former innkeeper."

"What did I tell you?" Dora's eyes were shining with pride as she paused her spoon in its back and forth journey from bowl to mouth. But she wasn't a bragger so changed the subject. "We had lunch at Kingshouse – such an amazing view from the restaurant. The meal was gorgeous and the current host seems totally different to the one when the Wordsworths were there…"

"We took our lunch under the rain," said Robert, "as our second clue suggested we search the Devil's Staircase."

The two young people did not look as enthusiastic as they had on previous days.

"So who won?" asked Dora, despite the fact Sue had already told her and Etta Professor Hobbs had taken over the lead today. "Are you still ahead of the competition?"

"In fact, we aren't," said Grace, her sweet face looking sad.

"Alastair knew exactly where to look. He found both clues first and he's well ahead now. Tomorrow's clue could decide who's going to win the inheritance – the solicitor hinted the final clue might turn things around, giving us all a chance."

Grace sighed.

The empty soup bowls were taken away, and then the young receptionist brought over large steaks with chips, onion rings and pan-fried mushrooms. Leon thought steak was just the right food after such a psychologically hard day for a poor doggie.

"You certainly deserve a long rest," said Dora, looking at the two tense young faces.

"Grace did go up straight after dinner…"

"I was so tired," she admitted, "but I was restless, so I decided to come back downstairs to have a little chat with Robert and relax before hitting the sack for a second time."

The storm outside had eased a bit, the rattling of the rain becoming gentler. The four friends were staring at the fire, absorbing the heat, as still as standing stones.

"We met Sue before dinner," said Etta eventually. "She was

also coming back downstairs, so I guess she couldn't sleep either. Too much adrenaline..."

"She didn't look that happy, though," said Dora, "considering Professor Hobbs is in the lead."

"No, but she did mention he was in a bad mood."

"Maybe he's wondering about the next clue," said Grace.

"We'll do our best tomorrow, Grace," whispered Robert gently.

"We have to; we can't let Tilda fall into the wrong hands." Her doe-eyed gaze hovered on him. Robert was about to reply when a sudden explosion resonated around the room and interrupted the low chatter in the bar.

"What was that?" said Mr de Beer.

"It didn't sound like thunder," said Robert.

"Still, it came from outside. A hunter?" asked Hope Hillock.

"At this time of night and in this weather?" said Robert.

All of a sudden, the treasure hunters were on full alert. Even the few other guests lingering in the bar for a drink had their interest piqued.

"It wasnae thunder, that's for sure," said one man, putting his beer down on the counter.

"I agree, definitely a gunshot," said his companion, nodding.

"Are we sure it came from outside?" Mr de Beer said, springing up from his seat and heading for the door. In a fraction of a second, everyone had followed suit, especially those whose friends or relations had already retired for the night. They wanted to check their loved ones were unharmed, while the others were agog with curiosity.

Dora, Etta and Leon followed Robert and Grace, Hope Hillock and Lloyd de Beer. In the hallway just before the stairs, they all encountered Sue coming out of the lounge.

"Did you hear that?" she asked. "Who could be hunting on a night like this?"

"Hunting?" asked Etta, eyeing Sue suspiciously as the group climbed up stairs.

"Hunting, shooting... I don't know. Whatever this madness is."

"We're not sure the noise came from outside."

"Well, I *am* sure," insisted Sue. "I was in the lounge and I heard the explosion outside quite distinctly, close to the window."

Despite Sue's conviction, she followed the others upstairs. The first-floor landing became awash with agitation, doors opening right and left so people could make sure everything was fine in their room, while those who had already gone to bed peered out, wrapped in dressing gowns, to see what was going on – they could hardly have failed to hear the explosive noise and the commotion that followed.

The young woman from reception and the bartender were there too.

"We're maybe panicking for nothing," the receptionist said.

"Better make sure everyone is OK," said the bartender, knocking on the few doors that remained closed.

"That's my room," said Grace. "And I'm the only occupant."

"And that's mine," said Robert. "Room 13."

"And that's ours," said Etta.

A guest from the northern wing arrived, announcing that everyone was fine there. Mrs de Beer and Faith Hillock appeared from opposite sides of the landing, opening their doors to reassure everyone that they too were fine. Now all the doors on the eastern wing were either open or accounted for, apart from Professor Hobbs's which remained resolutely locked.

"If I were you," said Sue to the bartender, "I wouldn't trouble him. He tends to get angry if he doesn't want to be disturbed – you know what Englishmen are like when it comes to privacy."

"It doesnae matter since I'm Scottish," and he knocked on the door even more energetically now he knew he might be disturbing an Englishman from his sweet dreams.

No answer.

The man knocked harder as everyone crowded round him.

Again, no answer.

"Is he pretending to be asleep and just ignoring us?"

Sue seemed to have lost some of her confidence, but what the man had just said made her smile.

"Maybe."

"I'll fetch the spare key," the bartender said. Disappearing downstairs, he was back in a minute. He tried to slip the key into the lock, unsuccessfully.

"Professor Hobbs's room key must be in the lock on the other side," he said, bending to look through the keyhole. "The light is on, maybe from the bedside lamp. I'm going downstairs to fetch something to push the key out of the lock. In the meantime, keep calling him; he must be sound asleep."

Sue called and knocked, then Lloyd de Beer joined in with his louder voice. But to no avail.

"Did he have a gun?" asked Etta.

"No!" answered Sue incredulously, then seemed to lose the courage of her conviction. "Not that I know of."

The bartender was back with a pair of long-nosed pliers. He managed to grasp and turn the key inside the room, then slid the second key in and pushed it through. The silence among the group was such that they all heard a soft *THUMP!* as the key inside with its heavy brass keychain fell to the carpet. The second key was now free to turn in the lock and the bartender threw the door wide open.

To the surprise of all present, the room was empty.

They stood perplexed, uncertain what to think. Then a strange smell hit Etta's nostrils. She went to move forward, but her legs felt as if she was wading through a thick swamp. Sue walked past her and into the room, her face expressionless; Grace instinctively followed her. They reached the opposite side of the bed, then Sue gave a cry, her hands flying up to cover her mouth. Grace staggered back as if she'd been hit by something so hard, she was struggling to stay on her feet. Reaching behind her, she felt for the windowsill and leant against it.

The bartender crossed the room in a few long strides and peered round the other side of the bed. Then he kneeled down briefly, only to get up with a shocked expression on his face.

"Goodness, the man is dead. Get out of here, immediately."

He led Sue away. All her strength seemed to have deserted her. Robert reached out for Grace, who was still leaning on the windowsill and crying silently into her handkerchief, and gently escorted her from the room.

"What's happened?" asked Etta, instantly regretting not having gone into the room when she had the chance. The bartender consigned Sue to Dora's care, locked the door, faced the crowd and spoke without mincing his words.

"The man shot himself. I'll call the police."

"But the shot came from outside," Sue whispered as if she still couldn't believe what she'd seen.

"No, it didn't; the gun is next to him," said the bartender gloomily.

IT WAS THE MIDDLE OF THE NIGHT BY THE TIME ETTA'S TURN CAME to be interrogated by the local police.

"Suicide?" she cried, taking charge as soon as the local constable outlined the facts as he saw them and asked her to relate what she had witnessed. "You're not buying that, are you?"

"Window shut, door locked, no sign of a break in," said the constable. He was obviously tired and not happy at all at having to deal with this belligerent Italian at this time of the night. "Unless you think it was a ghost who killed him, what else could it have been?"

"But this is the third strange or unfortunate incident that has, in effect, removed someone from this group of people. How is that coincidental?"

"Well, those people are stressed out, that is quite obvious. I would be if I were in their shoes! The competition is pushing them to the limits. One died of a heart attack, one decided to quit, and now one wasn't able to cope with the stress."

"The stress? This is a man who walked 20 miles and won both parts of the competition today. He was a step away from winning a fabulous inheritance, so why would he find it too stressful to sleep in a comfy hotel?"

"That's the meanders of the human mind."

"The meanders... nonsense!" cried Etta, leaving the room before she strangled the man. He'd clearly watched too many episodes of *Profiler* and experienced too little of real life.

24

WHY?

When she woke up the next morning, Etta could hardly believe her eyes. The sun was shining and from their room, Kinlochleven looked like the most cheerful of villages. But one impression remained the same: even in daylight, the sparkling dark-blue loch resembled a Nordic fjord.

Of course, Dora did her Dora thing and stood in front of the window, her mouth open, her hands clasped and her stare radiant. Her face took on the weird expression of unearthly pleasure that reminded Etta of one of Bernini's masterpieces, the *Ecstasy of Saint Teresa of Avila*. Mind you, the appearance of the sun in Scotland was such a rare event, she could almost understand her friend's weird rapture this time.

Leon, his head tilted, his face puzzled, was sitting on the floor, waiting for the sweeter biped to come back to reality. In fact, it took ages for Dora to return to her senses. Aware of her two friends staring at her, she laughed a little self-consciously.

"I'm sorry, but doesn't this make all yesterday's struggles and hardships worthwhile?"

"Had we saved that man from murder, then I would have said yes, our mad scramble was worth it," said Etta, feeling it was time to burst Dora's bubble of pleasure with a little reality.

"Murder? Do you still think it was definitely murder?"

"What else could it be? I just hope we won't be served another corpse for breakfast, which is highly likely if we're relying on that stupid policeman to protect the treasure hunters."

Now, Dora had her feet back on terra firma. Satisfied with the results of her reality check, Etta carried on.

"I'm positively starving. Let's get some food."

Leon, who had been unmoved by Etta's brutal words to the sweet biped, sprang to his feet promptly at the mention of his favourite trigger word.

The breakfast room was in the pentagonal eastern tower of the building. Four tall windows were kissed by the morning sun, while the inevitable pine-panelled wall, painted a cheerful bright blue, was almost hidden behind a generous buffet. The mantelpiece over the fireplace held a collection of porcelain ducks, and on each table, a small bouquet of bright fresh flowers welcomed the guests.

The hikers seemed too absorbed in their activities to pay heed to the welcoming touches in the room. They were walking from the buffet bar to their tables, carrying plates filled up with whatever was available to them, but their ubiquitous chatter was a few tones lower than usual. Their spirit may have already been walking the Way, but they clearly felt they needed to show some form of respect to the poor fellow who had decided to quit this world last night and miss such a glorious day.

"Lloyd, get me some more bacon, and another two or three fried eggs." Olive de Beer's strident voice rang across the room. "Not the ones that are all hard, but you know I like them fairly well cooked. And are there any crumpets to go with the eggs? I'll stay here and keep our table, otherwise these greedy people might come and eat everything we have fetched already."

Mr de Beer almost cleared the buffet, filling three large plates with food, indifferent to the glares of the people behind him. Not only were they to be insulted by the wife, but they'd also be left ravenous by the husband.

"I'll be back in a jiffy with more trays," whispered a waitress to the hungry queue, making sure Mr de Beer couldn't hear her.

"That poor girl must be feeling all alone in the world," said Dora. It was only then that Etta noticed, partly hidden by the large figure of Mrs de Beer, Sue MacDuff was sitting at the table next to the greedy pair. On her plate was an untouched slice of toast and her face looked tired. She seemed almost nauseated at the amount of food on the plates of the de Beers.

Robert came in, his face fresh. *Young folk recover from fatigue so quickly*, thought Etta, *bless them*. As usual, as soon as he spotted Etta, Dora and Leon, he asked if they'd like to share a table with him.

"Where's Grace?"

"I knocked on her door, she will join us soon. She said it took her an age to get to sleep last night."

The buffet restocked, Robert, Etta and Dora filled their plates before sitting down together.

"Did you stay up late chatting?" asked Etta, winking at him.

"Actually, Grace said she'd got a terrible headache. As soon as her interview with the police was done, she went to bed. I spoke to Sue instead; the poor woman was in shock."

"Sure she was," said Etta sarcastically.

"What did she say?" Dora, as usual, tried to soften Etta's words. "Did she have no idea of Hobbs's intention?"

"None at all. She told me he was quite enthusiastic after winning the day yesterday. He ate a hearty dinner, then went to bed early."

"Hmm," said Etta. "Did you notice what time he retired to his room?"

"Oh yes, around 8.30. Most people left the restaurant and went straight to their rooms."

"Who are most people?"

"Faith Hillock, Olive de Beer, Sue and Alastair. And Grace felt tired… but as you know, she came back down when she couldn't sleep."

"Quite. What about Sue?"

"Eh?"

"We met her on the landing just before 9.30. She was going to read in the lounge and she told us Hobbs was in a filthy temper… a drastic mood swing in such a short time."

"Maybe he'd received unwelcome news."

"In which case, the police will find out easily enough. Did Sue say anything else?"

"She said that if she hadn't seen the man with a gunshot wound to his temple, the gun still in his hand and the door locked from the inside, she would have thought it was some form of foul play…"

Etta lowered her voice, hoping the chatter of the walkers around her would muffle her words from curious ears.

"Don't you think foul play is exactly what did happen?"

Robert's eyes widened in surprise. "Why do you think that?"

"Did Sue know the professor was carrying a gun?"

"She knew he was familiar with weapons, but no, she never thought he'd carry a gun along on the West Highland Way."

"Doesn't that convince you there's something strange about all this?"

"But how? You saw the same as the rest of us: the door was locked, and the police said the window was latched."

"Yes, the locked-room murder, so beloved of crime writers. There's always a way out."

"Do you think there's a secret passage somewhere?" Dora asked Etta, her eyes twinkling. "After all, Mamore is such an old building…"

To Dora's surprise, Etta gave it some thought. "You might be right. The aristocracy has always needed secret entrances and exits, whether it's to flee from murderous rebels or to sneak a lover into a bedroom without being seen…"

At that moment, Grace came in. Dora whispered, "Please don't mention any of this to her. I'm afraid the sensitive girl might get upset if she knows you suspect murder." Robert and Etta nodded in approval.

"Good morning," said Grace, dark shadows around her eyes and her face tired. "It's so good to see your friendly faces. I can't believe what's happened." But with the resilience of the young, Grace placed a plate of food on the table and started to eat, nibbling at first, but soon devouring it with gusto.

"I've been wondering about the why," Grace said between mouthfuls. "I wonder if Sue might shed some light on it; maybe she knew he was depressed."

"He didn't look depressed to me..." Etta couldn't contain herself and Robert interrupted smoothly.

"In fact," he said, "I spoke to Sue last night and she hasn't a clue. We were wondering if Alastair might have received some bad news."

"That would explain it. Did the police find anything out?"

"Nay," said Robert. "That is, I mean... I haven't spoken to them, except when I was interviewed, and then they didn't say anything at all."

When Etta turned her head, she was surprised to see Sue staring across the tables at Grace with an enigmatic look on her face. Was she jealous of the dear girl?

"*Protect the two young ones,*" Rufus had said. Could Grace be in danger?

As quick as lightning, Sue's eyes flicked on to the solicitor, who had just entered the breakfast room. Mr Morlore reached Sue first and spoke to both her and the de Beers, then moved on to Robert and Grace. He greeted Etta and Dora by name, not forgetting Leon, who was busy licking his bowl that was now woefully empty of bacon. Life is an endlessly cruel list of pleasures that have to come to an end.

"Where are the Misses Hillock?" asked the solicitor.

"In fact, I was wondering about them," said Robert. "I haven't seen either of them since last night." He sprang to his feet, his face concerned. "I'll go call them," and with that brief announcement, he left.

"Should we follow him?" Dora asked, a little shyly in front of Mr Morlore.

"I'm sure they'll be fine," replied Morlore. "They must be taking their time; after all, yesterday was a long day. Anyway, I want to see you, Miss Jelly, and all the other heirs in the lounge once you've finished breakfast."

"Will you give us the next clue then?" Grace asked.

"Not really," said Mr Morlore. "I might as well inform you now: I've spoken to the police and they might have some more questions for you. As you're the only ones who knew Professor Hobbs, I'm suggesting you spend another night at Mamore Lodge. This, hopefully, will also give you a little more time to recover from this unforeseen tragedy..."

"The sisters!" Robert came back, his alarmed voice cutting across the solicitor's measured tones. "The sisters are not answering their door. I knocked quite a few times... and no one at reception has seen them."

His voice was unusually loud, so much so that the de Beers and Sue came over to ask what had happened. When they heard the news, so reminiscent of trying to raise a response from Professor Hobbs's room the previous night, their faces went pale.

"So no one has seen them today?" Mr Morlore asked for confirmation. The others all shook their heads. Her eyes filling up with horror, Sue started to tremble, so much so that Dora had to invite her to sit down.

"I'll tell the police," said Mr Morlore. "Please wait for me in the lounge."

"I ain't finished my breakfast," Mrs de Beer protested, careless of her companions glaring at her.

"Then wait for me here in the breakfast room," said Mr Morlore, unable to hide his disgust.

"Will do," said Mr de Beer defiantly into the face of the others' contempt. "And don't look down on my wife when you've all been stuffing your faces this morning. She can't be the only one who's hungry."

As Mr Morlore left, shrugging, the de Beers returned to their table.

"You don't mind if I wait with you, do you?" asked Sue.

"Of course not, dear," said Dora. "What are your plans from now on, if I may ask?"

"I guess I'll wait to speak to the police. I'm not sure if I should go back to England, or if they'd rather I stayed here."

"You're not going to finish the treasure hunt?" said Dora.

"I'm not one of the family, so I'm not included in the competition. I was only doing it to help Alastair… and now I want to go home."

Etta shook her head. As soon as she formed a theory, she learned some details that didn't fit. Motives – if only she could understand the motives behind the wickedness she suspected. Could greed explain it all, or were there other forces at play?

It wasn't long before Mr Morlore came back, his face pale, his voice broken.

"The police opened the room… the Misses Hillock aren't there."

"Have they left?" asked Etta promptly. "I mean, has their luggage disappeared like Mr Herrera's did?"

"No, everything is still in the room: their raincoats, their daily rucksacks and the other luggage. The beds have been slept in, but the two women have vanished. No one on the hotel staff has seen them this morning."

"Maybe they've just gone out for an explore," said Grace, puzzled.

"After a day like yesterday?" said Etta. "I don't feel like walking 100 metres. I wonder what has happened to them…"

"How is this possible?" cried Sue. "There were plenty of people about this morning, including the police, so how could they have gone out unnoticed?"

"Well," said Robert, "the police just sealed off Professor

Hobbs's room while they waited for further instructions, but they weren't guarding the hotel as a whole…"

The de Beers, who had finally finished their breakfast, came back over to rejoin the conversation.

"Are you going to give us the next clue so we can start doing some online research while we're stuck here?" Lloyd de Beer demanded of the solicitor.

"No, I'm afraid not. You won't get your clue until the day of departure, in accordance with the rules Sir Angus McGrouse set for you."

"But he wouldn't have foreseen that we'd be held up by someone in our party committing suicide, would he?"

"Certainly not, but we at Law, Lorr and Morlore are duty bound to comply with our late client's wishes. He was adamant the clues would be handed to the participants on the day of departure, with only a few exceptions," and Archibald Morlore looked in the direction of Robert.

"But us not being able to do online research means the Scottish contestants, who know the lie of the land and the history, are the most likely winners," Olive de Beer protested.

"Until last night's unfortunate event, the man in the lead was English, which rubbishes your argument," Mr Morlore cut the de Beers short before the husband could put his beak in. "Anyway, I've booked myself a room at Mamore Lodge too; I want to be available for the police anytime, so I'll be around if you need me. In the meantime, I want to understand more about the ladies' disappearance. This is indeed a puzzle on top of last night's tragedy."

25

THE SEARCH FOR THE HOTEL'S SECRETS

"I think we've finished our breakfast, haven't we?" Etta asked Dora.

Dora nodded.

"And the poor dog needs a little walk," Etta continued.

The 'poor dog' looked at her in shock. Walk? Now? When precious crumbs could be falling from tables? Here was a lovely walker already asking if she could feed the cute dog a little bit of...

An instant later, Leon was dragged from the breakfast room, too shocked to call upon his Basset superpower – his ability to increase his weight at least tenfold whenever a human was silly enough to attempt to force him to move when he had other ideas. Once the trio was outside, they found the sunny air was a little chilly, but it smelled of new green leaves, clear sky and good things. Leon immediately forgot his chagrin at being forced from his cleaning duties in the breakfast room and joined his bipeds in a few deep, long breaths.

"Why did you want to rush outside?" asked Dora.

"Just curious," replied Etta enigmatically.

"About what?"

"I want to see this building from the outside. Let's explore the right-hand side."

This meant walking the whole length of the beautiful southern façade. They passed the dining room, which was below their own room, and circled around the lounge in the pentagonal tower just below the Hillock sisters' room. Opposite the western side of Mamore Lodge was a charming one-storey cottage, partly hidden by a mass of shrubs.

"Such a romantic little building," said Dora, but Etta was looking in the opposite direction. The northern wing started with the games room at the back of the bar, which had to be an extension of the original building as it was terraced above. A flight of steps next to the terrace led to the first floor. Etta began to march up those steps resolutely.

"Where are you going?" whispered Dora. Etta stopped on the steps and turned to look at her friend.

"Just having a poke round. We need to be clear on the geography of the place. Why are you hesitating?"

"Isn't the room on the right of the terrace Professor Hobbs's?" said Dora, pointing to what little of the wall was visible from ground level.

"Exactly," said Etta.

"I'm not sure I want to peer in there," Dora said, horrified.

"We don't need to peer in, just understand if the room has access to the terrace. Also, these steps should lead to a door. If there was foul play involved, we need to know how the murderer moved around."

"The murderer?"

"That's what I call those who go about killing other people."

Before Dora could answer, Etta turned and climbed the rest of the steps, and Dora felt duty bound to follow her with Leon. Etta was right: the steps led to an emergency door on the first floor; they hadn't seen it before because it opened into the north wing. There were railings separating the emergency exit and steps from the terrace above the games room.

Four windows opened on to the terrace, two from a bedroom just opposite them, the others from the interior stairs. The bedroom windows had police tape across them, which told them that was Professor Hobbs's room.

"That's a convenient way out, isn't it?" said Etta. "I wonder if the police have checked whether the bathroom window was latched, too. Yesterday, the constable only mentioned the bedroom window."

"Etta, what are you doing?" Dora blurted out in a strange mixture of a cry and a hiss. Etta was climbing over the railing and walking towards the police tape.

"Hey, what do you think you're doing?" a policeman echoed Dora's words, looking out at Etta from Professor Hobbs's bedroom window.

"Really, nothing …"

"Aren't you the Italian teacher I interviewed last night?

"I am," said Etta, her face reddening beyond the colour of her hair.

"Are you trying to spy on a dead man's bedroom? You tourists are so incurably nosy! I told my superiors we should have cordoned off the whole terrace area from the ground, but we weren't allowed to close off the emergency exit. Just in case. Now, get out of here, but don't go too far – expect to be called in again for more questioning later."

Etta returned to her two companions, her tail between her legs. Dora and Leon glared at her with no sign of sympathy and 'we-told-you-so' expressions on their faces.

After that, Etta completed her tour around the outside of the hotel in silence. Leon made sure to mark any vertical surface so that the dogs of Kinlochleven and beyond would know he was without doubt the one and only master of Mamore Lodge.

RECEPTION WAS DESERTED WHEN THE THREE FRIENDS RETURNED TO pick up their room keys from the collection on the desk, which included the spare key for the Hillocks' room. The heavy brass keyrings worked wonders in ensuring guests would be unlikely to forget to leave their keys at the hotel.

Once they were upstairs, to Dora's horror, Etta passed their room and marched on decisively towards that of the Hillock sisters. Worse still, she slid a key into the keyhole and opened the door.

"Come on, quick!" she muttered, her determination too strong to resist. Dora and Leon scampered in after her, and Etta closed and locked the door behind two backs and one tail, laying the key on a bedside table.

"Are you mad?" hissed Dora, her usual gentleness deserting her. "What are we doing here? Wasn't it enough that the policeman told us off not ten minutes ago?"

"You're the one who's so keen on the idea of a secret passage. This room is the closest to Professor Hobbs's, the only one sharing a wall with his; the only one that could hide the secret passage."

Now Dora felt in two minds. What was she to do? Second her friend's madness or convince her to quit and return to their own room? But... could she really resist the unveiling of a secret passage?

"So, do you think the sisters might have killed him, and then run away when the police showed up?"

"That's one of two possibilities," Etta answered, busy exploring the wall on her right. Then she poked her head up the chimney.

"What's the other?"

"Someone used the sisters' bedroom to gain access to Professor Hobbs's – it's well-known that they are sound sleepers. When he or she thought they might have found out, the killer had to get rid of the sisters too."

"That's horrid!"

"Aye, it's full of ashes and cinders."

"Not the chimney! I mean it's horrid that two more people might have died..."

Etta didn't seem too upset by the idea, not when she was busy exploring the fireplace.

"There must be a lever or something here," she muttered, running her hand over the wall at the back of the chimney.

"But Etta," objected Dora, "the chimney wall doesn't give on to Hobbs's room. You remember what it looked like from outside? It must be the bathroom that joins with the professor's room," and she pointed to the door on their left.

"Och, I wish you'd mentioned that before," said Etta, her accent becoming more Scottish with each passing moment, her face and hands black with soot.

"You'd better have a wash," said Dora, opening the bathroom door to let her friend in.

A few products lay around, including toothbrush, toothpaste and a couple of threadbare beauty cases. For the first time, Etta looked as if she might be feeling guilty at intruding on the privacy of others.

"The wall behind the tub," whispered Dora. "That's the only one adjacent to Hobbs's room."

"Genius!" Etta climbed into the tub and carried on in her search for a lever without explaining whether the genius was Dora or whoever had designed the mythical secret passage. Minutes later, after a long series of failed attempts, she shrugged, got out of the tub and planted her feet firmly on the floor. Then, to Dora's astonished horror, she started to pull the whole tub forward.

"It must be hidden behind it."

At a loss as to what to do for the best, Dora gave her a hand. The sooner they were out of this compromising position, the better.

"This isn't getting us anywhere," said Dora after a few

moments, letting go of the bathtub and straightening up. "We might end up dragging the whole wall down if we don't stop."

Etta looked embarrassed, as if she realised she might have gone too far this time. Dora knew it was the right time to press her advantage.

"What if the police come in? And what if they take our fingerprints?"

"But no one knows for sure that something bad has happened to the sisters yet..."

"If they suspect foul play and do a search, we'll be in big trouble."

"So we'll clean up after ourselves."

"Forensic experts can gather evidence from all kinds of things: hairs, fragments of skin, droplets of saliva..."

"I'm sure I haven't dropped any parts of my body!"

Dora sighed and pointed at Leon, who had fallen asleep on the bedside rug. One of Leon's lesser superpowers was shedding fur with a generosity one could hardly believe from a short-haired breed like a Basset. And that was beside him drooling after his satisfying breakfast.

Etta glared at him. "I knew from the start he'd be the ruin of us."

"Don't blame him," in support of her beloved hound, Dora managed to sound uncharacteristically menacing. As for Leon, he yawned, stretched and sat up, moving his head from left to right as if he was watching a tennis match. He quite enjoyed the bickering between his bipeds, a renewed demonstration of how important he was. But they stopped arguing a little too abruptly for his ego to be completely massaged.

In fact, they stopped talking altogether.

And that's when the hound became aware of a number of voices coming from outside.

Etta and Dora crossed over to the window and peeped out. A crew of scene of crime officers dressed in white suits, masks and gloves and carrying overshoes were leaving a van and entering the hotel via the back entrance next to the games room.

"Let's get out of here!" said Etta, forgetting the need to wipe away the evidence of her fingerprints in an instant. But as the trio rushed over to the door, there came the sound of a key turning in the lock. Then the handle moved of its own accord and the door slowly opened...

26

A SHARP TONGUE CAN SAVE YOU

"AAAARGH!" A woman as ugly as a gargoyle, her messy long hair hanging limply either side of her face, screamed out in alarm. "What are you doing here?" she added, more in anger than fear.

"I almost had a heart attack," echoed a second equally ugly gargoyle, her hand patting her breast as if encouraging her heart back into her ribcage.

"What are you doing in our room?" repeated Faith Hillock.

Etta hesitated for a fraction of a second; probably only Dora and Leon, who knew her so well, would have spotted her uncertainty. Then she charged like a cornered bull.

"What are YOU doing here?" she asked, looking the sisters up and down.

"What? This is our room!"

"You mean this *was* your room."

"No, I mean this *is* our room."

"That's weird. They told us at reception that you had left, and as we want to spend one more night at Mamore Lodge, we were planning to take over this room. It is far larger…"

Etta's voice petered out and she looked at Dora for inspiration. Her friend didn't let her down.

"It's airier than ours and the furniture is much cosier. I like that old painting..."

"Enough!" Etta cut her short, her fists resting pugnaciously on her hips, doubling her width. Even Leon had to acknowledge that his feistier human was quite good at looking imposing. "We don't need to justify ourselves, Dora; *they* are the ones who need to explain what they're doing here!" Etta's eyes fixed on Faith; the other sister was in reality just a poor imitation of the first.

"We never left the hotel!"

"Of course you did; we've spent half the morning looking for you."

"I mean, we never checked out of the hotel. As you can see, our stuff is still here, but it's Sunday, so we went to church."

"In Kinlochleven?"

"Exactly. On Sunday, the church opens early for private prayers and dedication..."

"Most unfortunately," Hope finally managed to get some words in edgeways, "the service isn't until 10.30, which would clash with the day's treasure hunting..."

"But as faithful believers, we couldn't miss our Sunday prayer."

"Did you walk there?" asked Etta, still implacable.

"Of course not! Yesterday evening, we arranged for a taxi to pick us up at 6.45."

"No one at the reception desk at that time, I guess," said Dora.

"We actually left via the emergency exit in the north wing – it's closer to the parking area where the taxi was waiting for us. And we took our key with us."

"And you didn't think to alert anyone in your group? You know, they were all worried something might have happened to you."

"Alert anyone? They'd be the first to take advantage of our absence given half a chance. No, we did our best to leave unnoticed."

"How long did you stay in the church?"

"A good hour. On Sunday, we're always keen to reread passages in the Bible."

"God comes first for people as devout as us."

"Then we met the vicar and had a little chat with him."

"How impressed he was to have two good women like us in his humble church…"

"Now get out of our room," said Faith, regaining the upper hand. "We need to get ready to join the solicitor downstairs."

"They've already had their meeting," Etta informed them.

"But it was postponed!" said Faith. "It would be a little later because of all the trouble last night."

"All the trouble? That's what you call what could have been a nasty murder?"

"I hope that's true for the sake of his soul."

Etta and Dora failed to understand, and it must have shown on their faces.

"If it was a murder, Our Lord in Heaven will save his soul," Hope explained as her sister nodded in approval. "But suicide is the most grave of sins."

"You two are hopeless. If someone has been killed, there's still a guilty murderer somewhere, so the sinner count would be the same."

Faith considered this objection, then shook her head.

"I believe suicide is a worse sin than homicide. With suicide, you're not only a killer, but you also destroy the very gift God has given…"

"Enough!" said Etta again. "Anyway, for your information, the solicitor said you're to spend an extra night at Mamore Lodge. Maybe you'll continue the treasure hunt tomorrow, maybe you won't. Mr Morlore is staying here too, and I'm sure he'll be very pleased to know you're fine."

The trio left before the harpies could realise that Etta, by informing the sisters that all the treasure hunters would be staying, had just contradicted her assertion that she'd been told the sisters' room was vacant. Just before the door closed behind them, Etta heard one harpy make a comment to the other in a none-too-quiet whisper.

"Those Italians are so very nosy."

Once they were back in their room, Dora burst into a deep chuckle.

"Concetta Natale Passolina, you were simply wonderful. How did you come up with the idea of wanting to change rooms?"

"I guess storytelling comes naturally to me."

"I was paralysed with fear when that door opened – I thought it was the police and we'd be arrested straight away. You're one of a kind."

Leon barked out his protest: "WoRf, woRf, WORRRF!"

"Of course, my dear," Dora instantly corrected herself. "You're one of a kind, too."

"In the end, the two harridans saved us: now that they're back safe and sound, the police won't be checking their room for evidence."

"What a relief, no jail term for us this time. But why did you tell them about the solicitor and the outcome of his briefing? I didn't think you'd want to do anything to help them."

"It's not that – quite the opposite. I don't like those two, and yesterday night at the time of the murder, one of them was upstairs. It's completely out of character for one to do anything without the other, yet there was Hope, bold as brass, on her own in the bar. So what was Faith doing all by herself? I didn't tell them anything they wouldn't have found out soon enough, and hopefully it'll stop them from thinking too deeply about what we were really doing in their room."

"You're so sure it's murder, yet we found no secret passage. How could someone get in and out of a locked room with the keys inside and the windows shut?"

Etta walked to one of their windows and checked it. Of course, someone could close the window from the outside, but there was no chance they could fasten the latch. Maybe it really was suicide and the treasure hunt party was just cursed. After all, as the constable had said, when people are stressed, you never know how they might react. And what could be more stressful than knowing you're about to either become a millionaire or get nothing?

Except... Professor Hobbs had been leading the ranks yesterday evening. He'd seemed his usual self to his assistant at 8.30, but by 9.30, that same woman was saying he was shut in his room in a bad mood. What had happened in that hour to change his mood so dramatically? Was there a scandal? Had the police found anything out? Maybe Professor Hobbs knew he was about to be exposed as a fraud or a crook, and such a scandal would surely prevent him from winning the contest, wouldn't it?

"What are we going to do now?" said Dora. "I'm sure the dog wants to go out for a walk."

"You don't mean to visit Kinlochleven, do you?" Etta asked, knowing what her friend was like. "I can barely carry myself from here to the dining room, my knees, thighs, feet and ankles hurt so much. Actually, I don't think there's any part of my body that doesn't hurt this morning."

"The hotel staff were putting deckchairs out earlier," replied Dora. "It'd be a pity to stay inside when the sun is shining so pleasantly... what if we fetch a book, sit in the sun and take it easy before lunch? And Leon could make new friends and sniff the grass."

"Leon will pee on the grass, as if it hasn't been watered enough recently. But as for the rest, I believe it's a splendid idea."

Leon approved as well, happy to know he wouldn't be held captive in a hotel room all day long. Bassets have a great need to discover the wild world, especially when the rain stops.

Leaving their room, the two women and one dog met an army of SOCOs entering Professor Hobbs's room, their faces serious.

So, the police are not convinced it was suicide after all, thought

Etta as they went downstairs. What a stroke of luck that the two sisters had come back; Etta wouldn't have liked her hair, fingerprints and droplets to be collected and studied...

Why was it that the presence of the police made her feel not only apprehensive, but guilty, as if she had something to hide? The obvious answer was that trespassing in someone else's room wasn't exactly a nice thing to do under normal circumstances, let alone when an investigation into a mysterious death was going on. But this did not even cross her mind.

At reception, the two friends had just informed the smiling young woman that should the police need them, they'd be outside, when a velvety voice called from the corridor.

"Mrs Passolina... ahem... Etta."

27

YOU, AGAIN!

When Etta turned, she could hardly believe her eyes. Meanwhile, her treacherous heart started to pump an abundance of blood all around her body, including the places she never normally took any notice of like her earlobes, the tip of her nose, the side of her neck, the inner parts of her wrists. More than anything, she was afraid the strange reaction might be visible from the outside, so took refuge in a retort.

"Rufus, what the heck are you doing here?"

For an answer, he laughed his loud, intoxicating laugh. It was enough for Etta to lose a little more control over her body.

"Well, I actually dared to hope it would be a nice surprise…"

Etta blushed. As blunt as she'd managed to sound, this man had the power to disarm her, making her feel that her hostile ways – normally so natural, but right now so hard earned – were out of place.

"I mean, indeed, it is. A surprise… a nice one… I was hopin… I thought I wouldn't see you again until we arrived in Fort William?"

"You're right, this wasn't planned, but here in the Highlands, news travels fast. First of all, though, how's Leon?"

The man kneeled down before Leon, who always appreciated it when humans submitted to His Majesty. And the man knew how to touch a dog: gently, asking permission first and only proceeding once the Basset had wagged his 'Yes, you can' response. Then, he gave Leon scratches and massages in the right spots. Leon preferred women, of course, but a male masseur would do, especially when he acknowledged who was in command.

"Are you going for a walk?" Rufus asked, continuing to caress Leon.

"Not really, we were just going to sit outside on the deckchairs. Something bad happened last night... we need to stay around."

"I know – that's what I meant when I said news travels fast. I'll just have a word with the SOCOs, and I'll get back to you in five to ten minutes. That is, if you don't want to be left in peace. Do you?"

"Yes, of course. I mean, yes, you can join us, not that I want to be left in peace. Why would you being here trouble me? We have nothing much to do, Dora and I, so I might just as well talk to you. That is... no, what I mean is..."

The man looked straight at her.

"I'll return as soon as I can."

"Tha... thank you." Etta grabbed Leon's leash and hurried outside, wondering why she was making such a fool of herself.

Only once they'd found two deckchairs in the full sun, near to the hotel pond and close enough to a little bush that Leon could move at his leisure in and out of the shadow, did Dora mention Rufus's surprise arrival.

"Do you think he's here about the murder?"

"I suspect so."

"He's certainly come for you. I mean, if there had just been a mere murder, I don't think he'd have bothered. Didn't you say he'd retired from the force?"

"But he didn't know we were here."

"No, that's true. But he must have known we were due to arrive in Kinlochleven today."

"Yes, but I didn't mention Mamore Lodge to him."

"I have half an idea that, just as Rufus said, news travels fast in Kinlochleven. It's hardly the size of London, is it? So when he arrived here, he probably guessed he'd stumble into you at some point. I mean, look at just now – he must have arrived moments ago, but the first thing he does is make sure he can spend some time with you. Should I disappear, by the way?"

"Why would you do that? Please don't!"

"Concetta Natale Passolina," Dora said, chuckling, "don't tell me you're afraid of a fine Scotsman?"

"Of course, I'm not. It's just that... please stay."

Then Etta pretended to become absorbed in her book, but her brain was working furiously, trying to unravel the events of the previous day and the mystery of the so-called suicide. Was she imagining it all? How could anyone come in and out of a locked room? Why wasn't she accepting the obvious solution: that it really was suicide? Why dig for trouble when life itself was so very generous in supplying plenty along the way?

Truth was – and Etta was aware of it – she wanted to come up with a brilliant insight: some details no one had noticed; something no one would have paid attention to apart from this clever Italian. In all honesty, she wanted to impress Rufus, let him know she was no common woman. She could dance and enjoy life (at least, that's how she hoped he regarded her), but she had a powerful brain too. A woman not to be taken for granted.

But as hard as she tried, not even half a clever idea came to mind. The search for the mythical secret passage had proved useless. And the locked room puzzle was tying her in knots; for every step forwards, she seemed to take two steps back.

Before long, both Dora and Leon started glancing in her direction. It was as if they knew she wasn't really reading and were expecting a brilliant suggestion to come from her at any moment.

"Stop staring at me! I can neither read nor concentrate under your gaze."

"We're not staring," said Dora, looking down at her own book, while Leon simply sighed and turned his back on his bipeds, his most scornful look on his face.

～

FORTY MINUTES AND MANY AGONIES LATER, ETTA, GLANCING IN THE direction of the hotel from behind her book, finally spotted the cause of her distraction.

Five to ten minutes, he said. Typical man, never reliable. But what is a woman to expect from such a subspecies?

The man spotted them, despite Etta refusing to allow herself to wave at him. Instead, she pretended once more to be engrossed in her book.

"Hello, ladies; hello, Leon. I hope you're enjoying your rest in this glorious sunshine." Rufus spoke amicably enough, but his expression was serious.

"Oh, it's you," said Etta, as offhandedly as she could manage.

"Hello, Rufus," as ever, Dora was more welcoming, "what's going on inside?"

"I'm sorry I took longer than expected, but there have been some developments..." and he looked around as if to make sure no one was close enough to hear them.

"And what are they?" asked Etta, putting her book down face up. A twinkle entered Rufus's eye.

"Oh!" he said. "Do you often reread books straight after finishing them?"

"Of course not," but her eyes followed his stare and saw the book was open at the copyright page – she'd got no further than that! "I was simply checking the year the book was published."

"We were just discussing it," Dora was quick to back her friend up.

"I see," said Rufus. "So, Dora, can I safely assume you know what book Etta is reading?"

"Of course," Dora answered so resolutely, no one would have felt the need to ask her what the book's title actually was. Rufus grinned at her.

"You're a real friend, and there's nothing better in life than good, loyal friends." His glance included Leon, so the dog stretched himself out, grateful he didn't have to waste his energy to make a point. "Now, back to business, I'm afraid. I'm wondering if you could help me out."

"Sure!" said Dora, inviting Rufus to sit down in a vacant deckchair.

"With what?" said Etta at the same moment.

Rufus took a seat and looked around again, as if he was wondering where to start.

"It's not pleasant, so feel free to say no. I'll understand."

The two women nodded gravely, and Leon did the same, even if it was just an imitation.

"The last time we spoke, Etta, you mentioned a couple of unfortunate... incidents involving two people in the treasure hunting party. I spoke to some of the cops I know back in Glasgow and they got in touch with the solicitor, Mr Henry Law, who confirmed Law, Lorr and Morlore haven't heard a word from Mr Herrera since he left. His phone is simply dead. My friends in Glasgow did some research, but to no avail.

"However, early this morning, a farmer was taking his cattle out to pasture close to the Drovers Inn. He was surprised as the thirsty animals refused to go anywhere near the pond in the pasture; they'd approach it, then shy away. He thought it strange and went to check it out, fearing an animal may have drowned there... but he actually ended up fishing out a human body. It had no identification on it, but the sex, height and hair colour match Mr Herrera's description..."

"You want us to identify the body?" asked Etta gravely.

Rufus nodded.

"Why can't the solicitor, Mr Morlore, do it? Or someone in the treasure hunt party?"

"The officers inside thought of that, but they – we – don't want to disclose the news to any of them, yet. The deceased man had been hit hard on the back of the head with some kind of solid object before being dumped in the pond. Now, if we verify it's Herrera, we have a killer in the treasure hunt party. If that is so, the police here will immediately get in touch with their counterparts in the Netherlands and see if they agree to do an autopsy on Mrs van Wetering. Of course, this will take days, if not weeks. In the meantime, we – the police, I mean – don't want to alert the killer, but will keep a close watch on the heirs to make sure no more foul play takes place before they reach Fort William."

"Do you want both of us to come along to identify the body?" asked Dora.

"It would be better if just one of you came. It will take a good three hours to drive there and back, and for the identification. If only one of you comes, the treasure hunters are less likely to notice your absence."

As usual, Dora didn't hesitate.

"That sounds like a good plan to me. Leon and I will stay here and tell anyone who asks that Etta has gone to bed with a headache. She is the one who tends to notice small details that I'd miss, so I'm sure she'll be more help than I would."

The matchmaker in action, thought Etta, but a part of her felt like hugging her friend.

28

BACK TO INVERARNAN

In the car, a pleasant smell of lavender aftershave lingered in the air. Etta recognised it as the fresh, light perfume she associated with Rufus. He was driving fast, but smoothly, and soon they left Kinlochleven behind.

"What did the police say about Professor Hobbs? Was it murder?"

"Apparently, it wasn't. Or, at least, they'd have a problem explaining all the facts if it was anything other than suicide."

"Have they checked the bathroom window? The constable who interviewed me told me the latch on the bedroom window was fastened, but how about the bathroom?"

"So, you've been thinking an intruder could have used the terrace to get away. I'd heard you've been nosing... I mean, investigating."

"Just a little," Etta confessed, blushing again.

"No, the other window was also fastened, and it's impossible to do that from outside. At the same time, as I'm sure you know, there's only room for one key in the keyhole; if a key is inserted inside, no one could use another key to lock the door from the outside. Unless the bartender who tried was telling lies and the keyhole was clear all along."

"I guess not," said Etta, "as I and all the other people present at that time heard the key falling on to the floor inside the room."

"And the police have found no connection between the bartender and Alastair Hobbs, so why would he murder the professor anyway?"

"It would have been a great twist to discover the bartender was a long-lost relative of Sir Angus and a potential heir," said Etta, grinning impishly.

"Absolutely, although we'd have a hard time explaining how and why he was involved in the previous incidents."

"I've been thinking and thinking about that locked room, but I can't figure out what trick the killer used…"

"It doesn't really matter," said Rufus, although his expression was not that of someone who didn't care. He must have felt Etta's quizzical eyes on him because he elaborated. "Think of it this way: you're climbing the mountain by the toughest route. We need to concentrate on a different way up."

"Which is?"

"First of all, we need to do an accurate reconstruction of what happened that night. Can we really exclude anyone as a suspect?"

"Sure," Etta fired back without hesitation. "All the people who were in the bar at the time of the gunshot…"

"You've been thinking about this for quite a while, haven't you? Tell me everything you remember about that night."

And Etta described her arrival with Dora at Mamore Lodge; their fatigue; the thunder storm; the chance meeting with Sue on the landing. Their very welcome dinner in the bar just before they heard the shot.

"So we can definitely exclude Dora and me, Robert and Grace, Mr de Beer and Hope Hillock. As for Sue, she was alone in the lounge and joined us as we were heading towards the stairs."

"So among the people who could have committed the crime,

we have Mrs Olive de Beer, Miss Faith Hillock, and maybe Miss Sue MacDuff."

"Yes, I guess. Once Dora and I had gone into the bar, Sue would have had time to go round the building, enter via the steps at the back – maybe she'd already made sure to leave the emergency door open. It would not have been hard for her to persuade her professor to open the door to her; she shot him, and then... then we're stuck. How did she get out and leave the room locked from the inside?"

"Are you sure she joined you downstairs?"

"Of course!"

"Please don't answer mechanically; think back to the sequence of events before you got into the room. When exactly did you meet Sue after leaving the bar?"

"That's easy peasy. We saw her as soon as we entered the corridor leading to the stairs." As she answered, Etta noticed the disappointment on his face.

"Who went into the room once you managed to open the door?"

"Sue was the first one to step in, and then Grace followed her, I guess to offer support. The third person to go in was the bartender, but that was only when he heard Sue cry out."

"Just the three of them?"

"No; as the bartender led Sue away from the body, Robert stepped in to help Grace as she too was in shock."

"No one else was in the room?"

"No, just the four of them. I never went inside... but why are you so disappointed?"

"I was hoping it had been an illusion, a bit of smoke and mirrors..."

"An illusion?"

"Yes..." he sighed. "In the confusion of the moment, I wondered if you might have believed a person had walked into the bedroom from the door when in fact she'd been there all the time..."

"You mean Sue?" asked Etta. "No, I'm adamant she walked upstairs with us and no one was already in the room."

"I thought she might have something to do with the whole thing as she seemed to be the one most keen to establish an alibi for herself. It seems that the others were where they were as a matter of chance, but she actively made sure you noticed her going downstairs. I wondered if she might have waited for you on purpose so that you could confirm this. To the best of our – the police's – knowledge, there was no one else in the lounge at that time to confirm whether or not she was there."

Etta wanted to process all this information, but at that moment, they reached Glencoe. And before she knew what she was doing, she'd clasped her hands together and emitted a cry that was somewhere between wonder and a difficult-to-explain sense of awe. Again, she had the feeling of a dynamic Earth taking shape in front of her mystified eyes; something primordial set to the soundtrack of *The Rite of Spring* by Stravinsky, the Russian composer she'd discovered when watching Disney's *Fantasia* with the infant Maddalena.

"I'm sorry," she said almost shyly when she realised she'd been playing Dora for the second time in front of this man.

"Not at all. I've been living with these views for the past 20 years, but still I never get used to Glencoe's beauty; I simply try not to show it." He burst into one of his loud laughs, and Etta found herself laughing too. Wholeheartedly. Not at what he'd said particularly, but because of the strange sense of comradeship she felt with him.

"The Kingshouse!" she cried on sighting the familiar building. "It seems ages since we stopped here for lunch; I can barely believe it was just yesterday." Then, she turned serious. "I have two objections to the Sue theory. One: why? What was her motive? What did she have to gain from the murder, or maybe the series of murders? She wasn't an heir in her own right. Two, how did she manage to perform her trick at Mamore Lodge?"

"For the first point, I think we need to dig more into her past. As for the second, I suggest we use the black box approach."

"And what's that?"

"It might be too early to focus on the how of the locked room; we don't have enough evidence. Let's just assume it was a homicide and that the killer managed to perform a good trick to make an impossible crime possible while conveying the impression it was suicide. That's our black box. Now, let's look beyond the crime at the motives, just like you said: the whos; the whys. Let's leave the hows for later."

"From what she said, as soon as the police tell Sue she can go, she'll return home; she won't be walking the Kinlochleven to Fort William stretch tomorrow. She's no reason to do it; she has nothing to gain from this treasure hunt."

"So let's consider the other two suspects."

"Well, for Mrs de Beer, the motive is clear: she would do anything to get her hands on Sir Angus's riches. And she was already on the first floor a few rooms away from Professor Hobbs. Let's say she knocks on his door under some pretext, shoots him, and then walks back to her room undisturbed. There's just a little risk she'd be spotted by someone as she walked along the corridor."

"What about Faith Hillock?"

"It would have been an easier job for her because her room is next to Hobbs's, and she has an even better motive. She and her sister are higher up the leader board and have a realistic chance of winning the competition tomorrow, while the de Beers would have to be planning a massacre to stand any chance. They are last."

"So we might have our most likely suspect."

"There's one more thing: I found it very strange that Hope stayed in the bar yesterday night while Faith went to bed. Usually, she follows her sister everywhere; Faith Hillock is the dominant one and Hope just agrees with her on everything."

"You're saying Faith Hillock might have told her sister to stay put so Hope could keep an eye on what was happening downstairs?"

"Exactly."

29

WHAT A FACE CAN'T TELL... A HAND
MAYBE CAN

W hen a uniformed police constable barred their way along the little muddy country road, Rufus gave his name.

"Detective Chief Inspector Thomson should have let you know I'd be arriving with Mrs Passolina, who might be able to identify the victim."

The man had indeed been informed and he lifted the police tape to allow them to enter the cordoned area near the loch.

"Please, wait for me here," Rufus said to Etta as he approached a group of people, one of whom was bent over a body on the ground. There were still scene of crime officers trying to find evidence near the pond, with someone coordinating them.

"Hello," Rufus addressed the group around the body. "I've been sent by DCI Thomson with a woman who may be able to identify the victim."

"Rufus, don't you recognise me?" a bright voice answered from behind the face mask as the pathologist stood from her work and came over to greet him.

"Angela! No, I didn't recognise you. How are you doing?"

"I'm OK, but this poor chap..." her head moved in the

direction of the body on the ground. A powerful stench rose and Rufus wrinkled his nose.

"What happened to him?"

"As you know, I can't say for sure until I get him back to my lab," said Angela, "but the guy has been rotting in the water for three to four days, I'd estimate. Luckily, the water is still relatively cold, despite it being June. That has helped preserve quite a lot of evidence."

"The police in Kinlochleven mentioned he'd been killed…"

"Definitely. There's a deep wound at the base of the skull that would never have been caused by the man falling by accident. He was hit by a sharp object, I'd say, which would have taken a certain amount of strength from the assailant…"

"So it couldn't have been a woman?"

"It could have been a woman; what I meant was the blow was struck with the purpose of killing him, not knocking him unconscious. The killer then threw him into the water with a bag of stones tied to him to stop him from floating."

"But he entered the water after his death?" Rufus confirmed.

"That's correct. In fact, some time passed between the moment of his death and his body being submerged. Don't ask me how much time before I've taken the body to the lab, but you may ask me if there's anything else worth noting."

"Is there anything else worth noting, Angela?"

"Hmm, yes – the most gruesome part."

"The fish have eaten him?"

"I wish it had been the fish. Whoever killed him didn't want the man to be recognised; they've smashed his face awfully."

"Goodness!"

"Have you become squeamish since your retirement?"

"It's not that; I'm just thinking of the sensitivities of the civilian I have brought to identify him…" Rufus looked towards Etta.

"Oh, of course," said Angela, following his gaze. "Did she know him well?"

"Luckily, no; she and his party had just met up a few times while hiking the West Highland Way."

"All the same, I think you can spare her the trauma of seeing the body; there's nothing much she could recognise." And with that, Angela guided him over to the corpse.

~

"Etta?" Rufus called, finally coming back over to her. "I'm afraid I've wasted your time…"

"Have you found out the man is someone other than Mr Herrera?" replied Etta. "Are you sure?"

"It's not that," and he told her of the victim's condition as gently as possible. But he didn't get the gentlest of answers.

"Well, we half expected that, didn't we? If you want to make someone disappear, you cover all eventualities. I guess the body is naked as well?"

Matching her no-nonsense style, Rufus answered simply. "It is."

"I can't say I'm looking forward to seeing him, but as long as his hands are OK, I can almost certainly identify him. If he is Mr Herrera, that is." She paused, then added, "And I don't really need to look at the rest of him."

Rufus laughed, his joyful bark alleviating the tension of the conversation somewhat. "Are you one of those women who checks a man's hands for a ring before anything else?" he joked.

"Not generally. But if you've got hands like Amilcar Herrera, they're hard to ignore."

"How come?"

"He had hair covering them almost as far as the knuckles, and his fingers were all about the same size and practically rectangular."

"Again, you surprise me, Mrs Passolina."

"Glad to hear that, especially coming from a gritty Highlander." She grinned, but as they turned and approached the body, she became more serious, her mouth dry. Just like most people in Castelmezzano, Etta was used to seeing dead bodies; the villagers all knew one another and were expected to show up not only at funerals, but also at the home of the deceased to pay respects face to face before the coffin was closed. But a violent death was a totally different business. True, in the past year since she and Dora had started home swapping, Etta had seen more murder victims than she would have wished to in a lifetime, but she'd not yet grown accustomed to this kind of death. And no, she wasn't in any hurry to see one more.

"I really don't need to see any part of him but his hands," she repeated.

Rufus nodded. "Don't you worry, I will ask the pathologist to cover the rest." He took her by the arm close to the elbow. Despite her jacket and fleece, she felt that protective touch.

Moments later, she confirmed that the swollen, livid thing you could barely call a hand did, most likely, belong to the late Amilcar Herrera.

"And how's your dad?" Rufus asked Angela after having introduced her to Etta.

"Pretty well, I guess, except he's always trying to nose around whatever I do. You should know what he's like – once a copper, always a copper."

Rufus grinned. "I guess I do know... in part. Say hello to him and tell him I'll call him for a catch up one of these days."

"Please do, he might leave me in peace for a while," but her ready smile whenever she mentioned her dad suggested Angela was quite happy with the man as he was.

On the way back to the car, when Rufus asked Etta if she wanted to get something to eat, she had to admit the stench and the sight of the dead hand had upset her. But Rufus was clearly not a man to be discouraged. After they had put a few miles behind them, he stopped at a white cottage that had been converted into a nice café and suggested they use the facilities. By the time she came back from the ladies', he had a large bag of refreshments hanging from his arm.

"It's a little late for lunch, but we can have a light picnic in the fresh air when we get back to Kinlochleven. It will help."

Once they were back in the car, the smell of the warm food in the bag reconciled Etta's stomach, which gave a growl of approval. They stopped near a long pier on Loch Leven, the scenery peaceful and pastoral compared to the dramatic view from Mamore Lodge. Sitting at the end of the pier, their legs hanging over the water, they listened to the smooth swashing of the loch below and enjoyed the enchanting glistening of the surface under the sun.

"I can hardly believe this is the same place we arrived at yesterday," said Etta, contemplating the bright colours all around her.

"Scotland keeps changing all the time. A good metaphor for life, I guess."

"So is this why Scottish people know how to live?"

"Do we?"

"Yes! You go out and you don't mind if it's pouring with rain; you can dance and drink and spend time together; and you can make a joke… anytime."

"I'm glad my country has made such a good impression on you."

"Well, when I arrived, I thought it was a wild land, only suitable for coos, Highlanders and mad people. Then I realised there's a lot more to it…"

Their eyes locked and Etta felt a pang of pleasure she'd not experienced for years… make that decades. And she wanted to know more about this man: this joker and dancer, one moment gently quizzing her about her life, the next facing a cruel death without flinching. And now he was so contemplative as he faced the beauty of Loch Leven.

"You've asked me about my daughter and ex-husband, but how about you? Do you have a wife? Any children?"

"A wonderful wife," said Rufus, "and two beautiful children. And now I have four grandchildren too."

Etta's heart sank to the depths of the loch. She felt like running all the way back to Mamore Lodge to let Dora and Leon cheer her up.

"We had great plans to travel and see the world," Rufus continued, "and enjoy our grandchildren, and turn our wild garden into something nice. But such is life… when cancer hit, it took my Margot away in just over a year…"

"Recently?"

"Five years ago, though it doesn't seem that long."

"I'm so sorry," said Etta. "Does it still hurt?"

"I guess it does, but in a different way nowadays. At the time, I felt embittered, angry with life for dealing me such a bad hand… then I realised it made it harder on the children to see me like that. And I had a feeling Margot herself wouldn't be too pleased. You see, I indulged in alcohol for a wee while. I was never a heavy drinker, but I could easily have become one…"

"How did you give it up?"

"It was a Nigerian woman I arrested. Being a cop is a strange job: at times, you create a barrier between you and the people you arrest – the good chaps and the baddies – but there are times when the barriers fall. She was a good woman, a wise woman, but she had a very sad backstory. And suddenly, I realised how lucky I had been throughout my life; that I was letting myself down, and my kids and grandchildren deserved something better. For three years, I did not drink a drop of alcohol. Nowadays, I allow myself a drink as long as I'm in company; with others around me, I need not fear the old demon."

"You're a good man, Rufus McCall," said Etta, touched.

"And you're a good listener…"

"A *turnupstuffer*, as my grandson, Armando, would say." Etta smiled, remembering the favourite book Armando always wanted her to read him.

"Is that a Pippi Longstocking thing?"

"I see you know your children's literature…"

"Kids!" they said in unison.

"We've got so much to learn from them," Etta added. "But maybe it's time to go and see what's happening at Mamore Lodge."

Rufus got up, and then stretched out his hands to help her. She enjoyed the same firm grip as when they were dancing wildly at the cèilidh in Luss.

What are you thinking, you silly woman? she said to herself, at the same time wondering how long it had been since she'd last felt like this, all her aggressive barriers having dwindled away to allow her to show a bit of her real self. But it was too early to indulge in fantasies. Once they were back in the car – maybe it was the companionable silence between them; maybe the sun warming the windows; maybe the tiredness from the day before kicking in – in moments, she'd dozed off.

But not for long. She was rudely awoken by a sudden screaming roar as loud as thunder.

30

CONJECTURES

"What's happening?" cried Etta as the screaming continued above them.

Rufus smiled, then chuckled at her alarm. "It's only the RAF – the Royal Air Force – practising low-level flights in a mountainous area," he said, pointing to a couple of jets speeding away, now well ahead of them.

"Wow! It sounded like they broke the sound barrier. That'll be why they're so far away, but we're only hearing them now."

"Not quite the speed of sound," explained Rufus. "Jets are not allowed to reach supersonic speed over land, but I believe it has something to do with how the sound propagates…"

But Etta was no longer listening. "Stop the car," she said, pushing her red glasses up her nose.

"Here?"

"Here."

"What's the matter?"

"It's like with thunder and lightning," she said, not getting out of the car, but still watching the two white vapour trails left by the jets. "Unless the storm is right overhead, we see the flash, and only later do we hear the thunder."

"Is that important? It's a sunny day, after all…"

"Dora… Dora was counting the seconds…"

"What seconds?"

"The seconds between the lightning and thunder. The closer the storm, the shorter time between the two."

Rufus was trying to be patient, she could see that, but she also perceived a certain amount of doubt in his face. Could she blame him? She sometimes wondered herself if she was sane.

"Don't you see? If a killer counted the seconds between one flash of lightning and the related thunder, he would know when to fire his gun to ensure the sound was covered by the next roar."

"Well, he wasn't very good at it, was he? You all heard the shot in the bar. And you all agreed it came in a moment of silence, when the storm was long gone."

"That's right. How clever the killer was!"

"Clever?" he repeated carefully, as if dealing with a complete lunatic.

"Rufus! You're a detective – once a copper, always a copper, remember? Don't you understand? There were *two* shots; the first one – the one that actually killed Professor Hobbs – was hidden by a clap of thunder; I remember Dora commenting it sounded as loud as if a cannon had been fired in the corridor. As it would if a gunshot had occurred in Professor Hobbs's room, just across the landing from ours. But as it happened at the same time as the thunder, who would have distinguished between the two?"

"But what about the shot you heard later, when you were in the bar?"

"That was to make us believe the murder had just happened. The killer knew it would be some time before the village doctor could arrive at Mamore Lodge, so how could he say in absolute certainty the man had died an hour or so earlier than the gunshot we heard?"

Now Rufus's eyes widened in understanding.

"What time was it when you heard the thunder?"

"We had just arrived in our room... around nine-ish, I'd say."

"I wonder who was in the bar at that time?"

"We certainly weren't. Robert told us that at 8.30, Professor Hobbs, Sue, Grace, Faith Hillock and Olive de Beer all left the bar. Only Grace and Sue came back downstairs later..."

"Wait! You said you met Sue when you went down for dinner..."

"At around 9.25," said Etta.

"And you saw Professor Hobbs going into his room?"

"Actually, we didn't; we only have her word for that."

"Did she make it all up in order to create an alibi for herself?"

"Only half an alibi... why didn't she come into the bar with us?"

The question was left suspended in the air, then they both answered at the same time.

"Because she had to fire the second shot...

"She had to go outside unnoticed to fire the decoy shot..."

"But we need to find a motive for her to kill Professor Hobbs," said Etta. "The black box trick, although if she really killed the man at nine, she had far more time than we thought to arrange the scene of the crime at her leisure."

"This is all very interesting, but let's not concentrate on her yet. People tell lies for the most stupid of reasons – and she may have been telling the truth about when Hobbs went into his room. Let's keep an open mind and consider the others too, in particular the two sisters."

"Well, they each had a partner, which would have made the job easier. Someone upstairs to do the killing and someone downstairs to fire the second shot..."

"...or make sure whoever fired the second shot had time enough to get back to their room before everyone streamed upstairs. Remember, Hope was in the bar when you all heard the gun go off."

But Etta looked disappointed. There was something not entirely satisfactory in both hypotheses.

Gosh! For a second, it had seemed as if she'd got close to solving the mystery, seen a glimpse of the truth. But now, she was stuck once more in the same muddle of suspects, the same mystery of the locked room bothering her. Etta's own words *"We only have her word for that"* resonated in her head.

"It's gone," she said desolately.

"What?"

"For a split second, I thought I could see how this whole thing had happened from beginning to end, but now it's gone."

"It will come back, I'm positive. But in the meantime, you've probably unveiled one of the tricks used by the killer, or maybe the *two* killers."

When Etta looked at Rufus, she was dismayed to find a new expression of unease on his face; something more than simple determination. They were silent during the drive back, until they left the car in front of Mamore Lodge. Then Rufus spoke as they walked into the hotel.

"I'll speak to DCI Thomson, inform her about Herrera and suggest your theory of the murder having been committed earlier than we first thought. I'd also like to know if the police have dug anything up from the past about this group of people – anything that can help us shed a light on this mystery."

"Yes, of course. I'll see you later," and while Rufus headed towards the lounge, which had temporarily become a police headquarters, Etta stopped at reception. Both sets of keys for their room were there. Dora and Leon must still be outside.

ETTA WENT TOWARDS THE POND WHERE SHE HAD LEFT HER companions that morning. Not only were they no longer there, but a couple of people Etta recognised were occupying the deckchairs instead. Robert and Sue were talking conspiratorially, their heads close to each other.

When did those two become such good friends? Etta wondered. *And where does that leave Grace?*

She'd have given anything to know what they were discussing, but getting closer would give her away. Their talk seemed serious, but every so often, a smile appeared on their faces. Until…

"You don't mind us joining you, do you?" said Mr de Beer, approaching the young ones with his wife.

"Of course not," said Robert, startled. Raising his head, he spotted Etta, who smiled as innocently as she could.

"Hello, all," she said. "I was looking for Dora and Leon; I left them here earlier on…"

"How are you feeling?" asked Robert, appearing to be a little surprised. "You seem to be fine now."

Of course! Etta had forgotten she was supposedly recovering from a bad headache.

"Much better, thank you. Those migraines are a nuisance."

"Indeed, they are, but you're lucky," said Olive de Beer, stretching out voluptuously on her sunbed. "You don't have a husband. It's so hard to make a man understand what a woman goes through in her moments of pain."

As Lloyd de Beer protested, Robert informed Etta he had not seen Dora since lunchtime. Taking her leave of the treasure hunters, Etta walked round Mamore Lodge, wondering what her two friends were up to that was more important than hanging around the hotel, waiting for her. But the only people she found were Grace and Adam.

When Grace paused her conversation with Adam to greet her with a hello, Etta responded rather mechanically. She didn't want to be waylaid; she wanted to tell Dora all about her morning. But when she passed by the cottage they'd spotted earlier, she couldn't help but pause.

The two croaking voices were unmistakable: the Hillock

harridans. What were they conspiring about? Etta stood behind the only box hedge thick enough to hide her.

"What do you think she's doing?" one voice asked. Etta guessed it was Hope, as always looking to her sister for guidance.

"I've no idea, but if she's sticking to him, there has to be a reason."

"Do you think they suspect something?"

"Of course, or he wouldn't be here."

"Then we need to take precautions."

"Yes, let's go back to the hotel to make plans."

As Etta moved clockwise around the box hedge so as not to be spotted by the two hags, they left. But she had no time to wonder what their talk was all about before a loud "BOOO!" behind her made her jump like a liberated jack-in-the-box.

"Dorotea Rosa Pepe, what a stupid prank to play!" she cried, swinging around. Dora chuckled, and even Leon seemed to enjoy the humour of his gentler biped.

"WOOF!" he hollered, wondering if perhaps he should have synchronised it with Dora's battle cry.

"What a nice pair of jokers you are!" Etta complained. "Scaring the woman who couldn't wait to speak to you... but where have you been?"

"Just a short walk along the Old Military Road to help us digest our lunch. Now we're back, I want to explore this neglected patch of garden... it could be so pretty with a little care," said Dora, pointing to the cottage and smiling.

Surely she isn't dreaming of weeding, digging and seeding future flowerbeds? thought Etta grumpily.

When Dora paused in her list of things that needed doing to the garden – a list much longer than the patch of land itself – Etta took the chance to get a few words in edgeways and informed Dora about the body almost certainly being Amilcar Herrera and her theory about the gunshots.

"Goodness!" cried Dora, her salt-and-pepper fringe flapping

as she jumped back in surprise. "That was why the thunder seemed to come from inside the hotel, while Sue insisted the second shot came from outside."

"Exactly! Your observations about the thunder were very helpful. Trouble is, I still feel lost. I'm not sure where to go from here."

"That's easy peasy," said Dora, sitting on a low stone wall at the side of the cottage. "Let's start from the beginning – you can't go wrong by doing that. As Mr Herrera's death was murder, then we should really start with the cèilidh in Luss."

"You believe that Wilfrida van Wetering's death was also murder?"

"Well, if the killer managed to pass two murders off as a disappearance and a suicide respectively, why not pass another off as a natural death? Yes, I'd start from there."

And so, they went over what had happened that night again.

"I can't remember anything strange happening during the cèilidh," said Dora. "There's only Wilfrida's last words before she passed away…"

"What, about her heart rate?"

"Well, I've been wondering if she didn't say something different…"

"Like what?" said Etta, suddenly alert and curious.

"It's just," murmured Dora, looking at the floor, "that maybe I misunderstood her…"

Etta's eyes were devouring her friend, but she made a super-human effort to keep calm and give her an encouraging smile. Nonetheless, it felt more like a grimace.

"So what do you now think she said?"

"I'm not completely sure…"

"Just spit it out!"

"Well, I thought she was saying her heat rate had gone into overdrive, but the more I consider it, the more that doesn't sound right. Maybe… just maybe, she said, 'The portrait.'"

"What portrait?"

"Well, earlier on, during the cèilidh, Wilfrida had told me she was reminded of someone. That is, one of the men in a kilt reminded her of someone."

"Who?"

"She couldn't remember."

"I mean, which man in a kilt reminded her of this unknown person? There were plenty of kilts on show that night."

Dora flushed, her face screwed up in concentration, her brain running at the speed of light. But it seemed Etta's impatience was faster still.

"Spit it out, NOW!"

"Well... well... I'm sure it doesn't matter that much, but I think she meant..." Dora gulped, and then stuttered, "Ru-Ru-Rufus Mc-Mc... Rufus McCall. "

Etta looked at her friend with disbelieving eyes. She could not remember a single time in her whole long life when she had felt so gobsmacked.

"Rufus reminded Wilfrida of someone? And her last words could have been about him?"

"Maybe it's not that important..."

"A woman might have been murdered and her last words were about Rufus, and you say that is not important?" Etta took a deep breath. This didn't make any sense; it called for some deep thinking. A pity the thinking had to be fast, too.

How could Rufus have reminded Wilfrida of someone she'd seen earlier on? And if he had, what did it mean? How could she find out who?

Wait a second... the black box approach, Rufus had said. If part of a puzzle is too tough to solve, jump to an easier part. That was the gist of it, wasn't it? And Etta knew where to jump next.

"And when she first mentioned that resemblance, who was close to you? Who could have heard?"

"Well, we were all sitting at the table except for you and Rufus. You had just finished dancing and were returning to join us."

"*Dashing White Sergeant,*" murmured Etta, remembering each and every dance from that wonderful night.

"I'm afraid Wilfrida may have thought she was whispering, but like many people who are hard of hearing, she was actually rather loud. We all heard her…"

"What if someone felt threatened by that revelation and had to act immediately?"

"You think someone poisoned her?"

"More than likely, considering what we now know about Mr Herrera's disappearance. Could someone have injected her with something without her realising it?"

"Or maybe put something in her drink?"

"Whatever. We really need to find out who resembled whom. Where could she have seen a portrait – probably a portrait of a man in kilt?"

"I can't remember any portraits in the hotel in Balmaha, nor in the restaurant in Luss…"

"We don't know what she might have seen before we met her."

"Could she have meant a photo? But then, surely she would have called it that; if she referred to a portrait, she probably meant a painting…"

"But if she saw a painting in a random restaurant or pub, why would it have seemed so significant to her that this kilted man resembled the subject?" Etta preferred not to mention Rufus's name. Besides, how many people had been wearing a kilt that night? What if Wilfrida had meant another kilted man? What if Dora had misunderstood Wilfrida's words?

"Etta?" Dora's voice made her jump, so absorbed was Etta in her thoughts.

"Yes?"

"Do you remember the video the treasure hunters watched in the solicitor's office? The one Robert told us about? He said it featured Sir Angus McGrouse, sitting in Tilda Castle, explaining the rules. Could there have been a portrait behind him in that video?"

"You are absolutely right, you marvel of a woman! Castles are always full of paintings of ancestors..."

"Or ancestresses..."

"A *man* in a kilt," Etta reminded Dora, then returned to the thread of their conversation. "What if Mrs van Wetering noticed that *someone* bore far too strong a resemblance to an ancestor of Sir Angus – someone who had no reason to look like a member of the family? Someone like Lloyd de Beer, for example?"

The two looked at each other in both excitement and shock. There they were once again perched on the edge of the truth.

"Shall we tell the police?" asked Dora.

Etta thought about it for a while, considering who the man in the kilt might have been. Then she shook her head.

"No. Let's see if we can get our hands on that video first."

"We could convince someone back at Law, Lorr and Morlore to email us the video, or ask Mr Morlore... but how would we explain ourselves?"

"I was thinking of Robert."

"Of course! He said we could watch it any time, so we can ask him..."

Etta shook her head. "I'd rather not ask anyone, just in case. But it's so easy to pick up the wrong keys from reception..."

"What?"

"Wasn't the DVD in his rucksack with the map and guidebook?"

Dora banged her head with her hand, then resigned herself to her destiny. Such was life with an unscrupulous friend.

THE PLAN WENT MORE SMOOTHLY THAN DORA HAD FEARED. SHE distracted the woman at reception, while Etta picked up their room keys plus an extra one. Once upstairs, as Dora and Leon made sure no one was coming, Etta entered Robert's room and grabbed the DVD. Then Dora sneaked back downstairs to return Robert's key surreptitiously to reception before joining Etta and Leon in their room.

"But how are you going to return the DVD?" Dora asked.

"We'll just slip it back under the door. Robert will think it must have dropped from his rucksack."

Dora inserted the DVD into her laptop and the two friends finally met Sir Angus McGrouse.

"I like this man," said Etta. Gruff in manner and speaking in a cultured, commanding voice, the late nobleman had a flash of humour in his eyes that one could not help being drawn to. And yes, indeed there was a painting behind him. Dora paused the film and enlarged the picture. The painting portrayed a man in a kilt, but try as they might, they couldn't see anything in his facial features that reminded them of anyone in the treasure hunt party.

"But we're not looking for the obvious suspects," said Etta. "Keep playing."

The video was close to the end and they were about to admit defeat when Sir Angus got up and moved towards a fireplace. And above it was another painting of a true Highlander. Once again, Dora paused the film and enlarged the painting, zooming in on the man's face.

The two women gasped. Take away some of the beard and the sideburns, and there was their answer!

It took some time for the revelation to sink in, then Etta realised the implications of what they had just discovered. The times she had seen them talking a bit too intently came back to her, "*We only have her word for that*" echoing through her mind again and again.

Etta spoke at length with Dora, reviewing the whole trip: the various incidents – the sudden death of Wilfrida van Wetering and murder of Amilcar Herrera; the details of Professor Hobbs's death. Finally, all the lies and deceit became clear. The black box had become the clever illusion, as Rufus himself had called it. An illusion that had been performed majestically. And as with all the best tricks, it had been executed right in front of their eyes without raising any suspicion.

Now they had the truth, it was no longer time for indulging and thinking. Now, it was time for action.

31

THE LETTER

They were sitting in the moonlight on a bench near the pond. It had come as a shock to learn that someone lived in the cottage; all along, they had been sure no one was there, no one could see them. But it had been late in the night, so there was still hope. Maybe the inhabitant was used to cars coming and going to and from the hotel. What if the inhabitant had peeped from behind a curtain, though? Protected by the darkness within, they could have seen exactly what was going on.

No! They couldn't be found out now, not when they were so close. They could no longer assume they had covered their tracks well enough. But another mysterious death would mean the police would take the investigation more seriously. And yet, they had been discussing that very thing over and over for the past 20 minutes: they had to make sure the inhabitant hadn't seen anything.

If she had seen something, surely she would already have approached the police and told them, wouldn't she? If she had kept silent, it must be because she had slept soundly all night long and not noticed anything weird at all.

And yet… something had been slipped beneath the bedroom door back at the hotel. In the uncertainty of the discovery that the cottage was occupied, they had forgotten about it until now.

They took out the envelope and tore it open. A letter. Handwritten on Mamore Lodge paper. The notepaper was unfolded by impatient hands. It was clear from the first line they had not been wrong to be worried.

"HELLO,

I just wanted you to know the remedy you suggested for a good night's sleep hasn't worked at all. Not only that, but it seems to have made me have all sorts of hallucinations. I hear voices and see people doing the meanest things.

Like last night.

I'd like to have a word with you about this. Come to the cottage at midnight – I like my privacy, so don't come any earlier, in case someone sees you. I hope you can explain what I saw. Otherwise, I will have to report the incident to the police.

To recover one's sleep can be a lengthy, difficult process, and rather expensive too. Don't come empty handed. After all, if you can't explain what I saw, it would seem you're dealing in hallucinogenic drugs, and I'm sure you wouldn't want me to tell the police about that.

Sincerely yours,

Penny."

"WHAT IS THIS REMEDY ALL ABOUT?"

"Can't you see?" The reply was stiff and cold. "It's coded in case the message ended up in the wrong hands, letting us know she was wide awake last night. She saw it all."

There was no time to waste. They agreed on a plan – it was risky, but they had no choice. At this point, they couldn't sacrifice it all.

Win or lose. No other option.

32

THE COTTAGE

At five minutes to midnight, two shadowy figures approached the cottage. Most cars in the parking area had gone; the bar closed at 11pm, and the people who weren't staying at Mamore Lodge had left. For their part, the guests had retired to their bedrooms.

Well, most of them, anyway.

The figures crossed the little garden that separated the cottage from the hotel and stopped in front of the door.

"Shall we ring?" a voice hissed.

"Knock, gently. She should be expecting visitors," was the reply.

"The door is ajar…"

"So she's waiting for us. Let's go in."

The hall was in darkness, but a soft light was coming from the room at the end. A fire was flickering cheerfully in a small fireplace, beside which someone was sitting on an armchair. Still. Completely still.

Then the person – a woman – spoke.

"I'm glad you've come," she said, her voice calm and cold, its accent unidentifiable. "I hope you don't mind if I don't offer you any tea or coffee."

"There's no time for pleasantries."

The two visitors stood on the threshold, as if uncertain what to do, then crossed over to sit on the sofa opposite the armchair.

"Quite right, this is the time for sleep. Unfortunately, I can't, so I sit here and stare into the fire. Or sometimes, I look out the window until the early hours of the morning..."

She looked out at the western façade of Mamore Lodge. The windows of the Hillock sisters' room were clearly visible, as was the terrace... and Professor Hobbs's room

"So, what do you want?" Impatiently, one of the visitors stood and took a threatening step towards her. She remained calm and unmoved.

"Sit down," she snapped. "Do you really think I wouldn't have taken precautions?"

The visitor stopped abruptly.

"You see, I knew you'd come, so I wrote another letter and gave it to someone to open in the event that anything... let's say, *unfortunate* happened to me. Like a sudden disappearance. Or maybe a heart attack."

The visitor stepped back abruptly as if punched in the stomach.

"But we were told you were half-witted," blurted the other visitor. "At dinner... they said you were just some foreigner who'd lost her marbles... is this a trap?"

"Don't be so stupid!" The standing visitor rounded on their partner, gesturing wildly at the woman in the armchair. "It's obvious she has a price." Then the visitor turned back to the woman. "How much do you know?"

"Sit down," she commanded again. "Let's discuss a few things. Because I tend to be curious, I did a bit of research and found out more about this treasure hunt of yours. What a lot of misfortune your group has suffered."

The tension in the room rose. The visitors' eyes locked on to the woman's flashing ones.

"Let's take that handsome young man from Argentina, shall

we? The one who disappeared from the Drovers Inn. I bet he was easy to dispose of, wasn't he? All you had to do was tempt him from his room – how did you do that, I wonder? Did you tell him you had the next clue? Then you hit him over the head, got rid of his luggage from his room, and dumped him in the pond, naked and disfigured. Did you think no one would recognise him?" The woman's face took on a look of mock distress. "Big mistake, that."

"What are you blabbering on about?" The more brazen of the visitors dismissed her with a contemptuous smile.

"Did you know that yesterday, the police found a body in a pond near the Drovers? No, of course you didn't; the news hasn't been made public yet. But you know, in the Highlands, someone always has a friend of a friend who's in the police force. What'll be headline news tomorrow has clucked from the tongues of gossips today. But why him? He couldn't have been that strong a competitor, as he wouldn't be familiar with the local terrain."

The visitors shook their heads, clearly reluctant to speak in case they gave away more than they wanted to.

"I can see why *you*…" the woman fixed her eyes on the more aggressive visitor "…wanted to get rid of that Dutchwoman. It was at the cèilidh in Luss, wasn't it?"

"If you mean Mrs van Wetering, she died of natural causes."

"Yes, the heart attack… she'd mentioned her heart condition more than once, I believe; what could be simpler than helping her on her way? Especially as she'd been so struck by the uncanny resemblance you bear to a portrait in Tilda Castle when she saw you wearing a kilt."

"She'd never been there."

"No, but Sir Angus McGrouse had. And during the video where he explained the rules of the treasure hunt, that portrait appeared behind him in a couple of sequences. Wilfrida van Wetering was an anthropologist; her eyes were trained to read the features of a face beyond beard or sideburns, and so she was struck by the resemblance."

"Who the hell are you? How could you possibly know about Sir Angus's video?"

"You see, in order to gather the information I need, I speak to people. They see me as a harmless, lonely old woman, so even strangers tend to tell me more than they'd say to someone they know."

"Harmless? You want to extort money from us – is blackmail a profession for you?"

"No, listening to people is my profession."

The two visitors shared a sarcastic smile.

"But last night," said the woman in the armchair, "was a real stroke of genius. Professor Hobbs had to die, didn't he? He was close to winning the competition, and the thunderstorm gave you the chance you'd been waiting for..." she looked at the second visitor, the one still sitting on the sofa.

"Plenty of witnesses will tell you I was in the bar at the time of the gunshot."

"No, you weren't. Because the real shot – the one from inside the hotel – happened a good 40 minutes before the fake one outside. The storm was raging near the hotel; all you had to do was count the seconds between the lightning and the thunder. You called at Professor Hobbs's room, chatted to him, maybe pretended to congratulate him on winning the day. After all, that would tie in with the caring persona you'd portrayed up until then. But as soon as you saw the lightning, you started counting; the gun was loaded and ready in your hand, so when the thunder roared, you fired. Then all you had to do was use the bedside lamp to signal from the window to your partner, who was waiting in the car near this cottage, letting him know everything was going according to plan.

"Having seen your signal, he walked over to Mamore Lodge. Then he entered via the emergency door – the one you'd conveniently left open for him – and picked up the room key, also left by you. Dressed like Professor Hobbs – which meant a simple black suit and a false goatee beard – he wanted at least one person to see him entering the man's room. And there was Sue MacDuff, ready and waiting. It was dangerous, but at the same time, a good opportunity to cover your tracks. You did not answer her greeting; just walked in and closed the door behind you, leaving a witness to testify that Professor Hobbs was still alive a good twenty minutes after his death.

"Once in the room, you made sure the crime scene looked like suicide. Then you left the key in the lock and escaped via the bedroom window. Outside, you fired a shot into the air with another gun, making sure everyone heard it this time. This second shot was to mark the time of the death in the eyes of the witnesses, and even if someone did suspect foul play, your partner would have the perfect alibi – she was in the bar, surrounded by people. From this window, I saw it all, and what I didn't see, I can imagine."

The man jumped up and grabbed the woman, shaking her violently, his hands tightly round her neck. "I will torture you until you spill the beans, including the name of who you gave the letter to. And you know I will do it – as you've just said, we've already killed three people."

The woman tried to cry out, but all she could do was choke, her face going as red as the coals in the fireplace.

"Don't, you'll kill her!" the second visitor cried, grabbing his hands. "We need to know more, especially who's got that letter. No one can know the truth of how we got away with murder."

"She will speak," the man said. "Better to pass away quickly than endure a night of torture."

"Stop right there!" a voice cried from the door. The lights were switched on and the three people in the room were momentarily blinded. Then the killer recognised the woman he'd been trying to strangle, disguised though she was beneath a curly white wig and a mass of shawls around her neck.

"But that's Mrs Passolina."

"That's correct, Adam," Etta said, reverting to her usual Italian accent, but her eyes were fixed on the young woman beside him.

"The police are here! It was a trap! A trap!" she said, looking like she was unable to believe what she was seeing.

"Well spotted, Grace," Etta said. "Shall I continue?"

Rufus McCall looked at DCI Thomson, and the DCI nodded as if to say, "Please carry on."

"Well, once we heard the shot in the bar and rushed upstairs, all Grace had to do was be one of the first people to enter the room." Etta looked directly at Grace again. "Then you faked being sick or fainting or something and leaned against the windowsill. Using the tissue in your hands, all you had to do was gently push the bolt down on the window behind you. With that simple action, you created the perfect locked-room murder."

EPILOGUE

The treasure hunters' table at breakfast was not much smaller than usual as it included the remaining participants – the de Beers, the Hillock sisters and Robert – along with Sue MacDuff, Dora and Etta, and Mr Morlore. Rufus had been called in as a consultant by his former colleagues at Police Scotland.

Needless to say, the conversation was all about the two murderers.

"Mrs Passolina," asked an unusually subdued Mr de Beer, "what made you suspect Grace?"

"I didn't suspect her for a long time; I actually suspected Sue..."

Etta looked apologetically at the young woman, who nodded as if to say, "No offence taken, please carry on."

"But I ended up against a brick wall: a complete lack of motive," Etta continued to address Lloyd de Beer. "My brain kept telling me it had to be one of the heirs, and a likely winner of the treasure hunt had a stronger motive than one lagging behind. That's why I pretty much excluded you and Mrs de Beer and looked mainly at the Misses Hillock. My apologies to all parties concerned."

Olive de Beer glared at her husband, who shrugged. To Etta's amazement, instead of getting mad at her, the sisters not only nodded in approval, but winked at each other and chuckled. Relieved she had for once caused no offence, Etta carried on.

"The sisters were present at the cèilidh in Luss, while Grace was not. Miss Faith Hillock was alone in her bedroom the night Professor Hobbs was killed. Then I thought how strange it was that not only did Grace always seem to have an alibi, but we'd had to take her word for what happened on a number of occasions. For example, when she told Robert that Sue had never informed her about the cèilidh."

"That's a lie! Of course I told her," Sue protested vehemently.

"It wasn't her only lie. You maybe don't know that she pretended to have an accident at Inversnaid Falls. But here, she slipped up slightly as she said the sisters had tricked her into believing the clue was hidden at the waterfall."

"We never even saw her at Inversnaid," said Faith.

"We were far faster than the others," added Hope.

"Exactly," agreed Etta. "You sisters were a long way ahead of her – Dora and I know because we saw you. And you didn't want to be seen by your competitors, so you would never have stopped near the hotel in full view. And anyway, the pace you were going, you must have got there much earlier than Grace."

The two women agreed they had passed through Inversnaid quickly and stopped for a quick lunch further north, nowhere near the hotel restaurant.

"And Grace was the only one near Robert when someone attacked him on Beinn Dòrain."

"But she was attacked too," said Robert.

"Again," said Etta, raising and dropping her shoulders, "we only have her word for that. I bet she grabbed your rucksack to pull you off balance, and then pretended to have been attacked herself; in the fog, you couldn't see what had really happened. She didn't want to hurt you, just make sure all suspicion was deflected away from her."

The others looked at Etta in surprise. Now, the truth seemed all too evident.

"But in all frankness, what caused me to review my thinking was when we started to consider that Professor Hobbs might have been killed earlier than we'd at first believed. Then I realised the whole scenario had been staged, though it took me a while to understand the implications of this. Who could have benefited from fooling us into believing the murder had happened later? Just one person, but I admit I couldn't see that in the beginning; a part of me kept excluding Grace, telling myself maybe it was Sue MacDuff, Faith Hillock or Olive de Beer.

"What a fool I was! But when I finally considered that it could have been Grace, I saw that she was the perfect fit. Certainly, that meant she needed a partner in crime: someone to fire a gun outside while she was back in the bar; someone who was at the cèilidh in Luss while she very conveniently stayed in Balmaha; someone who could have helped her out at the Drovers. And the more Dora and I thought of Luss, the more Dora recalled Mrs van Wetering mentioning how similar *he* looked now that *he* too was wearing a kilt. But who was *he*? Which particular kilted man of the many present that night at the cèilidh? And similar to whom? I realised I had to take those words more seriously; Mrs van Wetering had seen something of such extraordinary significance, and unfortunately had announced it in so loud a voice, the poor woman had to die there and then.

"We never thought of Adam; we had become so focused on the treasure hunt party that he – allegedly one of the staff – went under the radar. But when we saw Sir Angus's video, it finally struck me that Adam too had been wearing a kilt in Luss, and that Michael had mentioned he was a new face among the guides. When we quizzed Robert last night, he told Dora and me that the solicitor had mentioned Adam had to stand in at the eleventh hour as the regular porter had fallen suddenly ill. I suspect that was down to Adam making sure the porter was indisposed so he could take his place. It's high season on the West Highland Way, so it would be difficult to replace anyone at such a short notice.

"But one question remained: if Adam was so similar to the man in the painting, was he too one of the relatives? If so, why wasn't he an heir? Why wasn't he called in to join the treasure hunt by Sir Angus McGrouse's solicitor? Well, in a way, he was. You see, Adam is the real Amilcar Herrera."

"*What?*"

"Yes, the police have received a full confession. Adam Brains, aka Amilcar Herrera, had moved to Manchester under his new identity years before, having served time in prison for robbery in his homeland. There, he looked up his distant relation Grace Jelly, who was working as an estate agent; we think that she maybe passed him information about houses for sale and absent owners who often became the victims of burglaries, but this is a thread the police are investigating. More relevant to us is that when he heard from friends in Argentina, telling him about the letter inviting him to come to Scotland to claim his inheritance, and when Grace was also invited, Adam sprang into action.

"He called one of his former contacts in Argentina – probably another criminal he held some power over – and told him to take up his old identity and present himself in Glasgow. But that wasn't enough for Adam; he decided he wanted to know first-hand what was going on in Scotland. It must be recognised he is a very resourceful man; imagine my surprise", here Etta's voice was heavy with sarcasm, "when I found out he had recently finished a relationship with a secretary for Law, Lorr and Morlore. The silly woman told him all about the treasure hunt Sir Angus had prepared for his heirs, and that her bosses would use the services of the Travel Light company for luggage transport.

"A couple of nights before departure, he followed the driver to a pub, slipped something into his drink that would knock him out for a few days, and presented himself at the company as a stand-in driver, most likely with fake references. That way, Grace would have full support from day one in case anything went wrong."

"But why kill Herrera if he was in on the scheme?" asked Faith Hillock.

"Yes, why?" echoed Hope.

"At some point, the guy probably felt the odds were stacked against him and feared his two accomplices' ambitions. Why would they want to split the inheritance in three, especially as he had no claim to Sir Angus's wealth. It was easy to make him disappear, after ensuring he first confessed to being an impostor; they probably told the poor man they'd let him live and Adam would release him from whatever hold he had over him if he did so… who knows? Even if Law, Lorr and Morlore looked into the claims, all they'd discover is that the real Herrera could not be found in Argentina. Adam and Grace would sell Tilda Island as soon as the five years were up, split the money and live happily ever after. Or at least until the next fraud."

"But weren't they afraid someone might recognise Adam?" said Lloyd de Beer.

"How would you recognise Adam? You don't strike me as the type of family who have regular get-togethers. And once Grace had won, she would probably have changed her solicitor as soon as the inheritance procedure was over, split the money with her partner in crime, and then they could both disappear and reinvent themselves somewhere new."

"But what if Robert had won?"

"He trusted Grace so much, he kept handing the woman the clue with the higher rating; that was his life insurance. Had he not done so, she would probably have killed him just after he got them to the last clue, but before he could claim his inheritance."

Sue's face had gone from cheerful to sombre in seconds, but Robert winked at her and made a little gesture. Then her face lit up again.

"Well," said Mr Morlore, "all of this is very interesting, but I need to remind you that today's stretch is the one that will decide who the winner is. If Robert or the Hillock sisters do not manage to get their hands on the last treasure, the de Beers could still win…"

He distributed the sealed letters and the treasure hunters tore them open instantly. Then they all went to fetch their rucksacks.

"We'll see you all in Fort William where the winner will be announced," Mr Morlore continued, but there was no one left to listen but Etta, Dora and Leon.

The hound got to his feet. After listening to all these boring human explanations, wasn't it time to go?

DORA AND ETTA FETCHED THEIR RUCKSACKS AND ETTA DID NOT even grumble about the light rain.

"It's dreich," said Dora, enjoying the sound of the Scottish word while contemplating Loch Leven from the entrance porch at Mamore Lodge. Etta smiled, then her face turned serious.

"I'm afraid I'm not really cut out to be a matchmaker; I believe I'm much better at sleuthing…"

"That's not a minor thing. Without you, justice would not have been served."

"But when I think how hard I tried to push Grace into Robert's arms…"

"Well, it wasn't just you; I mean, she was determined to do that herself!"

"But I helped her in her devious plan."

"No one is perfect," said Dora.

"Poor Robert will be broken hearted and it's partly my fault."

"Now, don't imagine things as being worse than they are. I have my reasons to think Robert was merely acting kindly towards Grace…"

"Kind? He was more than kind; he was spellbound by her."

"Do you really think so?" said Dora, disappointed.

"Of course! Didn't you witness it at all? How he was falling in love, getting more and more involved with her?"

Dora smiled strangely. If one could ever use the word in the same sentence as Dora, one could even have called it a wicked smile.

"Yes, I witnessed it. I saw the interest they had for one another growing day by day, and the more interested they were, the more they felt unable to speak to each other. Love doesn't always know what route to take, but theirs was definitely original…"

A bell rang in Etta's head. Surely Dora couldn't mean that…

Robert and Sue passed through the door at that moment. Sue stopped as soon as she saw Leon, and the dog was happy to run into her arms and be scratched and played with. For the first time, Etta noticed that Leon and Sue had always got along well, and he was a very discerning dog. She was also a pretty nice woman, now she was out from under the shadow of her domineering professor.

"I need to thank you for all your help," Sue said, looking at the two women. "At one point, I started to fear I would be framed for murder at any moment."

"But you had no motive," said Etta. "And that was your salvation."

"But I could have been another heir in disguise."

Etta shook her head, but didn't comment. "What will you do now?" she asked instead.

Sue blushed, something the two women had never seen her do before.

"To start with," said Robert, just as red as Sue was, "we have one more piece of treasure to hunt for."

"But Sue's not in the treasure hunt party, or what's left of it," Etta said bluntly. Dora hit her in the stomach with her elbow.

"I asked Sue," Robert carried on, "to accompany me today and maybe stay with me in Fort William for a while…"

"That is only if you don't win the inheritance," said Sue

quietly. "If you do, you'll have plenty of women determined to catch a rich husband for themselves. But I won't be one of them as I'm no gold digger!"

At that point, Robert did something totally out of character. "There comes a moment when a man can't wait any longer to deal with this kind of nonsense," and he pulled her to him and kissed her, passionately and deeply. She struggled a little at first, but her resistance didn't last long.

"Is she kissing him back?" asked Etta while Dora uselessly tried to silence her.

"I think she is," Dora whispered.

Robert now had control. "Now, as I said, Sue, you'll come to Fort William, and of course we have to win. You don't want to hand Tilda Island to a couple of selfish sisters or two disasters from South Africa, do you? That place needs protection and care."

Sue looked at him with strange – were they loving? Etta conceded she was far from being the expert – eyes.

"I'm afraid I will have to get used to your commanding ways," she said, laughing, something resembling shyness tempering her usual bluntness.

Unlike Etta, Dora was an expert on affairs of the heart. "Sue, can't you see? Robert badly needs you and your practical ways to manage Tilda Island and turn his dreams into something real," she said.

"You always knew, didn't you?" asked Sue.

"Yes. Your eyes spoke the truth." Dora winked. "But now you'd better go or the sisters will be ahead of you."

Sue hugged the ladies, kissed Leon on the head, and then followed Robert outside.

"See you in Fort William tonight," she called over her shoulder, "where we will celebrate the end of the West Highland Way and the treasure hunt."

Etta looked at Dora who was smiling, her eyes following the couple. Now walking at speed, but with a comfortable, companionable rhythm to their strides, they were rapidly disappearing into the distance.

"Robert said today's treasure is on Ben Nevis," Etta said. "It will be a tough day's hike. Do you think they stand a chance of winning?"

"I'm sure of it!" And if Dorotea Rosa Pepe had no hesitation, who was Etta to doubt?

～

LEON LED THE WAY AS IT TOOK A WHILE FOR ETTA TO THINK THINGS over. Then she stopped in her tracks, dumbstruck.

"What's up?" asked Dora.

"There's a mystery I've not been able to solve," Etta admitted, her face pained. "It's the one about the Hillock sisters."

"What about them?"

"You remember the conversation I overheard at the cottage when I was looking for you and Leon?"

"Oh that," Dora said with a chuckle. "My dear sleuth, those two might be hags, but they have a brain…"

"Yes, at least one between them."

"I believe they too suspected foul play… and you and Rufus were top of their suspect list. After all, you have to admit, Mr McCall has kept turning up: in Luss; the day after Herrera disappeared; and then, here he was again after Professor Hobbs's death. Not to mention that you and I have been following the group all along…"

"Go figure – me, a suspect? And Rufus?" Etta gave a snort, then a lightbulb glowed brightly in her brain. "That'll be why Hope was alone in the bar the night Professor Hobbs died: the cunning old harridans were setting a trap for me." Etta laughed loudly, her eyes sparkling with the irony of it all. "If I had done anything suspicious, maybe sneaked off somewhere, good soldier Hope was to follow me and catch me in my devious act. Well, well, who would have thought the sisters would give me the best belly laugh of the holiday?" And belly laugh she did, Dora joining in as her friend rocked back and forth on her feet and clutched her sides, tears of mirth running down her face.

"Come on," said Etta, finally calming down after five minutes of hilarity, her voice still wobbly with laughter. "As you said to Sue, we'd better go. I want to get to Fort William and find out who wins the treasure hunt."

"The end of the Way, but the beginning of all sorts of new things to come," said Dora, giving Etta a strange look. "So, will Mr McCall be there waiting for you?"

"Well, there happens to be a cèilidh in Fort William tonight..."

"Are you kidding me?" said Dora abruptly, sounding more like Etta. "You want to dance after a 96-mile walk?"

"We're starting off so early," said Etta, blushing as they walked through an area the map called Tigh-na-sleubhaich, "we'll have plenty of time for a shower and rest before hitting the dance floor..."

But Dora was no longer listening; she had stopped dead in front of the ruins of a cottage. A ray of sunshine made its way through as the clouds cleared and hit the feet of the mountain and part of the walls, illuminating them in amazing shades of green and reviving the ancient stones.

Leon sprang forward, eager as ever for new adventures; Etta took her camera out and captured a snapshot of a woman with clasped hands and open mouth and a Basset with his tail up. And those gorgeous colours that only Scotland could offer: a sky now an immense stretch of blue; the fields so green. True, the West Highland Way was coming to an end, but they had one more home swap to look forward to – one in a castle on the north coast of this most extraordinary nation.

~

I REALLY HOPE YOU ENJOYED THIS BOOK. **IS THERE ANY WAY A reader may help an author? Yes! Please leave a review on Amazon, Goodreads and/or Bookbub.** It doesn't matter how long or short; even a single sentence could say it all. We might be in a digital era, but **this old world of ours still revolves around word of mouth**. A review allows a book to leave the shadow of the unknown and introduces it to other passionate readers.

GRAZIE :)

AUTHOR NOTE

The West Highland Way and Me

I lived in Scotland from 1994 to 1999. It was there I learned the ropes of hiking using a compass and map, along with getting a deep understanding of what life is like as an amphibian. In fact, it was in Scotland that I bought my first pair of gaiters and learned how useful they could be in the local wilderness, even if I wasn't hiking in the snowy season.

There is water everywhere in Scotland. Not only in the lochs and brooks, rainfall and rivers, but when you walk on the moor, water literally springs up from beneath your feet at every step. It's like walking on a damp sponge. Nothing could describe it better.

Oh, and how could I forget? When you're not wrapping up against another rainstorm, when the sun peeks through the clouds and illuminates the majestic beauty of the landscape, you have the dubious pleasure of dealing with midges. These tiny biting beasties fly *everywhere* whenever the sun is shining and I experienced for myself what a pest they are.

Despite all of this, or maybe because of it, by 1996, I was ready to take up the challenge of walking the West Highland Way solo. I mean, it wasn't *that* solo; the Scottish people are friendly, Scottish hikers even more so, which meant I never felt lonely along the way or in the youth hostels or other accommodation I used.

MAMORE LODGE

Back in 1996, the internet was in its infancy, so when I booked my room at Mamore Lodge, it was only on the basis of a wee picture in the single tourist brochure I'd had found and I didn't really know what to expect. When I finally arrived in town, damp, tired and hungry after the rainiest and coldest day of my adventure, and asked for directions, my heart sank when an old man pointed to a little white spot up on the mountains. Almost two more miles to go, and my soaking wet rucksack was getting heavier by the minute. Much like Etta in *Death on the West Highland Way*, I was tempted to stop for the night in every B&B I passed.

But if there's one thing you learn when you hike, it is that things always happen for a reason. So up I went through the storm and arrived at Mamore Lodge, and what a delight was waiting for me. A beautiful mansion perched high above the town of Kinlochleven, and in the morning, I would awake to the most amazing view over Loch Leven.

I loved that my pine-panelled room had once welcomed Captain RH Britten. Unlike Etta, Dora and Leon, I had no cheerful flames flickering in the fireplace waiting for me, but the room was warm and cosy while I listened to the fierce northerly wind whistling around outside the lodge. There was a fire in the lounge, and the food served in the friendly pub was superb. I enjoyed a feast, accompanied by a chat with a bunch of fellow walkers.

I was just a student at the time, so a hotel room and a proper dinner (instead of canned food cooked hastily in a hostel kitchen) was a real luxury for me. I wished for that evening to last as long as possible as I enjoyed every bit of it, and as a memento, I kept the Mamore Lodge brochure in my journal. And there I found it 26 years later.

I learned during my research that Mamore Lodge closed in 2000. What a shame; it was such a legendary hotel. If you search on the internet, you are likely to find it mentioned as a weird abandoned place only fit to be included among the strange facts listed on Atlas Obscura. It's a sort of anachronism to feature the Mamore in my book as Etta, Dora and Leon's adventure takes place well after it closed in 'real life'. Still, I'm proud and happy to have been able to bring this special place back to life once more, using Mamore Lodge as it lives on in my memory, the only change being to stretch the terrace on the first floor (strategically) a further couple of metres to take in the victim's room in the southern wing.

As for bringing the Mamore back into business... well, that's one of the privileges of being a creative: you can do whatever you want, regardless of economic recession, business crises, expensive maintenance or natural disaster. These are just some of the reasons for Mamore Lodge's closure I read in various blogs and articles. However, none of these posts was convincing enough to persuade me to share the links with you.

I'm far more interested in another point altogether: wouldn't it be great if someone really brought Mamore Lodge back to life?

Scottish language

I lived in Scotland – actually, Glasgow – for six years, and at the end of those years, I was amazed that I still couldn't understand a single word the local taxi drivers spoke. And Glasgow cab drivers are very sociable, so they'd talk uninterrupted from departure to arrival point. I always felt bad that my being Italian was hindering me from fitting in with the local people and their language.

Then I spoke to a friend from Surrey who had lived in Glasgow for almost ten years, and he confessed that he couldn't understand most Glaswegians either, particularly the taxi drivers. You can't imagine how much joy and relief I felt; if a native English speaker couldn't understand Glaswegian, what hope did I, a poor lost Mediterranean soul, have?

Anyway, I had to make a choice for this book: how much Scottish vernacular would I use? And here I stumbled into two problems. FIRST: the story is told by Dora and Etta – with a few shrewd observations from Leon, of course – so would they catch on to all those inflexions that make the Scottish accent so melodious, but so hard to decipher for a foreigner? I doubt it, but I also doubt that even the most faithful of transcriptions would do justice to the musicality of the Scots; the weird cadence of their language that endears it to one's heart from the outset. If you're already familiar with the Scottish accent or, even better, a Scot yourself, perhaps you can play the words in your head to "listen to it" as you read.

SECOND: were I to drop too many distinctly Scottish terms into the book, how about the others in the series? I can't imagine using German, Polish, Swedish, Czech, Danish expressions in my books; even though some of my readers might enjoy that (if they come from or have relatives in one of these countries), the majority – including me – might be distracted from the story. And the story is the most important thing; I want my readers to feel that they're part of the adventure, not be puzzling over the words I'm using. Language should be as "user friendly" as possible.

So for the sake of clarity, I decided, with a tinge of regret, not to use much Scottish in *Death on the West Highland Way*, simply dropping in the few words we international visitors – like Dora and Etta – soon pick up such as "wee", "lassie", "lad", "dreich". As for Leon, well, he's in another league. Dogs can pick up any language in a matter of minutes, reliant as they are on clues, from context to inflexion to body language. They're born multilingual.

. . .

Tom Weir's statue

In the early chapters set in Balmaha on the bonnie banks of Loch Lomond, Dora mentions the statue of Tom Weir. Tom was a keen climber and lover of the outdoors, and for eleven years (1976 to 1987), he hosted *Weir's Way*, a TV programme that celebrated the Scottish wilderness and local traditions. His passionate voice, bushy moustache and iconic hat made *Weir's Way* popular among the young and old alike.

In Balmaha in 2014, 100 years after his birth, Tom's statue was unveiled to the public. His wife, who'd shared many of his adventures, was there to witness the ceremony.

You can see part of one episode of *Weir's Way* dedicated to Inchcailloch, the island Etta and Dora visit in the book, here:

https://www.youtube.com/watch?v=VcIqPxYGJaE

(paperback readers, search for: "Weir's Way: Inchcailloch and select the YouTube video).

I hope you'll love his accent as much as I do.

For the touching and fun statue-unveiling ceremony with all the guests wearing red beanie hats in honour of Tom (and an 8-minute video about Loch Lomond viewed from above as Tom floated over it in a hot-air balloon), you want to head here:

https://www.seelochlomond.co.uk/discover/tom-weir-statue-balmaha

Cèilidhs

Searching on the internet, I found that a cèilidh is simply a social gathering; it doesn't necessarily involve any dancing. This is kind of weird as when I lived in Glasgow and when I worked in Dufftown as a tourist guide in a whisky distillery, cèilidhs always involved music and dancing. That's what I looked forward to! I found it fascinating that you'd get young and old all mixing together, equally determined to have fun. I've never been a good dancer, but that didn't discourage the Scots from leading me on to the dancefloor and encouraging me to follow their moves.

I only attended one cèilidh during my West Highland Way hike and that was in Fort William to celebrate the end of the walk, but I was extremely happy to allow Etta and Dora to experience their first ever cèilidh in Luss, a quaint little town on Loch Lomond. I wish I could have travelled with them to get there by boat at night. If at all possible, I'd skip the part involving a sudden death, but alas! In life, you don't always get to choose.

You can learn what a Scottish cèilidh looks like by following the link below. I do apologise in advance because the Scottish comedian Danny Bhoy does use some swear words, but swear words from the mouth of a Scot are never meant to offend anyone; they're simply there to emphasise the point. Enjoy his accent and appreciate how tired you can get just simulating a cèilidh, let alone surviving the real thing.

https://www.youtube.com/watch?v=1msu8iQT3kw

(For those of you reading the paperback edition, search for: "Danny Bhoy's hilarious description of a Scottish cèilidh dance" and select the YouTube video.)

Or you can look at this wedding cèilidh. There's no foul language here, and you can see the various types of dances:

https://www.youtube.com/watch?v=62sim5knB-s

(Paperback readers, search for: "Traditional cèilidh dancing at a Scottish wedding".)

The Drovers Inn and its Bogles

I deeply regret that I did not sleep at the Drovers Inn. I'm not sure how this oversight could have happened; maybe as a student, I was just looking for youth hostels to spend the night, and without the help of the internet, I didn't realise the Drovers had regular visits from its very own ghosts. So yes, the inn is a real place, but all the staff and the unfortunate incidents that appear in *Death on the West Highland Way* (especially the guest disappearing from his bedroom) are a product of my imagination.

Nowadays, if you want to know more about the Drovers' beds, food or ghosts, please head here:

https://www.droversinn.co.uk/about-us/ghosts/

As for me, I can't wait to visit, enjoy a good ghost story near the fire in the cosy pub, and thank the owners for allowing me to use their premises for my book.

Tilda Island

Tilda Island is an imaginary place, but people who undertake large complex projects in order to restore and preserve part of the rich Scottish heritage are very common. On a visit to Scotland, you're likely stumble in a number of these modern resourceful heroes. So Tilda is to me both a pretext (in the sense of excuse) and a means to thank them all.

The West Highland Way Logo

Thanks to Stuart Davies from NatureScot for allowing me to use the West Highland Way logo on this book's cover. Featured on all the poles along the route, it's not just a simple logo; it's a memento all West Highland Way hikers treasure during and after their walk.

The West Highland Way – Guidebook

Thanks to Jacquetta Megarry, a really passionate walker, for helping me find out who is actually responsible for the logo and, more importantly, for writing books and guides about the adventurous hikes she's taken all around the world. In particular, her West Highland Way guide has helped me rekindle my memories. It's a treasure trove of information, maps and stunning pictures; any errors that crept into *Death on the West Highland Way* are entirely my own. If you fancy following Etta, Dora and Leon, be it with a real rucksack, boots and, of course, waterproofs, or from the comfort of your armchair, you can do so with a copy of Jacquetta's book: West Highland Way.

WANT TO TELL ME SOMETHING?

Have you enjoyed the book? Please let me know at me@adrianalicio.com. I've done my research, but errors, pretty much like the Drovers Inn bogles, can creep in unexpectedly.

FREEBIE: AND THEN THERE WERE BONES

And Then There Were Bones, prequel to the *An Italian Village Mystery*
series, is only available by signing up to
www.adrianalicio.com/murderclub

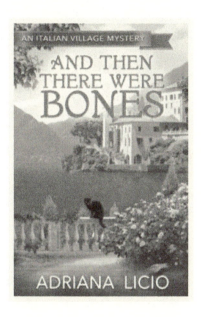

**A Murder Mystery along the lines of Agatha Christie's *And Then
There Were None*.**

When feisty travel writer, Giò Brando, receives an invitation to join her
long-time friend on an island in Calabria for a Murder
Mystery weekend, she is excited by the prospect.

To run away from the grey London weather for a while; to escape her
stubborn fiancé – and even better, her mother-in-law-to-be – meet her
family in her Italian hometown by the sea, and enjoy the Murder
weekend with some celebrity guests sounds too good to be true.

In fact, some of the guests are just as temperamental as you would expect from celebs. But when one mysteriously disappears, and strange things befall...

Gosh, what's happening?

Is a madman trying to repeat the Ten Little Indians Saga or there's a method to this madness?

As the storm ravages the island, cutting it off from the mainland,

Giò has very little time to find out what is going on and save herself as well as the surviving guests from certain death.

MORE BOOKS FROM ADRIANA LICIO

THE HOMESWAPPERS MYSTERIES SERIES
Travelling Europe one... corpse at a time!
0 - Castelmezzano, The Witch Is Dead – Prequel to the series
1 - The Watchman of Rothenburg Dies: A German Travel Mystery
2 - A Wedding and A Funeral in Mecklenburg : A German Cozy Mystery
3 - An Aero Island Christmas Mystery: A Danish Cozy Mystery
4 – Prague, A Secret From The Past: A Czech Travel Mystery
5 – Death on the West Highland Way: A Scottish Cozy Mystery

AN ITALIAN VILLAGE MYSTERY SERIES
0 - And Then There Were Bones. The prequel to the *An Italian Village Mystery* series is **available for free by signing up to www.adrianalicio.com/murderclub**
1 - Murder on the Road Returning to her quaint hometown in Italy following the collapse of her engagement, feisty travel writer Giò Brando just wants some peace and quiet. Instead, she finds herself a suspect in a brutal murder.

2 *A Fair Time for Death* The annual Chestnut Fair brings visitors from far and wide to the sleepy village of Trecchina. This year, one will be coming to die.

3 - A Mystery Before Christmas A haunting Christmas song from a faraway land. A child with striking green eyes. A man with no past. A heartwarming mystery for those who want to breathe in the delicious scents and flavours of a Mediterranean December.

4 - Peril at the Pellicano Hotel – A group of wordsmiths, a remote hotel. Outside, the winds howl and the seas rage. But the real danger lurks within.

5 - The Haunted Watch Tower – The doors are locked, the windows shuttered, but still he comes. Dare you set foot in the haunted watchtower?

More books to come!

ABOUT THE AUTHOR

Adriana Licio lives in the Apennine Mountains in southern Italy, not far from Maratea, the seaside setting for her first cosy series, *An Italian Village Mystery*.

She loves loads of things: travelling, reading, walking, good food, small villages, and homeswapping. A long time ago, she spent six years falling in love with Scotland, and she has never recovered. She now runs her family perfumery, and between a dark patchouli and a musky rose, she devours cosy mysteries.

She resisted writing as long as she could, fearing she might get carried away by her fertile imagination. But one day, she found an alluring blank page and the words flowed in the weird English she'd learned in Glasgow.

Adriana finds peace for her restless, enthusiastic soul by walking in nature with her adventurous golden retriever Frodo and her hubby Giovanni.

Do you want to know more?
Join the **Maratea Murder Club**

You can also stay in touch on:
www.adrianalicio.com

Made in United States
Orlando, FL
18 August 2022

21179741R00168